The Wildman

The Wildman

A Novel by

RICK HAUTALA

FMP
Full Moon Press 2008

The Wildman
Copyright © 2008 by Rick Hautala. All rights reserved.

Dust jacket and interior illustrations Copyright © 2008 by Alan M. Clark.
All rights reserved.

Lettered Edition art Copyright © 2008 by Josh Thompson.
All rights reserved.

Signature page art Copyright © 2008 by Alex McVey.
All rights reserved.

Interior design Copyright © 2008 by Desert Isle Design, LLC.
All rights reserved.

First Edition

ISBN 978-0-9814748-0-9

Full Moon Press
17 Village Gln
Dallas, GA 30157

www.thefullmoonpress.com

—Dedication—

To the Booths—Mary, Bob, Dan, and Sarah ...

As Stan Wiater says:
"Some people have a life ... We have *NECon*."

And special thanks to Doug Wright for his eagle eye ...

"De goat never know de use of him tail
'till de butcher cut it off."

—Jamaican proverb

Chapter One

B.F.F.

YOU COULD SAY it all started with a late-night phone call in July, but that wouldn't be strictly accurate.

Pre-conditions can be set, and unseen forces are set in motion long before we become aware of them. It's rather egocentric or, we might say, "human-centric" to declare that *anything* starts at any particular point in time simply because that's when we first notice it.

And we should never forget that there are always things we don't know, buried secrets that might eventually come to light with or without our help. Like it or not, there are things that will knock us down long before we see them coming.

That's life, and, as they say, "Life moves in mysterious ways." Like an underground river slithering silently through dark caverns deep within the earth, we never know when something long hidden is going to boil up suddenly into the light. Worst of all, we never know what might be drifting on those dark, mysterious currents until they sweep us away.

So to say all of this began about twenty minutes before midnight on a humid night in mid-July last year when Jeff Cameron got a phone call from someone he hadn't heard from in so long that it might just as well have been a ghost on the other end of the line is as good a point as any to say this is the moment when *this* particular story begins.

It was Wednesday night, in July.

As usual, Jeff had had a hard day at work at the real estate agency. Every day was tough. At least today was Wednesday—"hump day." Just two more days on the downhill slide to the weekend. Of course, Jeff's prospects for the weekends weren't all that thrilling either, but at least he wouldn't have to put in any time at work. His assistant, Betty Schroeder, was more than eager to cover the few showings they had scheduled on Saturday and Sunday.

Susan, Jeff's wife, had left him almost a year ago, and Jeff still hadn't adjusted. The house seemed unnaturally large and empty without her around. More and more, Jeff found himself wondering why he even stayed at his job when he no longer needed to maintain such a high standard of living, much less a big house like this—especially now that Matt, their one and only child, was off to college. He could probably have made a killing if he sold now, but the real estate market, which had been booming in southern Maine for the last ten-plus years, was—like the rest of the country—finally going a soft.

Soft?

How about house prices and sales in free fall?

It figures, Jeff thought bitterly. *Just when I'm thinking about bailing out, prices drop through the floor.*

For the last six months or more, he had been forced to admit he didn't really enjoy the peace and quiet at home the way he thought he would. With Susan and Matt both gone, this place with its four bedrooms, huge living room and dining room, family room, and game room in the basement, wrap-around porch, two and a half baths, and three-car garage was much more than he needed or, the ways things were looking, would ever need.

So why not just get a shack somewhere out in the boondocks and stash away some bucks?

As always, Jeff had eaten supper alone. Tonight, it had been take-home… Massaman curry with tofu from the Thai restaurant downtown. As usual, he watched the evening news, which was as depressing as ever, and then settled down to read a little before taking a hefty shot of rum—but just *one* shot … to help him sleep. Then he went to bed.

He had been sleeping soundly when the phone rang, shattering the quiet.

Confused and disoriented, Jeff sat up in bed and reached for the phone as he glanced at his bedside alarm clock. He'd already taken out his contacts, so the numerals were a bright smear of glowing red lines. Leaning closer, he was finally able to make out the time.

His heart jumped.

11:52!

Shit! … Something bad's happened … Someone's died!

His throat felt suddenly constricted as he mentally flashed through the short list of people who might have died or been injured.

Dad's heart finally gave out … mom's had another stroke … or maybe it's the town cops in Ithaca … Matt's been out partying with his college buddies … he drove after having a few too many … or maybe it's Barry … Susan's new husband

The Wildman

... Susan had a heart attack ... or has cancer ... or she's killed herself ... or she started drinking again ... or ... or ...

"H'lo?" Jeff said, licking his lips. His stomach was churning as he readied himself for whatever load of bad news was about to drop on his head.

There was a long pause at the other end of the line. If there had been a dial tone instead of the long, hollow silence, Jeff might have thought he had dreamed the phone had rung, but then…faintly….someone on the other end of the line took a deep, whistling breath.

Jeff's panic rose, and he kicked away the sweat-soaked bed sheet that was tangled around his feet. Then he swung his legs over the side of the bed, barely restraining the impulse to get up and start pacing just to be doing *something* to relieve the tension inside him. In spite of the heavy humidity in the air, a chill wrapped around his shoulders like a drape of thin cloth as he straightened up, preparing to tell whomever this was to *fuck off* and then hang up.

"'S that you, Jeff?" a man's voice he didn't recognize said.

"Yeah, it's me." Jeff realized his hand not holding the phone was balled into a fist. He consciously relaxed it. "Who the hell is this?"

Another pause, shorter this time, was followed by a faint, nervous chuckle.

"Sorry," the voice said. "I was just lighting a cigarette. You'll never guess in a million years."

That was all the person on the other end of the line needed to say. A sudden rush made Jeff feel lightheaded. In an instant, he was whisked back more than thirty years to when he was a kid.

"Tyler?" he said, incredulous. "No way. This can't be Tyler Crosby."

Jeff was amazed to hear himself say the name. A tight smile spread across his face.

"Fuckin'-A straight it is," the voice said. "How'd you guess so fast?"

Feeling dizzy from the momentary flood of relief because no one was hurt or dead, Jeff let his shoulders sag as he sat down on the edge of the bed and took a shallow breath. He stared into the darkness as long-forgotten memories filled his mind. When they were kids, Tyler Crosby was always saying a million this or a million that …

"I told you a million times" … "I'll bet you a million bucks" … "You'll never guess in a million years" …

Back then, Jeff had jokingly said to him: "If I told you once, I told you a million times—you exaggerate," but Tyler never got the joke.

"Easy as pie," Jeff said with a faint chuckle as he dredged up a mental image of his childhood friend. Short, dark-haired, with pale blue eyes and a Pillsbury Dough Boy physique. He couldn't imagine how much Tyler had changed over the years. A moment later, though, his shoulders stiffened again, and he shivered when he wondered why Tyler Crosby was calling him after … how long had it been?

"'S been a helluva long time," Jeff said, trying to sound a lot more at ease than he was feeling. "And—Christ! It's late. What's up?"

"Oh, yeah," Tyler said. "I forgot. You're three hours ahead of me. Sorry."

"I'm guessing you live on the West Coast?"

"Yeah. L.A. I'm a lawyer. Mostly I do entertainment law."

"No shit." Jeff was painfully aware of the snap in his voice. Making small talk at this hour was already starting to wear thin. He had to be up at six o'clock to get ready for work. The last thing he needed to hear was that someone he hadn't spoken to or even thought about much-if at all in the last thirty years- was some hot shot lawyer to the stars.

"I just got an email from someone," Tyler said, "a mutual friend, and was wondering if you'd gotten the same one."

"An email? I dunno." Jeff scrubbed his face with the flat of his hand. His skin was oily with sweat. "I—uh, I won't check my email again until I get to the office in the morning."

"I'll bet you this one's gonna interest you."

"Bet me a million bucks?" Jeff asked, but Tyler didn't get that he was poking fun at him. Maybe he wasn't as conscious as Jeff was of how much he used the expression.

"It was from Evan."

The instant Jeff heard the name, a dash of cold rippled through him. The surrounding darkness pulsed and subtly pressed in on him, making it hard to catch his breath.

"Evan Pike?" Jeff thought his voice sounded like a faint echo, reverberating hollowly in the darkness.

"Yeah. *That* Evan. And guess what?"

"I couldn't guess … not in a million years," Jeff said, barely aware this time that he was imitating Tyler.

"He wants to have a reunion."

"A what?"

"A camp reunion."

"A camp reunion."

Jeff didn't like the way he kept repeating everything Tyler said, but the shot of rum he'd had before bed, and being awakened from a deep sleep, had thrown him off. He was a little embarrassed that Tyler had caught him off guard like this. He liked to think he was always on top of his game.

The Wildman

"What do you mean, *a camp reunion?*"

"At Camp Tapiola," Tyler said, "on Lake Onwego."

Jeff sucked in his breath with a loud *whoosh*, but as hard as he tried to focus, his mind was a roaring white blank.

He had no idea how to respond.

The first, most reasonable thing would be to read the email tomorrow, assuming Evan had sent one to him, and see what he thought. Evan had to have invited him if he invited Tyler. There was no reason to think otherwise, but then, knowing Evan—or at least Evan the way he had been when he was twelve years old—he couldn't be sure without actually checking his email.

"I—ah … I dunno," Jeff finally said. "Camp Tapiola—Jeeze, I haven't thought about that place in … ages … not since … well … you know—"

He sighed as he ran his hand across the slick sheen of sweat that sprinkled his forehead. It wasn't just the humidity, he knew, because an icy chill had formed in the pit of his stomach. He felt like he'd swallowed a snowball.

"I know," Tyler said breathlessly. "Me, neither."

Why does he sound so excited about this? Jeff wondered.

"He's inviting all of us from the tent."

"All of us?"

There's that echo again.

"Who does that include?"

"I assume he means him, you, me, Mike, Ralph, and Fred … all of us guys from Tent Twelve."

"Fred Bowen? Jesus, I've always wondered what happened to him. You have any idea?"

"Not a clue, but Evan says he wants to have all of us out there if we can make it."

"To the camp, you mean."

Jeff couldn't imagine why he was suddenly so cranky. Was it just because he'd been awakened so late, or was it because of the memories this phone call was stirring up?

"I—uh … Jeeze, Ty, I dunno. Like I said, I haven't seen any email yet, so I have no idea what you're talking about." He made an effort to keep the pique out of his voice, but he was sure he wasn't doing a very good job of it.

"Yeah … Sorry," Tyler said, lowering his voice and sounding truly apologetic. "My bad."

It was just like Tyler to blame himself. Maybe he hadn't changed all that much in the intervening years. Jeff narrowed his eyes and tried to picture his childhood friend now. It was difficult...no... it was impossible to imagine Tyler Crosby a grown man, a successful Hollywood lawyer, no less.

"No need to apologize," Jeff said, hoping he hadn't hurt his old friend's feelings.

"I probably should have called you in the morning, huh?" Tyler said. "I definitely should have, but I was so excited about the idea I didn't even think about the time difference, but after I got the email ... I just started thinking, you know? Remembering the good ole' days, and I just ... you know ... I thought it was a really cool idea."

"Yeah ... No, I understand," Jeff said.

He was still having trouble focusing his thoughts as he stood up and snapped on the bedside light. He squinted in the sudden burst of yellow light that made his eyes start to water. He cleared his throat and rubbed his eyes, forcing back the sleepiness. He had never liked waking up too fast.

"It's just that ... it's been so long, you know?" Tyler said. "I mean ... we haven't been very good, none of us have, about staying in touch. I—" He sniffed with laughter, and Jeff could picture him shaking his head at the thought. "Remember how we had that whole BFF thing going?"

"BFF?"

"Best Friends Forever."

"Oh, yeah ... right. I remember." Jeff didn't like how this conversation was so one-sided. Tyler might just as well have been talking to himself, dredging up reminiscences about the good ole' days at Camp Tapiola.

"I checked you out on the internet, so I know you're still living in Maine. You're still in Westbrook?"

"Uh ... Yeah. Westbrook. I'm a real estate agent at a firm in Portland."

"You married? Got kids?"

That question, so innocent, gave Jeff pause because the last thing he wanted now was to get into all of that, especially with someone who was all but a perfect stranger. He still had more than enough emotional baggage to deal with, and this was not the time to get into it with Tyler or anyone.

"I got—uh, divorced a while ago. 'Bout a year. Got one kid in college. At Ithaca."

"That's in upstate New York, right?"

"Yeah. Just south of Syracuse."

"Gotcha. But you're doing all right, aren't you?" The genuine note of concern in Tyler's voice touched Jeff. Once again, he pictured him the way Tyler had looked when they were kids. That was the only memory he had of him with his long, dark hair framing a round face that remained pale no

The Wildman

matter how much time they spent in the sun, and his blue eyes that always glistened like wet marbles. It struck Jeff as strange how, all of a sudden, he experienced a wave of nostalgia for his childhood. He must miss those days with his best buddies in some way.

BFF, indeed.

"I'm doing all right, I guess," Jeff replied. "You know, the usual complaints at our age—gaining weight…losing hair."

"Tell me about it," Tyler chuckled softly. "I mean—it's weird how I don't feel like I've changed all that much, but a couple of years ago, I went to my high school reunion in Danvers, and a lot of people didn't even recognize me. It's weird, you know?"

"For sure," Jeff said, but as he said it, he stifled a yawn behind his hand. Glancing at the clock, he saw that it was **12:04**.

Damn!

He had to get up in six hours.

"Look," Tyler said. "I got your phone number and can call you tomorrow."

"How'd you find me, anyway?"

"Google. It's amazing what you can do on the Internet these days."

"It sure as hell is."

"So I'll give you a call tomorrow," Tyler said, "after you've checked your email. But let's make sure we stay in touch, okay?"

"Uhh—yeah…yeah. Sure. It'd be cool to reconnect after all these years."

"It's been *way* too long," Tyler said.

A million years, Jeff wanted to say but didn't.

"We'll talk tomorrow."

Jeff said "Good bye," but he wasn't sure if Tyler heard him or had already hung up. When the dial tone started buzzing in his ear, he replaced the phone. For a long time, he sat there on the edge of his bed, staring off into space, his mind filled with memories and images from long ago.

It wasn't long before the phone call took on a cast of unreality. Jeff checked the caller I.D. just to make sure he'd really gotten a call from California and not imagined it.

Sure enough, there was Tyler's name and phone number.

Jeff thought to jot it down before he forgot about it, but he was too exhausted and a little dizzy from the rum, so he turned off the light instead and flopped back onto the bed.

It took a while, but he finally drifted off to sleep.

A few hours later, he awoke again with a start. This time it was because of a dream he had about Camp Tapiola, but upon waking, he couldn't remember any of the details. All he knew was, the dream left him with a cold hollow feeling deep in his stomach in spite of the humid night air.

The only thought circling around in his mind as he tried to drift off to sleep again was that maybe having a camp reunion at Camp Tapiola wasn't such a good idea. As nice as his memories of it were, there were also things he'd just as soon not think about ever again. And now Tyler's late night phone call had dredged them all up.

❈ ❈ ❈

Over the next few weeks, Jeff received a slew of emails, not only from Evan Pike and Tyler Crosby, but also from Mike Logan and Fred Bowen. It was beginning to turn into "Old Summer Camp Week."

It wasn't all fun, though. Jeff learned that two of the people he thought might be included—Ralph Curran and their former counselor, Mark Bloomberg—had both died. Mark had been a high school Phys. Ed teacher who had a heart attack at the age of twenty-nine, while Ralph, a life insurance salesman in Boston, had been stabbed to death a few years ago in a barroom brawl following a Red Sox game at Fenway Park where the Sox had lost to the Yankees.

As soon as he answered the first email from Evan, he started getting several messages a day at his work account. It wasn't long before it began to feel like an invasion of privacy, but the upshot of it all was this…

Evan Pike had become an entrepreneur of sorts. He had his fingers, if not his whole hand and arm, in a variety of deals—mostly real estate, but some manufacturing and industrial development as well as property management. He told Jeff about how a corporation called Willow Creek was in the process of buying and developing huge tracts of land in western Maine on the northern shore of Lake Onwego and the surrounding area, including Lookout Mountain. Their plans ultimately called for two eighteen hole golf courses, a ski slope, a huge marina, luxury homes for both summer and year-round residents, a shopping mall, and numerous outfitters for rustic activities such as hiking, camping, boating, fishing, and hunting.

Although the deal didn't include Sheep's Head Island, the small island in the southern part of the lake where Camp Tapiola was located, Evan had learned through some insider information that the camp property was up for sale as well. It had been abandoned for the last thirty-five years following the death of a camper, Jimmy Foster. Because of the lawsuit brought by the Foster family against the camp's board of directors and the attendant bad publicity, Camp Tapiola had been forced to close. That was also the last summer Jeff

The Wildman

and his buddies had been campers. It was also the last time all five of them—Jeff, Evan, Tyler, Mike and Fred—had been together...until now.

Through the magic of the internet, they had reconnected or were in the process of reconnecting.

And now that Evan had bought not just Camp Tapiola, but the whole island, he'd come up with what he thought was the fantastic idea of having all five surviving Tent 12 campers get together. The only hurdle was finding a weekend that worked with everyone's schedules so they could meet at Camp Tapiola for a long weekend of drinking and reminiscing.

Maybe it's the kind of thing that only looks good on paper, Jeff typed in response to the third email he'd received from Tyler the day after that first phone call.

Jeff had a mountain of paperwork to do because, finally, the Howlands were closing on a house they'd been dithering about for the last three months. He wanted to make sure he had at least three estimates for the cellar wall repair the couple had requested, no, *demanded* before they would sign on the dotted line. The last thing he needed was to be wasting time *IM*-ing and emailing Tyler or anyone else he hadn't seen or talked to in the last thirty-five years.

BING.

The computer flagged a new email, and Jeff groaned when he saw that it was from Tyler, not the contractor who had promised he'd have his estimate done before lunch and here it was, almost three o'clock.

Reluctantly, mostly because he had nothing better to do, Jeff opened the email and read it.

U always were the cautious one. Time 4 you 2 have a little fun. Com'on. It'll be GR8, trust me.

Jeff sighed and shook his head. He winced when he took a sip of his coffee, which had gone cold more than half an hour ago. It was one thing for his son Matt and his college buddies to butcher the King's English with their abbreviations and "emoticons," but Tyler was a bit old for such juvenile shorthand.

He hit *reply* and quickly typed: **I'm just saying late October's probably not the best time for this. Why not wait until next spring or summer when it's warmer? As it is, I'm swamped with work.**

Without editing, he sent the email, and moments later his computer signaled another new message. This was a reply from Tyler, not the contractor, so he closed the screen, got up from his desk, and wandered out into the front office. His time might be better spent flirting with Debbie Hendricks at the front desk, but then again, the way Debbie had been treating him lately, he was beginning to think he didn't really have much of a shot with her anyway.

By the time he got back to his desk half an hour later, there were more emails from all of his former friends—Evan, Tyler, Mike, and even Fred, who was replying to Evan's email for the first time. Rather than deal with any of this now, Jeff forwarded all of the letters to his home account and tried to settle back into work. The contractor didn't get back in touch with him until almost five o'clock. By the time Jeff replied to him, it was too late to set up an appointment with the Howlands for today. It would have to wait until Friday. Jeff put any thoughts about a camp reunion out of his mind until he got home that evening.

That's when Evan called.

❦ ❦ ❦

"So what do you think?" Evan asked after he had laid out his plans in detail to Jeff, pausing every once in a while to get an affirmative grunt from Jeff before pushing ahead. After a couple of minutes, Jeff felt as though he had already agreed to go to the reunion even though he had never said as much.

No wonder Evan's so successful in business, he thought. He had a smooth, low-pitched voice…the kind of voice people would call "mellifluous"…and he had a way of making you feel as though you and he were on the same side of an issue with no opposition.

Very slick.

And truth to tell, it didn't surprise Jeff that Evan ended up like this. He thought back to when they were at summer camp—it had only been for two weeks a summer from the time they were nine to twelve. Just three years. It seemed much longer, but in that short period of time, even though Jeff had been coming to the camp since he was seven, Evan took right over, acting as though he had always been the unquestioned leader of their little group.

There had always been an unspoken rivalry between Jeff and Evan, and Jeff had never accepted that he was usually demoted to second in command.

Even after thirty-five years with little or no contact among any of them, a sense of competition was still there. Jeff felt it in the way Evan was trying to "sell" him on his idea of a reunion. As detached as Jeff felt from his job in some ways, especially after the divorce, he knew sales techniques when he saw them, and he cringed at how he was falling for the subtle ways Evan had of "closing the deal." He didn't like the pressure Evan was applying, and it irritated him to no end to think Evan was so confident he'd fall for it.

"Yeah … sure," Jeff heard himself say although he wasn't exactly sure where *that* had come from. "It sounds like it'll be a gas."

A gas? … Christ! I'm already sounding like a goddamned twelve-year-old!

"I'm thinking we can't really get this together until October or maybe early November," Evan said.

"That's kind of late, don't you think?"

"Yeah, but my schedule's filled solid right through September."

"I'm just not sure about camping out that late in the year."

Jeff could tell he was grasping at anything to find an excuse to back out now that, apparently, he had given his tacit approval to the idea.

"The cabins aren't there any more," Evan said, "but the dining hall's still in pretty good shape…at least it was the last time I saw it."

"When was that?"

"I was out there this summer when they did some percolation tests on the septic system. There's been a bit of vandalism over the years, of course, but being on the island and all, it's not as bad as you might think. And there's the fireplace in the dining hall. Remember that? It's still in good shape. We can use it for heat and cooking."

"What are we gonna do about taking a crap?"

"I've already arranged for a Port-o-Potty, but com'on. We can take a dump in the woods if we have to. I own the whole damned place."

Jeff was all too aware of how Evan kept switching from possible objections to appeals to nostalgia, but he closed his eyes for a moment and pictured the huge fireplace in the dining hall. It was made of large, rounded granite beach stones and had a mantel made from a thick, rough-cut log, probably some driftwood that had washed up on the shore. Over the years, campers and counselors had carved their names into the wood.

One year, Jeff remembered, it had rained for a week straight, so the campers couldn't take their traditional overnight hike into the mountains. Mark Bloomberg, their counselor, had arranged for the boys from Tent Twelve to camp out in the dining hall. They had cooked hot dogs and, later, when it was time for a scary story, toasted marshmallows and S'mores over the coals.

Good memories, indeed.

But remembering that night also brought back a cold, stark memory of Jimmy Foster. In spite of the warm evening, a sudden chill took hold of Jeff.

Jimmy Foster … Jesus Christ!

That night, after their counselor Mark had told them a particularly frightening story before bedtime, Jimmy had awakened, crying because he was scared. Jeff had heard him sobbing and had talked to him until he finally calmed down.

"Jesus," Jeff whispered. His eyes widened as he looked around the living room. He half-expected to see his childhood friend in the shadows. He was unaware he had spoken out loud until Evan said, "What's that?"

"Huh…? Oh, nothing." Jeff shook his head to clear away the memory. "I was just…You were saying?"

"I was saying we can have a fire in the fireplace and stay warm and dry. We'll drink beer all night. Smoke cigars. Shoot the shit. Come on, it's gonna be a blast."

Jeff chuckled, but it was a short, dry chuckle, and he suddenly found that he couldn't get the mental image of Jimmy Foster out of his mind. Jimmy had been small for his age, and in spite of the summer tan he always had even before he got to camp every year, there had always been something a bit sickly and feeble about him that had worried Jeff even back then. He remembered feeling sorry for the kid because he knew Jimmy's father had died when he was little and that he lived with his mother and younger brother in Randolph, Mass.

But maybe Jimmy had always known, even back then, that his life would end prematurely. Whatever it was, there had been something sad, almost pathetic about Jimmy Foster, which only made it worse because of what happened to him.

Jeff considered mentioning that he was thinking about Jimmy, but he decided not to put a damper on Evan's enthusiasm. Even if he ultimately decided not to show up for this reunion, he didn't want to ruin it for anybody else by reminding them about what had happened to Jimmy.

It struck Jeff as a bit odd that he hadn't thought about Jimmy Foster all that much over the years. His death was definitely something he didn't dwell on, but now that Evan and Tyler had stirred up these old memories, Jeff was surprised to discover how close to the surface his grief and fear, even outright terror, was.

The memory made him more than a little uncomfortable. He shifted on the couch as he cast his gaze nervously around the living room again, not sure what he expected to see.

"Looking at my calendar," Evan said, "I'm thinking the third week in October is our best bet."

Over the phone, Jeff heard a series of faint clicking sounds. He had a mental image of Evan scanning the electronic pages on his PDA. Busy, busy, busy.

"Yeah. I can pencil it in," Jeff said even as, in the back of his mind, a tiny voice was telling him he could always dig up some excuse so he could back out at the last minute. He didn't even bother to get up and write down the date on his calendar. It would be best to wait until Evan had firmed up their plans so once he *did* back out, it would be difficult if not impossible for everyone else to reschedule.

Jeff wanted time to think about what he was agreeing to. Like any buyer, he didn't like being pressured to decide. He saved the hard sell to use on his clients…like the Howlands. Now that the memory of Jimmy Foster had been reawakened and was sharp in his mind, his second thoughts were getting the better of him.

"So we'll get together on Friday, October twentieth," Evan said, and then he hissed and said, "Oh, shit. No. Wait a second. Damn it! I have something else that weekend. How does the weekend of the twenty-seventh sound?"

Without his calendar in front of him, Jeff had no idea if that weekend was open for him. Chances were it was, but what did it matter? It's not like his social life was humming at high speed. Besides, now that he was thinking about Jimmy Foster, he couldn't help but feel as though this reunion idea wasn't such a good idea.

Why go back there and dig up all those old memories?

Sure, there were good ones as well as bad, but there were reasons the camp had closed and none of them had stayed in touch after that last summer.

"Works for me," Jeff said, hoping Evan didn't catch the hollow tone in his voice that clearly signaled his utter disinterest on his part.

You're not closing the deal here, buddy, Jeff thought smugly and wanted to say even though he sensed—no, he was *sure* after only fifteen minutes of talking to Evan that Evan was much more successful in life than he was, at least on the material side of life.

But Evan either didn't notice or, if he did, was savvy enough not to acknowledge Jeff's hesitation. He wasn't going to leave a hole for him to wiggle out of.

"Excellent … excellent," Evan said. "I'll throw this date out to everyone else in an e-mail tomorrow. Do I have you home addie?"

Addie? Jeff thought, smiling that Evan used lingo Jeff usually only heard from his son. He was starting to sound like Tyler. Maybe next he was going to say he'd bet a million bucks they'd have an incredible weekend.

"My work email's fine," Jeff said. "I check it all the time."

"Yeah, but why don't you give it to me anyway, just in case," Evan said.

"Sure. It's **J**—the letter **J**, followed by *came running* … one word—*camerunning* at Yahoo.com."

He listened to a few faint clicking sounds over the phone, and then Evan said, "Okay … Gotcha."

Gotcha!...Jesus, Jeff thought, *maybe he never grew beyond twelve years old either…at least mentally.*

"We'll be in touch, then," Evan said. "I'm really glad this is falling into place for us. It's something I've been thinking about doing for a long time. I'm glad I finally just said 'goddamn it, I'm gonna do it'."

"How about women or significant others?" Jeff asked. "Are we gonna include them, too?"

"Naw. This weekend is just for us guys."

"You never told me- are you married?"

Evan chuckled softly and said, "Sure. Have been for the last twenty years. My wife will shoot me for not remembering exactly how long, but we've got two great kids, and we're doing really well."

"And you live in Massachusetts, right?"

"In Medford. Right outside of Boston," Evan said.

Jeff bristled and was about to mention that he wasn't stupid; he knew where fucking Medford was, but he realized he was getting a little edgy… maybe because Evan was so much more successful than he was.

Always taking second place after Evan, he thought bitterly, but he forced a cheerful note into his voice when he said, "I'm glad you set this thing up. I really appreciate all your efforts."

"Hey…no problem at all," Evan said. "Catch'cha later then."

The phone clicked off, leaving Jeff with a steady buzzing dial tone in his ear. He was mildly surprised that Evan hadn't said something like '*Later, dude.*'

After a second or two, Jeff replaced the phone and eased back on the couch. He exhaled slowly as he closed his eyes and rubbed them until he saw colored patterns swirling in the darkness. A shiver worked its way up his spine when he thought again about what had happened to Jimmy Foster that summer day thirty-five years ago…

Jesus! Jeff thought. *Thirty-five years ago…almost to the day.*

He'd have to check a calendar to be sure, but as he sat there listening to the dense silence of the house, broken only by the distant chirring of crickets outside, Jeff couldn't help but wonder if there was any chance Evan had picked this particular time on purpose.

Had he purposely waited until it had been thirty-five years since Jimmy died before planning this gathering, or was it just coincidence?

The Wildman

"Either way…screw it," Jeff muttered, trying to push such thoughts from his mind.

It was getting late, and he had to be at the office first thing in the morning to finalize that meeting between the Howlands and the contractor. Telling himself he might be getting just a wee bit paranoid about Evan's motives, he eased off the couch, padded into the kitchen, and poured himself a healthy shot of rum. He shivered when he took his first sip and felt the burn rush down into his stomach.

Rum in hand, he shuffled back into the living room and, heaving a sigh, sat back down on the couch. But no matter how much he tried not to think about it, now that his memories of that long-ago summer had been stirred up, there was no way he could stop himself from thinking about Jimmy Foster and what had happened exactly thirty-five years ago.

"BFF," he muttered as he leaned back, closed his eyes, and took a huge gulp of rum. "Best fucking friends."

Chapter TWO

The Last Day of Summer

BEFORE HE WAS twelve years old, Jeff had never seen a dead person. Not a real one, anyway. He'd seen plenty of corpses pile up on TV and in movies and comic books, but the only two *real* deaths he could remember in his immediate family were when his mother's mother, "Grammy Parsons", died of a stroke when he was eight, and his father's brother, Uncle Billy Cameron, a railroad man, who drank himself to death.

Both deaths had affected Jeff deeply, especially Uncle Billy's because, drunk or not, Uncle Billy was one hell of a funny guy. In both cases, however, his parents hadn't allowed him to attend either the visiting hours at the funeral home or the funerals themselves. His mother told him she wanted him to remember the people he loved the way they were when they were alive, not how they looked when they were dead and all made up by the undertaker.

It seemed like a good idea at the time, but now that he was older, Jeff saw how it might have created a warped attitude toward death and grieving on his part. Death had always held a strange fascination for him, and he thought it was in part, anyway, because his parents hadn't let him confront it head on, as a normal and natural part of life. He had been denied the opportunity, if that's the correct word, to deal with seeing a dead person—a real corpse—up close and personal.

That all changed on a hot July afternoon following rest hour when everyone in camp went into panic mode because Jimmy Foster had gone missing. As soon as he heard the news, Jeff knew something really bad had happened because of the cold, sinking feeling of dread in his gut.

"I'm tellin' yah," he said to his tent mates as they huddled in the sun-dappled protection of the brown canvas tent they all slept in. He was sitting Indian-style on his lower bunk with his tent mates gathered around him like he was holding court.

"He didn't run away, and he's not hiding. Jimmy would never do something stupid like that."

"You sure?" Evan asked. His pale, thin eyebrows arched like twin commas above his eyes. He seemed to resent that Jeff was the center of attention. "If you're so smart, where is he?"

"I have no idea," Jeff replied, reacting as if Evan's question was a veiled accusation that maybe he knew more than he was saying. "When did *you* see him last?"

For a tense moment, Evan stared straight back at him, not even blinking until—finally—he cleared his throat and said, "Last I saw him was when we all did. At the softball game."

"So what do you think happened?" Tyler asked, wedging his way into group the way he always did. "I'll bet you a million bucks he ran away."

"And—what, is swimming for the mainland?" Mike Logan said.

"Why would he do that?" Jeff asked.

Both he and Evan stared at Tyler until he backed up a few steps. Then Jeff said, "Last I remember, he said he had to take a dump and left to go to the crapper."

"And he didn't come back," Mike said, "'cause he's a *pussy*. He's probably hiding in the woods somewhere, cryin' like a little baby 'cause he struck out 'n is afraid I'm gonna pound his sorry ass."

"Hey! Watch the language in there!" Mark Bloomberg, their counselor, shouted. He was standing out in front of the tent, talking to several other counselors. Jeff had thought he was far enough away so he and the other counselors couldn't hear them, but that was obviously not the case.

"No way," Jeff said, lowering his voice and shaking his head in such firm denial someone might have thought Mike had called *him* a pussy.

Mike was a head taller than the other boys and was the "jock" of the group. For him, it was all about winning. Not just in sports. In life, too. Everything was a contest to see who was fastest and strongest and best. He always made a game of things, even stupid things like who would get dressed and be first in line for breakfast, or who could finish cleaning his section of the latrines before anyone else finished with even one sink or toilet, or who could carry the most baseball equipment out to the ball field from the storage shed when it was game time. Everything was a competition for Mike, which

The Wildman

wouldn't have been so bad if he was a good sport. But Mike hated losing, and he never accepted it when he or his team lost. If another tent beat their tent, Mike took it personally. And he always lost his temper because when his team lost—which was rare—it was never *his* fault. It was *always* someone else who had blown the game.

"'Sides," Jeff said, eyeing Mike cautiously, "we had a man on first and third, and you were on deck. We were gonna at least tie the game."

"A tie ain't good enough," Mike said through clenched teeth. His dark eyes gleamed with a strange light as if not winning was a personal affront.

"The question is, where the hell—" Tyler tensed and cast a wary glance at the counselors to see if any of them had heard him swear. Lowering his voice, he finished his thought. "So where the *heck* is he?"

"*Someone* must have seen him … wherever he went," Jeff said.

Again, Jeff eyed Evan, looking at him as though he didn't quite trust him. There was an odd blankness in Evan's expression, and Jeff had the impression he knew more than he was letting on.

"So what're we gonna do about it?" Fred Bowen piped in. Fred had an edge of nervousness about him that never went away. When he was really upset, he even stuttered, but the kids felt bad for him and never made fun of him.

Fred didn't speak much. Maybe, it was because of the stutter. Or it might be because he lived in Chelsea, right outside of Boston. He had a shy quality that had always made Jeff feel sorry for him. The first summer they met at Camp Tapiola, when they were eight, Fred had confided in Jeff, telling him about how his stepfather, who was a drunk who worked at the docks, beat up on him on a regular basis—especially when he was drunk, which was most of the time. The two weeks at camp, he said, were the only time all year when he felt as though he could actually breathe. Jeff couldn't imagine living with such fear in his life, and it bothered him that, even with the safety of his friends at camp, Fred never seemed to relax fully.

"We can't *do* anything," Evan said, straightening up and drawing everyone's attention away from Jeff. "The counselors and staff are gonna organize a search party. 'Sides, he couldn't have gone far…certainly not off the island."

"How do we know he didn't take a canoe or try to swim?" Jeff asked. "Has anyone checked to see if all the boats are in?"

Evan pursed his lips and shook his head.

"Do you think maybe he got, you know, like, homesick and took off?" Tyler asked.

Jeff snorted with derision. "He lives in freakin' Connecticut, f'rchrissakes. What do you think he's gonna do, walk home?"

"I think we should be in the search parties," Evan said. "The more people involved, the better chances of finding him."

Tyler's blue eyes suddenly lit up. "You mean like a camp-wide hide 'n seek?"

"Island-wide," Mike said. "There's no guarantee he stayed on the campgrounds."

"This is freakin' serious," Jeff said, feeling a surge of anger at Tyler and Mike. He wanted to tell them about the bad feeling he had, but he wasn't quite sure how to explain it. He didn't want any of them to think he was nuts or something, either, especially if Jimmy showed up later and was perfectly fine.

But he's not *perfectly fine,* Jeff thought. *He's not fine at all because he's dead.*

He had no idea how he knew that or even why he would think it, but he was convinced it was the truth. It was just a matter of time before everyone else at camp found out.

The boys fell silent when Mark broke away from the other counselors and walked back to the tent. He stared down at the ground as he walked, and it bothered Jeff to see him looking so upset. It was obvious the adults in charge had begun to realize just how serious this situation was. Jeff had the distinct impression the counselors weren't sure how to handle it.

"All right," Mark said, standing a short distance from the tent and rubbing his hands together as he looked from one boy to another. "We're not sure what's going on here, but until we locate Jimmy, we've decided to ground everyone to their tents." A collective groan went up from everyone in the tent.

"That's not fair," someone behind Jeff said. It sounded like Mike, but Jeff didn't turn to look. He kept staring at Mark, unnerved by how frightened he looked.

"You ask me what I think?" Mark continued, his head lowered. "I think Jimmy's hiding someplace, maybe thinking this is a game or something and how it's real funny, but this is *serious*. If he's in any kind of trouble, we have to find him as soon as we can."

"So how come we can't help?" Jeff said. He got up from his bed and walked toward Mark. Once he stepped out of the shade of the tent, the sun was warm on his back, but it wasn't enough to drive away the chill twisting like a knot of snakes in his stomach. "We could form teams, maybe by tent, and search the whole island from one end to the other if we have to."

"Like a camp-wide game," Mike said. Most of the other campers scowled and shook their heads when they looked at him.

"What?" he said, looking from face to face. "You're looking at me like I got poop on my face."

"Be a first if you didn't," Evan whispered.

"This isn't a goddamned game," Mark said, apparently unaware that he had sworn in front of his campers. "If Jimmy thinks he's playing a joke on us, it's not funny, and I'm sure Mr. Farnham will notify his parents and have them come and pick him up and take him home. But if he's in any kind of trouble…"

Jeff didn't like the way Mark left the thought unfinished. It meant that maybe Mark already knew, too, that something really bad had happened to Jimmy.

"Okay, then," Mark said, rubbing his hands together. "Tell you what. You guys hang here for a bit, and I'll talk it over with Mr. Farnham." He clenched his right hand into a fist and shook it for emphasis. "Until then, though, you guys have to promise you'll be cool and stay in the tent. Can I count on you?"

There was another chorus of moans and complaints, but everyone agreed.

"You can read or sleep or write a letter home," he said, and with that, he turned and walked away. He and the group of counselors headed toward the camp director's cabin.

"Farnham don't know dick," Fred said as the boys watched Mark go. "I say screw it. One of our pals is missing, and he might be in trouble. I say we do something about it *now!*"

Jeff shot Fred a questioning look. It wasn't like Fred to be defiant like this.

"We just promised Mark we'd be cool," he said, but he also knew that, no matter what anyone did, in the end it wasn't going to matter.

It was already too late.

Although he had never seen a real dead person, when he closed his eyes, the pool of blackness he saw was like staring into Jimmy Foster's cold, blank, lifeless eyes.

♣ ♣ ♣

As it turned out, the boys spent the rest of the afternoon in their tents. As the sun began to set, a few counselors—not including Mark—came back to the tents and collected the boys to bring them to a late supper. None of the counselors and older staff spoke much, and other than the clank of plates and the clatter of silverware, the evening meal was much quieter than usual.

Throughout the day, the knot of nervous tension in Jeff's stomach only got worse. He found he didn't have much of an appetite, but he forced himself to eat anyway because the care package his mother had sent him during the first week of camp had long since disappeared. He didn't want to wake up in the middle of the night hungry.

"So what d'yah think happened to him?" Evan asked, leaning close to Jeff across the table. His mouth was full, and he made loud sucking sounds as he chewed.

Jeff bit down on his lower lip, shrugged, and shook his head. He didn't dare say what he knew was on everyone's mind. They all should just admit they knew Jimmy was dead.

"No fuckin' clue," Jeff said, not realizing he had just sworn. He didn't know what the problem was when the counselor at their table—a guy named Ferguson or "Ferggie"—glared at him.

Years later, Jeff could never remember what the cook had served that night for supper. Probably Spam, but whatever it was, Jeff knew he didn't eat much…if anything. The knot in his stomach got so bad he thought he might never be able to eat again. He'd probably end up in the infirmary, where Mrs. Stott, the camp nurse, would force him to eat. All he knew was eating wasn't what he needed.

What he needed was to find out what had happened to Jimmy. He wished he could block out the terrible thoughts and images that filled his head. But the tension came to an end when Mr. Farnham, the camp director, entered the dining hall just as the designated campers were clearing the tables before dessert.

The ashen look on Farnham's face and the fixed, blank stare in his eyes said it all as he walked to the front of the room by the fireplace and, grabbing the nearest chair, leaned against the back of it with both hands clutching the top spindles. Jeff was close enough to see that Farnham's lower lip was trembling, and his eyes were filmed with tears.

Oh Jesus, Jeff thought, shrinking into his seat. *I knew it!… I knew it!*

Mr. Farnham cleared his throat, but when he began to speak, his voice choked off. Any other time, this would have gotten a ripple of laughter from the boys, but the room remained stone silent.

"I—ahh…" Farnham's voice choked off, and he lowered his head and wiped his eyes. After taking a deep breath, he squared his shoulders and raised his head. After scanning the assembled campers in silence for a moment, he said, "This is perhaps the most difficult thing I have ever had to do."

It was obvious he was struggling to maintain control.

"After searching the campgrounds and the immediate area, we have—we have found Jimmy Foster."

Almost everyone in the room either sighed or gasped, but Jeff's throat closed off with an audible click. He knew what was coming.

"Unfortunately—" Once again Farnham's voice cut off, making him sound like someone was strangling him, "Unfortunately he…uhh…he's had an accident…a serious accident."

Now a collective gasp went up from the campers. Someone, Jeff had no idea who, started to cry.

"Apparently he came down to the swimming area while it was unattended, and he—uh, he fell into the lake. I—I'm sorry to say this, but unfortunately he…he drowned."

Another, louder gasp of shock and surprise went through the crowd. Mr. Farnham's words echoed in Jeff's ears like a rolling thunderclap. He clenched his hands into fists as the blood drained out of his head. Tiny white dots of light spun crazily across his vision, and all he could think was: *I knew it!*

As stunned as everyone else, he looked at his friends, all seated around the table. A feeling of desperate sadness all but overwhelmed him. He locked eyes with Evan for a moment and felt compelled to say something, but he had no idea what he would say or even if he'd be able to speak.

The thought that his friends…every single one of them—Evan and Fred and Tyler and Mike…even himself—were going to die froze his voice in his throat. He barely had control of his eyes as he shifted them back and forth from friend to friend and tried to comprehend this horrible thought. The coldness that had gripped him all afternoon settled deeper into his stomach, sending tendrils into his chest.

He wondered if this feeling of dread would ever go away.

In that instant, something fundamental had changed in him.

This was the moment he first realized that life is all too real, and we're all going to die some day. Even then, he knew it was something he would never be able to ignore or forget.

"Oh my God," one of the counselors at a table behind him said in a hushed, broken voice. "I can't *believe* it."

When Jeff turned to see who had spoken, all he could see was a sea of blank, shocked faces with wide-open eyes and mouths that gaped open in stunned amazement and horror.

Mr. Farnham was still talking. Jeff was vaguely aware that he had been talking all along, but he hadn't heard a thing he said. He was going on and on about how he would have to contact all of their parents and ask them to come and pick them up as soon as possible. The camp season was over.

This was the last day of summer.

As soon as what Farnham was saying registered on Jeff, he glanced at Fred and saw a glaze of tears in his eyes. He suspected Fred was thinking, not about

Jimmy being dead, but about how horrible his life was going to be as soon as he got back home.

Mr. Farnham acknowledged that closing camp early would cause problems for many of the campers, since there were still four days left in the season, but he assured them that he would make arrangements for anyone who had to stay the full time. Otherwise, tomorrow morning, he would begin making phone calls to their homes, and they should start packing.

"Man, this sucks," Evan said, leaning close to Jeff.

Jeff couldn't look at his friend. He was only dimly aware that he was crying.

When he turned and looked away, his gaze shifted to the windows facing the lake. The sun had dropped behind the mountains to the west, and long shadows stretched across the campgrounds. Blue light suddenly flashed so fast Jeff's first thought was a bolt of lightning had struck somewhere nearby. He stared at the gathering darkness, waiting for the clap of thunder to come. Instead, a split second later, another flash lit up the darkening landscape.

Jeff's next thought was that someone was outside taking photographs, and their flashbulbs were lighting up the area. But as he stared out the window, more flashes came until he saw they were in a regular pattern. It was the flash of police emergency lights.

Jeff suddenly knew exactly what was going on.

The police and probably an ambulance boat from the mainland were here to pick up Jimmy's body.

Mr. Farnham was making such a big deal in front of the campers because he wanted to divert their attention from what was going on outside so they wouldn't see what was happening.

Jeff shifted his eyes back to Mr. Farnham and then, without a word, slid his chair back and stood up.

"Where you going?" Ferggie asked.

"I—uh, I have to go to the bathroom." Jeff kept his voice low because Mr. Farnham was still detailing their plans for tomorrow.

"Make it quick," Ferggie said, scowling.

Jeff nodded and, ducking low so he wouldn't draw attention to himself, wove his way between the tables down the short corridor to the bathroom. A few steps past the bathroom door on the left was an exit.

With a quick look to see if anyone was watching him, Jeff pushed the screen door open and stepped out onto the small porch. He eased the door back carefully so the spring wouldn't snap it back too fast and make it slam. After another glance to make sure no counselors had noticed what he was doing, he jumped off the landing and started running toward the beach and the flashing blue lights.

As he got closer, he slowed down and, keeping to the darkest shadows of the pine trees that lined the beach, approached the scene with caution. As Jeff had expected, a police boat was pulling up to one of the docks that defined the beginner's swimming area. Two other boats had stopped and were waiting further out. It looked like the entire police force of Arden, the nearest town, was here along with several volunteers.

What caught his attention was the group of people gathered on the beach. The searchlight from the police boat was directed on the beach, illuminating four men who were struggling with a stretcher with a sheet draped over it. The sheet had a slight bulge in the middle that had a sharply defined shadow, cast by the harsh glare of the searchlight.

Jeff knew exactly what was making that bulge.

"Oh my God," he whispered, trying to comprehend that Jimmy was under that white sheet.

Jeff's knees had turned to jelly, and he had to lean against a pine tree to keep from falling down.

The men struggled a bit in the sand as they made their way with the stretcher to the dock. They were going to load it and its burden onto the ambulance boat and leave. After that, he would never see his friend Jimmy Foster again.

No…this can't be happening, he thought as he stared in stunned amazement at the activity on the beach.

He glanced over his shoulder at the dining hall and the row of cabins that lined the pathway behind it. Everything looked so ordinary…so quiet…so safe, but then the sound of someone speaking over the police radio on the boat snapped his attention back to what was happening on the beach. Pressing the side of his face against the pine tree, he watched the men as they approached the water's edge with their burden. One of the policemen in the boat got out and walked down the dock toward them.

Without making a conscious decision, Jeff pushed off from the tree and, moving mechanically, like a robot, started walking toward them. The muscles in his legs were trembling violently as he headed in a straight line that would intersect the men before they reached the dock. Everyone on the scene was focused on what they were doing, so they didn't notice Jeff until he was less than twenty feet away from the men carrying the stretcher.

"Hey! Kid! You ain't supposed to be here," one of the men shouted.

Jeff looked at him with a blank stare. The town cop was moving toward him, so he broke into a run.

"He was my friend," Jeff said in a high, strangled voice. Tears streamed from his eyes, blurring his vision and turning the late afternoon light into a smear of shadows and darkness, pierced by the blue flashing light.

Another man who was closer to Jeff reached out and snagged him by the arm, but Jeff twisted out of his grasp and kept running without breaking stride.

"He was my friend," he said again before his voice climbed into a wild, ragged scream. Once he was close to the stretcher, he lunged forward. Before any of the men could react, he grabbed the sheet and tore it away.

What he saw staggered him.

He let out a loud, barking bray that echoed from the nearby forest.

Jimmy was lying on his back with his eyes wide open. Unblinking. The glassy surface reflected the flashing police light with an unnatural brilliance. His head was turned to one side, probably from the men trying to move away from Jeff as he ran toward them. Jimmy's thin, dark hair was wet and plastered to his skull in tiny curlicues. Except for the dark bruises under his eyes, his skin was as white as the sheet that covered him. It looked like someone had smudged his face with soot from a campfire. His arms and legs looked like sun-bleached sticks with tiny blue lines under the skin, but it was his throat that caught and held Jeff's attention.

That night and years later Jeff tried hard to convince himself it had just been a shadow cast by the police lights…or maybe some water weeds still clung to his skin, because it was obvious Jimmy had been pulled from the lake.

Whatever the cause, there was a dark slash that angled across Jimmy's throat just below his jaw line.

"Come on, kid," one of the volunteer firemen said. "Get the hell outta here."

The man didn't sound all that angry, and when Jeff looked at him, there was an expression of sadness in his eyes.

"He…" Jeff started to say, but he had to stop and take a watery breath. "He was one of my friends."

There was no way he could absorb what he was seeing, but one of the men quickly covered up Jimmy's body again, and they stepped up onto the dock.

Taking Jeff gently by the arm, the volunteer fireman led him up from the beach. The feeling of abandoning his friend overwhelmed Jeff. All he could think was he couldn't let them do this. He had to stop them from taking Jimmy away. They shouldn't be putting him on that ambulance boat and leaving. He and Jimmy were best friends.

They were B.F.F.

He should stay with him so Jimmy, who always got scared when Mark told them a scary story at night, wouldn't be alone.

"There's nothing more you can do, son," the man said, his voice low and comforting.

Jeff knew he was right, but he couldn't stop stammering, "But he's my best…he's my best—" until, finally, his voice choked off.

A heavy wave of darkness spread across his sight as he looked up at the sky. High overhead, the first few stars glittered. A crescent moon shined down on the beach, its reflection rippling like white ribbons in the dark water. The pine trees were all leaning inward. The dark slashes of branches looked like widening cracks in the sky. Jeff was afraid that any second now pieces of the sky were going to break off and come crashing down on him.

"You okay there kid?" the man beside him asked. His hand rested lightly on Jeff's shoulder, but his voice seemed to be coming from someplace far, far away.

Jeff turned and looked at him, but it felt as though his head didn't stop moving. It kept turning, spinning around on his neck like a child's top. The world became a kaleidoscope of flashing blue light, smeared faces, dark figures of people moving around him, and tall, black trees that writhed like snakes. Shimmering pools of bright yellow and white light dazzled his vision. And then, with a loud whooshing roar, everything went black.

❦ ❦ ❦

Some time later—he had no idea when—Jeff regained consciousness.

He was lying on something soft, but he knew it wasn't his bunk in the tent or his bed back at home. When his vision cleared a bit, he found himself looking up at Mr. Farnham's face. He was bending over him with an expression of genuine concern.

"Hello there," Farnham said in a whisper. "How are you feeling?"

Jeff licked his lips to answer but couldn't. His mouth was dry, and when he tried to speak, the only sound that came out was a strangled croak.

"Would you like a sip of water?"

This was a woman's voice, and Jeff finally realized he was in the camp infirmary. Mrs. Stott, the camp nurse, appeared at the bedside and held a glass with a straw up to his mouth. Jeff pursed his lips and sucked, amazed at how refreshing the tiny sip of water was on his parched throat.

"Whoa. Not too much," Mrs. Stott said. She slipped the straw out of his mouth before he could protest.

"Wha—what happened?" Jeff asked.

"You fainted," Farnham said. For an instant, his expression hardened, but then he sighed and rubbed his forehead, wincing as though suffering some deep, internal pain.

The Wildman

"You know," Farnham continued, "you shouldn't have gone out there. I was hoping the police would take care of things so you campers wouldn't have to see what was going on."

"What *was* going on?" Jeff asked. He was surprised that he would actually challenge an adult—the camp director, no less. "What happened to Jimmy?"

Mr. Farnham looked away and shook his head slowly from side to side.

"That's up to the authorities to determine," he said. "My responsibility is to protect my campers."

Protect us like you did Jimmy? Jeff wanted to ask, but he remained silent. It frightened him to see the obvious confusion and hurt in Mr. Farnham's expression.

"I have a lot of phone calls to make tonight and tomorrow so you boys can go home." Farnham paused and took a breath. When he swallowed, his throat made a funny gulping sound. "This has been a terrible, *terrible* thing, but we can all pull together and get through it. Right?"

Not entirely sure why Mr. Farnham needed his reassurance, Jeff nodded slightly. The slight motion sent a blaze of pain through his neck.

"Mrs. Stott will take good care of you, Jeff. I have a lot of things to attend to." Farnham reached down and patted Jeff on the shoulder before turning to leave.

Raising himself up and supporting himself on his elbows, Jeff watched Farnham walk out of the infirmary. The spring on the screen door made a loud *twang* as it stretched out and then pulled the door back, slamming it shut with a bang as loud as a gun.

Somehow, although he hadn't been there to see or hear it, Jeff associated that sound with the slamming of Jimmy Foster's coffin lid as it locked away one of his best friends in total, eternal darkness.

With these and other disturbing thoughts in his mind, Jeff closed his eyes and let out a long, slow moan. Falling back onto the bed, he settled his head on the pillow. The single clearest thought he had was—

There...at last...I finally saw a real dead person.

Chapter Three

Arrival

"**SO YOU'RE NOT** even a little bit creeped out about going back there?"

Standing in his kitchen, Jeff hunched his shoulder to tuck the phone against his ear as he poured himself a generous shot of rum. This was his second one tonight. He never had a second shot, but he was pretty sure he needed one tonight because of the direction this conversation with Tyler was taking.

"Not really," Tyler said after a short pause that made Jeff suspect he might really feel otherwise. "It was so long ago, you know? I can't say as I've really given it all that much thought."

"Seriously?"

Jeff narrowed his eyes and took a sip of rum, luxuriating for a moment as he swallowed. The liquor warmed his throat and stomach, and he had no doubt it was going to go to his head fast. He was already a bit unsteady on his feet.

"Really. I mean…Come on. We were just kids, and it was what? Like, thirty-five years ago."

"Yeah, but—"

"It's not like any of us really *knew* Jimmy Foster or anything. He wasn't an important part of our lives all the time or anything. He was just like the rest of us—some kid from some town we'd probably never even heard of who showed up at camp for two weeks, and then went back home for the rest of the year."

"Hmmm…" Jeff said. "He was gone, all right."

"We came from all over New England. It's not like we lost our best friend from our school or neighborhood or something."

"I know, but—"

Jeff interrupted himself to take another swallow of rum. He knew he was getting good and buzzed, and should stop now, but he convinced himself this was a good thing. It would blunt some of the more unsettling memories this conversation was dredging up.

"Look, Jeff. I didn't see what you saw." Tyler's voice dropped to a low, calm pitch…or maybe, Jeff thought, the rum was hitting him a lot harder and faster than he realized. "None of us saw what you saw. And I can understand how you might be a lot more freaked out about the whole thing than the rest of us. Christ, you were practically a celebrity because of what you did."

"But I didn't *do* anything."

"Bull. You actually got to *see* Jimmy after he was dead. Do you have any idea how pissed off Bloomberg and some of the other counselors were?"

"It wasn't that big a deal," Jeff said, but even as he said it, he knew he was lying. The image of Jimmy Foster lying there on the stretcher—cold, pale, and *dead*—was seared into his brain. He had carried it with him his whole life, but it was something he simply didn't like thinking about.

"But you can't say it didn't creep you out." he said, lowering his voice as he stared at the rum in his glass. "Even after you found out what had happened?"

Tyler sniffed over the phone, and Jeff could just imagine him shaking his head.

"No one really knows what happened to him. My parents never told me what, if anything, they heard."

"You ever ask them?"

"Hell, no. They both died quite a few years ago, in a plane crash. I never got the chance to… if I had wanted to. I never thought about it."

Jeff didn't hear even the slightest hesitation in his friend's voice, and he wondered how deeply his parents' death had affected him.

Is it something—like Jimmy Foster's death—that he never thought about?

Or had it affected him so deeply he doesn't allow himself to think or feel anything about it?

"But the police came to your house and talked to you about it once you got home from camp, didn't they?"

"Of course they did. As far as I know, they talked to everyone who was at camp when it happened—campers, counselors, staff. You must know what happened to Mr. Farnham."

Jeff was in the middle of taking another sip of rum, and he started to choke on it when he tried to speak. The liquor burned the back of his throat and nasal passages.

The Wildman

"I know that was the last summer Camp Tapiola was open." Jeff's nose was still stinging, and his eyes started to water. "They closed the place down, but my parents told me they'd never let me go back there no matter what. Years later, I heard that Farnham was sued by Jimmy's parents."

"His mother, anyway," Tyler said. "His father had died a few years before Jimmy did."

"Really? How do you know that?"

"Jimmy told me."

It surprised Jeff that Tyler knew something about Jimmy that he didn't.

"Anyway," Jeff said. "From what I understand, things got so messed up because of the legal shit-storm surrounding Jimmy's murder he had to—"

"Whoa. Hold on a second, bucko."

"What?"

"You just said Jimmy's *murder*."

"I did?"

Tyler grunted.

"Yeah. I guess I did." Jeff hesitated a moment and sneaked another quick sip of rum. "But he *was* murdered. I saw his throat, and it was cut wide open."

"As far as I know, no-one official ever concluded that's what happened."

"Come on, man."

Jeff wondered why he was getting so heated. Was it because Tyler's a lawyer and has to have a mountain of substantiated, verifiable proof? Or was it simply too unnerving to think about Jimmy's death, even after all these years?

"His friggin' throat was cut, Tyler. I know what I saw!"

"He maybe had a wound on his throat," Tyler said. "But there was never anything about his throat being *cut*. He went down to the swimming area, fell in, and drowned."

"Yeah. That's what my folks kept telling me," Jeff said, "but I checked it out later. Some Maine newspapers labeled it murder. A murder that's never been solved."

"I thought you said you didn't think about it. When'd you do all of this?"

Jeff realized he had said too much already, but now that it was out there, he knew Tyler wasn't about to let him off the hook.

"A long time ago," he said.

"So this *has* been an issue for you," Tyler said, his voice fairly dripping with accusation.

Or is he trying to piss me off? Jeff wondered.

"Sure. It's something I've paid attention to some. But I wouldn't say it's been an *issue* for me, exactly."

"Well…" Tyler sighed deeply. "I can't say as I'd blame you. Like I said, the rest of us never saw what you saw."

Someone else did…the person who killed him, Jeff was about to say, but he kept quiet and took another swallow of rum instead. The glass was already half-empty, and Jeff was definitely a "half-empty", not a "half-full" kind of guy. He reached for the bottle to top off his drink.

"The way you're talking, though," Tyler said. "Maybe you're right. Maybe you shouldn't come to the reunion. It might dredge up too many of these memories for you."

"I never said that, but…well…I dunno. I just asked if the whole idea creeped you out, and obviously it doesn't."

"But it *does* creep you out."

"A little…yeah."

"Good. At least you admit it."

Jeff could easily imagine that this was the tone of voice he used when he knew he was winning a case in court.

"And I, for one, would be really bummed if you didn't come."

"Oh, I probably will."

Jeff glanced at the clock and saw that it was already past eleven. Six o'clock came early. He had to get to bed, so he said a quick goodbye to Tyler and hung up. He staggered a bit as he made his way slowly up the stairs to the bedroom, turning lights off behind him as he went. His head was spinning, but that didn't stop the rush of thoughts and memories and images that filled his mind when he lay down to sleep.

Thanks to the rum, though, he drifted off quicker than usual. Still, his sleep was thin and disturbed.

❦ ❦ ❦

Over the next several weeks, scores of emails and a few telephone calls went back and forth among the friends. Jeff kept going along with the plans, but he was more and more determined to ditch the whole thing once it got a little closer.

July passed into August with another long stretch of scorching, humid weather. Then, toward the end of the month, the days began to get shorter, and the nights cooled off noticeably. Good sleeping weather, people called it.

During this time, work at Bayside Realty remained steady if not hectic, and Jeff felt a growing agitation. Maybe it was the upcoming reunion, but he had begun an exchange of hostile emails and telephone calls with Susan concerning child support for Matt. She had married someone she had known and dated back in high school, and she had relocated to California. Jeff argued that, if he was going to have full custody of Matt, she was going to have to start paying him child support.

Susan wouldn't yield.

She insisted their divorce agreement was finalized, and it fully covered her commitment regarding joint custody and child support. There was no provision about any changes based of either one of them remarrying. Jeff countered that it had never crossed his mind either one of them would ever remarry, especially so soon, but Susan insisted that it was *his* and his *lawyer's* fault for not planning for that contingency. No matter how many times he told her he had trusted her to do what was fair and reasonable, if only because the welfare of their son was involved, she wouldn't budge.

"If I'm ever gonna get married again, I'll find a woman I hate and give her a house and car," Jeff said more times than he cared to remember. It usually made his friends at the office laugh, but he was half-convinced he meant it.

The difference was, in his case, *he* had kept the house and car. He wanted to keep them if only to provide Matt some illusion of stability while he was off to college, even if the house *was* much too big for him, now that he was living alone. The cost of upkeep made it so he had little to no discretionary income; not that having a kid in college allowed much discretionary income.

As the weekend for the reunion drew closer, Jeff began to think how it might not be such a bad idea after all to hook up with some old friends. He could really use a weekend away, drinking and reminiscing with people who had known him long before he married Susan. Evan had finally settled on a weekend, the last weekend of October, a few days before Hallowe'en. Everyone agreed this was a good time for them, and they began to make their plans to rendezvous at the landing dock on Shore Road, where Evan would meet them with a boat and take them over to Sheep's Head Island and Camp Tapiola.

For a while, Jeff had argued that going out so late in the year might be a colossal mistake. The way he remembered it, the temperature had dropped close to freezing on a couple of nights when they were there in the middle of July.

Imagine it in October? ... a lake in western Maine? ... sleeping in an uninsulated, unheated building?

That didn't sound very appealing.

If they were still kids, it might be an exciting adventure, but at their age? No way.

The other guys, especially Evan, scoffed at him via email for sounding like a pussy and for lacking imagination. The problem was, Jeff could imagine all too easily how things could go wrong. If, and if was still a big *if*, he even went to the reunion he would be sure to bring plenty of rum to keep him warm and pleasantly buzzed for the entire weekend. Hell, maybe he'd even see if he could score some weed. That would certainly make for a fun weekend.

The month of September was rainy and much colder than usual. Jeff hoped Evan would finally see reason and call the whole thing off until next spring. But Evan insisted that, as soon as the ice was out of the lake come spring, his construction company was going to bring in bulldozers and other machinery to start tearing apart the old campgrounds. By June of next year, the island would be unrecognizable. If they wanted one last chance to see where they had spent a short but significant time of their lives…if they wanted to recapture some childhood memories, this was their one and only chance.

Do I really need this? Jeff wondered, but somehow in the end, he wasn't really sure why, he made the decision to go.

Jeff offered to meet Tyler at the Portland Jetport when his flight from LA arrived. It might be a good idea not to face this entirely on his own. Besides, it would be nice to drive out to camp with one of his friends and catch up, one on one.

Tyler nixed all that, telling Jeff he planned to come to Maine a few days earlier and spend some time driving around coastal Maine before heading over to the camp. Jeff couldn't afford to take any extra time off work, not if he wanted any vacation time when Matt was home from college on Christmas break, so that Thursday night he got packed. He made sure he took Matt's down-filled sleeping bag along with plenty of warm clothing.

As it was, on the Friday of the reunion, Jeff had to go into the office in the morning to take care of some last-minute paperwork, so he was late getting started. The drive out of Portland was pleasant enough, even though the foliage was a few weeks past peak and the "blue-crested leaf peepers" had gone back south to their retirement homes in Florida. When he got to Gorham, he stopped at the local *Shop 'n Save* where he picked up his share of the groceries for the weekend. They had all agreed who would bring what, but as he wandered up and down the aisles, Jeff kept picking up impulse items that it wasn't his responsibility to bring.

Just in case, he kept telling himself.

He also bought a few more bottles of rum at the agency liquor store next door to the supermarket. He had already packed three bottles of Myers, but he wanted to have a few more just in case the other guys wanted to partake. He was looking forward to this weekend with a curious mixture of anticipation and dread, and he definitely didn't want to run out alcohol.

The Wildman

From Gorham, he drove west on Route 25 to Limington and then headed north along winding back roads toward Alden and Lake Onwego. The posted speed limit was never above 35 MPH, but there were long stretches of open road where he nudged it up closer to sixty. Late in the day, he finally reached the turn for Shore Road which led down to the boat landing where, just like when he was a kid, he would meet the boat that would take him over to Camp Tapiola.

This far away from civilization, Arden being the nearest town, cell phone service was spotty at best, but earlier in the week, Jeff had arranged for Evan to meet him at the landing at four o'clock. Surprisingly, even though he'd gotten such a late start, he was only fifteen minutes late.

As his car bumped and rattled along the rutted dirt road leading down to the lake, a cold rush of tension started building up inside him. He was concerned that he might not recognize Evan or anyone else after all these years. They had talked about swapping photos online, but Evan had argued that it would be a lot more fun and surprising if they waited to see how everyone looked when they all met in person.

Besides, who else would be out here in the willy-whacks this late in the year?

Jeff was self-conscious about his receding hairline and the extra girth he carried around his middle, but he told himself not to worry. Chances were, Evan and the rest of the guys had all gained more weight and lost more hair than he had. All things considered, Jeff thought he'd held up fairly well over the years.

Lost in thought as he was, he missed the turn to the landing and drove past it when it came up faster than he had been expecting. The road that had seemed so long when he was a kid now struck him as short and actually rather pathetic.

Embarrassed by his mistake, even though there was no one there to see it, he drove a short way down the road, turned around quickly, and drove back to the turnoff. It was another half-mile or so to the landing.

When he pulled into the parking area, there were already four cars parked there—a green Volvo, a black Prius, a rusted Chevy pickup truck, and a small blue Toyota, which was obviously a rental. As he pulled to a stop beside the Volvo, Jeff tried to guess whose was whose. The only one he was sure of was the rental, which had to be Tyler's.

Down by the lake, a person was standing on the dock next to the boat launch where a small motorboat was tied up. The sun reflected off the water behind him, so it was hard for Jeff to see the person's face.

That's got to be Evan, Jeff thought.

The person silhouetted against the lake looked up and raised one hand. He waved it wildly as he started walking up the slope to where Jeff had parked.

"Christ on a cross," Evan called out, his voice light and tinged with merriment as Jeff killed the engine and got out of his car. He was parked on the crest where the steep road led down to the water.

"I swear to Christ…who'd a thunk it?"

"Evan?" Jeff said tentatively as he pocketed his car keys and walked down the hill to meet his friend. They shook hands vigorously and then just stood there for a long moment, staring at each other. Neither one of them seemed to know what to say or do next until Evan slapped Jeff on the shoulder and asked, "So how was the drive out? You find the place all right?"

"Oh, yeah. Only a couple of wrong turns," Jeff said. He smiled as he stroked his chin and took a deep breath while looking out over the lake. The powerful scent of pine resin, just like he remembered when he was a kid, filled him with a powerful surge of nostalgia. A stiff breeze was blowing in off the lake, churning the blue-gray water and making the waves sparkle like diamonds in the slanting sunlight. There was a chill in the air. Jeff shivered and hugged himself to try to stay warm. Off in the distance, already darkened by shadows because of the mountains to the west, he could discern the outlines of Sheep's Head Island and the camp, about a mile out on the water.

But as nice as this initial impression was, once again—as he had so many times right up until this moment—Jeff wondered why he had agreed to come out here. The prospect of being essentially stranded on an island for the whole weekend with people he hardly knew and hadn't seen in so long they might just as well be strangers didn't seem all that appealing.

"So…everyone else seems to have made it already." Jeff nodded at the line of parked cars.

"We're getting settled in just fine," Evan said with a wide smile. He chuckled and shook his head as though privately amused at something. The slanting sunlight illuminated his face, deepening the thin, dark wrinkles around his eyes and mouth. "I've been out here for a couple of days, getting things set up for you, but I gotta tell you, man, the place has really gone to shit."

"After thirty-five years, what do you expect?"

"Yeah, but…still, just wait 'till you see it. It's so freakin' weird to be back here."

"It looks a lot smaller than I remember," Jeff said simply.

"Of course it does. Everything was bigger because we were kids. I swear to God, there are times when I'm out there, I half-expect Bloomberg to come running down to tell me to get my butt back to the tent." Evan's eyes took on a distant glaze as he looked out across the water and sighed. "Remember Mark Bloomberg?"

"Who could forget him?"

Jeff gave him a twisted smile. The only image that sprang to mind was the look of worry and near panic he had seen on his counselor's face the afternoon he told his campers Jimmy Foster was missing. Even then, Mark must have known, as Jeff had known, that something terrible had happened.

"I wish he was still alive so he could have come, too," Jeff said. "Would've been nice to see him." He shivered and knew it wasn't just from the chilly breeze. "I can't believe he's dead. It seems so…I dunno…surreal."

"I know," Evan said as a dark frown flashed across his face. "I Googled him and found his obituary."

A strange tightness constricted Evan's voice and grabbed Jeff's attention. He assumed it was because Evan was as upset as he was about the death of someone who had meant a lot to all of them back when they were so young and impressionable.

"He never got married and was living in Lowell, teaching Phys Ed. at the high school. His obit said he was really active in Boy Scouts, too."

"Makes sense," Jeff said with a shrug. "He was a great counselor. I'm not at all surprised he ended up working with kids. How'd he die?"

"I'm not really sure," Evan said. "The obituary said he 'died unexpectedly', which I've always assumed means either suicide or overdose or something. You know, it's either that or 'died after a courageous struggle with cancer' or whatever."

"Shit," Jeff said, lowering his gaze and shaking his head.

For some reason, the thought that Mark Bloomberg was dead was really getting to him. Granted, Jeff had only been twelve years old the last time he had seen Mark. He figured his counselor must have been, what, maybe eighteen or nineteen years old that summer? But Jeff and the other guys in the tent had idolized Mark, and the idea that someone like Mark Bloomberg was mortal sent a shiver of frisson through him…especially, God forbid, if he had killed himself or overdosed. It just goes to show how you never really know.

"Count no man happy until he is dead," Jeff said.

"What's that?"

"Something from *Oedipus Rex*."

"Yeah…well. Whatever," Evan said, rubbing his hands together against the chill as an excited glow lit up his eyes. "You have a ton of stuff to carry?"

"A fair amount."

"Then let's get going."

"Did you check the weekend weather forecast?" Jeff asked as they walked back to his car. He popped the trunk open and started to grab stuff.

"Haven't had a chance for the last few days," Evan said. "Why?"

Jeff shrugged. "They're saying we might have a storm coming through later in the weekend, Saturday night. That's what they were predicting for the Portland area, anyway. They said there's a chance of showers that might be heavy on into Sunday. You know what that means."

"What?"

"We might get snow this far north."

"In October?" Evan scowled and waved his hand dismissively. "I doubt it. And anyways, we'll be fine…as long as you brought snowshoes."

When Jeff drew back and gave him a funny look, Evan swatted him on the arm.

"I'm just fuckin' with you," he said, but Jeff couldn't help but think how strange this whole encounter was. He couldn't deny the odd dissonance he felt, trying to relate to Evan as an adult while all he could do was try to see the twelve year old boy he had once been. The bottom line was, when they were kids, even though he and Evan had shared a deep and, at least they said so at the time, lasting friendship—

BFF.

—it had been so long ago it felt like it had happened to someone else.

He had no idea who this person was. Looking at him carefully now, Jeff thought Evan could be just about anybody. It took a real stretch of imagination to see the person Evan had once been. Jeff wondered if he had changed as much in Evan's eyes. He didn't feel much different, but you never knew…

"Well…one thing's still the same," Jeff said.

Evan shot him a quizzical look as he leaned into the trunk and grabbed some bags of groceries.

What's that?"

"None of the other guys bothered to show up to help. Are they still the same old lazy crew?"

Evan indicated the boat tied up to the dock.

"Boat's too small for all of us at once, anyway, not with all your stuff. When we leave on Sunday, we'll have to ferry people and luggage back and forth."

"Just like the old days," Jeff said with a grin.

"Yeah…just like the old days."

It took them a couple of trips from the car to the dock to get all of Jeff's supplies and luggage loaded into the boat. As the sun started to set, the wind picked up, carrying with it a biting chill. Jeff was glad he had packed some winter clothes. All he could think about was how he was probably going to freeze his sorry ass off, trying to sleep tonight.

Just like the old days, indeed…

The Wildman

Finally, once the boat was loaded, Evan fired up the engine, and Jeff cast off. He was glad he sat back down right away because Evan gunned the engine and cut a couple of sharp curves that would have thrown him overboard if he hadn't been sitting.

It wasn't long before the pounding of the boat on the water got to Jeff. He definitely didn't have his sea legs back, if he'd ever had them. Gripping the gunwales, he narrowed his eyes against the wind as Evan opened up the engine, pushing it as hard as he could.

Jeff didn't see any point in trying to carry on a conversation with the boat's engine whining so loudly and the cold wind whistling like a banshee in his ears. He felt self-conscious, knowing Evan, who was at the back of the boat, couldn't help but look at his back.

Maybe he was studying Jeff the way Jeff had looked at him, trying to see his childhood friend in this man he didn't really know.

Maybe he was trying to dig past all the years and see the little boy Jeff had been back then.

Or maybe he was studying him the way he was today, trying to figure out what kind of person he was.

With the cold wind tearing at his face, making tears stream from his eyes, Jeff stared straight ahead and watched as they approached the camp. A flood of memories swept through him as he scanned the shore from left to right. It struck him as funny how the horizon hadn't changed a bit after all in these years. There were the same sloping hills to the west and the same towering pines.

Some things never change, he thought, *or, if they do, it's at a pace too slow for anyone to notice.*

Further out on the lake, the water was a lot choppier. It banged the bottom of the boat hard enough to rattle Jeff's teeth, but he kept his jaw clenched tightly. It wasn't long before the chill worked its way into his bones.

When they were more than halfway to the island, Evan said something that Jeff couldn't hear above the roaring engine. Turning around and leaning closer, he shouted, "*What's that?*"

Evan smiled and, with a wave of one hand, indicated the shoreline to the right.

"This will all change soon," he shouted. "This coming spring, we'll break ground for the first houses and condos. Eventually, we'll have tennis courts and a swimming pool."

"Why do you need a swimming pool when the lake's right here?" Jeff shouted.

Evan either didn't hear him or else was ignoring him, so Jeff smiled and nodded as if what Evan had said was a terrific thing. The truth was, he couldn't deny a surge of sadness and even a bit of anger at Evan for everything that was going to be lost once the construction crews came in and started altering the landscape.

It was foolish, he knew, to feel so protective about a place he hadn't bothered to visit in the last thirty-five years. If it meant so much to him, why hadn't he come out here to have a look around? It wasn't all that far from Westbrook, a day trip, easily.

Regardless, his childhood memories were so tied up with this lake and the camp and the land around it that he was convinced what Evan was planning wasn't such a good idea.

"You ought to think about investing out here," Evan shouted.

He had to say it twice before Jeff made out what he said, but Jeff just smiled and shrugged.

Here comes the sales pitch already...

He had seen it coming.

Living in Portland and working in real estate, he had known all about Willow Creek's plans for the Lake Onwego area. He had also seen on the news that some of the locals and some environmentalists weren't so enamored with the plans. Since the project had first been announced three years ago, it had gotten tangled up in court with assorted land disputes. For the last year or so, there had been several instances of vandalism where the Willow Creek offices had been broken into and ransacked. Last spring, someone had tried to burn down the main office building, and many of the signs advertising the project in the area had been defaced with paint-ball shots and, in a few cases, shotgun blasts.

"Be a nice way to ensure you have a good retirement," Evan shouted, but Jeff shrugged again, pretending he couldn't hear him.

He turned and stared out over the churning gray water. Just like when he was a kid, it seemed to take forever to get to the island, and the closer they got, the more anticipation built up inside him. The pines were darkening, casting long shadows across the water now that the sun had dropped behind the mountains. The strip of sandy beach in front of the dining hall and what used to be the swimming area—

Where Jimmy drowned...was murdered!

—showed up like a white slash against the dark backdrop. Thirty or so feet up from the beach was the dining hall. When he saw it, Jeff couldn't ignore the cold lump that formed in his throat.

The Wildman

"Amazing, huh?" Evan called out as he cut the engine and brought the boat around so he was heading into the small cove where the swimming docks used to be.

Once they were out of the direct wind, Jeff tilted his head back and inhaled the aroma of the pines. The smell instantly brought back another rush of memories. It was all too easy to imagine he was a kid again who was arriving for a two-week stay at the camp. If it had been a little warmer and if there had been leaves on the trees, the illusion would have been complete.

But there was something else hanging in the air.

Something unsettling…maybe even menacing.

Jeff had no idea how he knew it was there, but he sensed a palpable presence hovering close to him in the gathering gloom. His eyes widened as they darted back and forth, scanning the cleared areas where the other buildings—the cabins and tent platforms and the old meeting hall—used to be. But his eyes were continually drawn back to the woods where deeper shadows lurked. The feeling of a presence lurking in the woods was overpowering.

Jeff's reverie was broken when the front door of the dining hall swung open, and three figures came out onto the porch and then started down the short flight of steps leading to the beach. Jeff raised his right arm in greeting, and the three men, now on the beach, waved back to him. He knew they were Tyler Smith, Fred Bowen, and Mike Logan, but in the deepening gloom, he had no idea who was who.

"Ahoy there, captain," a thin, dark-haired man who looked trim and physically fit called out.

Evan cut the engine, and the boat glided up onto the beach with a soft crunching whisper of sand and pebbles against the keel. It came to a sudden stop that jolted Jeff and would have thrown him forward if he hadn't been keeping a grip with his left hand on the gunwales.

The thin, dark-haired man waded out into the water and grabbed the bow of the boat. Leaning back, he dragged the boat further up onto the sand.

"Well I'll be a son of a bitch," the man said, smiling as he regarded Jeff. "I never thought in a million years you'd really make it."

"And here I am." Jeff said as he stood up, caught his balance, and then took the man's proffered hand and shook it. "How's it going, Tyler?"

Tyler had a good grip, firm and dry.

"'S gonna be one helluva weekend," Tyler said, his smile widening as he stood back and let Jeff clamber out of the boat and onto the beach.

Jeff didn't realize how tense he had been on the boat ride over until he was on solid land again and stretched to his full height. Hard knots tightened in his back and between his shoulder blades. He groaned as he leaned back and pressed his fist into the small of his back.

"Apparently I'm getting old just like the rest of you reprobates."

Everyone laughed at that as Fred and Mike approached the boat. Jeff's assumption had been right. The fat guy was Fred. The scrawny kid he had once been was all but unrecognizable beneath his fleshy adult features, but there was a youthful glint in his eye that indicated the old Fred was still in there somewhere. Mike had gained considerable weight, too, but his bulk looked more muscular than fat. He had a crushing grip when he and Jeff shook hands.

"Jesus H Christ," Mike said. "I hardly recognize yah."

Jeff sniffed with laughter, knowing if he had passed any of these men on the street, he would have walked past them without giving them a second glance. It was strange to think how these men, total strangers now, had once been his best friends, at least for two weeks every summer.

"Looks like you brought enough shit to last a week," Fred said, glancing at Evan, who was already unloading the boat, piling Jeff's things up on the sand.

"You never know," Jeff said with a chuckle. "We might get stranded here for days, if the weather forecast is right."

"How's that?" Fred asked, a look of concern in his eyes. "What'd you hear?"

"Storm might be moving in later this weekend," Jeff said. Realizing he didn't want to start the weekend off on a bad note, he added, "But I doubt it'll be much. If it is, you'll be grateful I brought as much stuff as I did."

"Long as you got plenty of beer," Mike said.

The bag Evan had just put down on the sand made a loud clinking sound, obviously bottles, and Mike's face brightened.

"Come on, you slugs," Evan said once the boat was empty. "Let's get this up into the dining hall."

"So that's where we're staying?" Jeff asked.

"Unless you want to sleep out under the stars."

"We got here early," Tyler said, "so we're already set up. I hope you brought a pad like one of them egg shell thingies or something for your sleeping bag, because that floor's gonna be hard as hell otherwise."

"It sure hasn't gotten any softer over the years," Mike said with a chuckle. He made a point of grabbing more stuff than anyone else and started back to the dining hall.

"Remember that night we missed the overnight because it was raining?" Fred said. "'N we 'camped out' in the dining hall and cooked S'mores?"

"How could I forget?" Jeff said.

The Wildman

With everyone helping, it only took them one trip to get all of Jeff's stuff and supplies off the beach. They deposited it in the semi-circle of everyone else's luggage and supplies. As he went about organizing his things, Jeff couldn't get past the sense of total unreality that was gripping him.

'Who are these people…and what the hell am I doing here?' He kept asking himself.

The sky was already pitch-black when they went back out to the beach so Evan could secure the boat for the night. It was much colder, too, but Jeff stopped and looked around at the old campgrounds, lit only by the stars and the wandering beams of their flashlights.

It seemed like a dream. He felt completely dissociated from himself, and he couldn't help but question who he really was and reflect on everything he had been so stressed out about lately. Everything seemed so far away now. It was like his life up until this instant had happened to someone else, and—finally—he was back where he truly belonged.

All in all, no matter how creeped out he might feel about being here with these people, this was definitely going to be one *hell* of an interesting weekend.

Chapter Four

Hobomock

LOGS CRACKLED, AND firelight cast a warm orange glow that filled the dining hall all the way up to the shadowed rafters where thick, dark cobwebs hung down like splashes of black ink. The shadows shifted crazily, and as Jeff eased back on his sleeping bag with drink in hand, he couldn't help but wonder how many bats or mice or *something* else were up there, scuttling around to avoid the light.

There was no electrical service on the island yet. It had been cut off years ago and hadn't been restored. Evan said he had to get the power back on in the spring, once construction started. Other than a handful of candles he had brought and the flashlights they all remembered to pack, the fire in the fireplace was their only source of light through the night. Evan promised, once the development got going, there would be cable TV and a microwave tower for cell phone service. It wouldn't be long before Sheep's Head Island and Camp Tapiola had all the amenities of civilization.

"Do we have a working toilet?" Jeff asked.

"A two-seater," Evan said.

There was a bathroom at the end of the short hallway, but it had obviously been out of order for decades. Jeff had poked his head in just long enough to determine that the room was off limits for the duration.

"There's a Port-a-Potty just outside the side door," Evan said. He sounded a bit defensive, as if he didn't like Jeff or anyone criticizing his accommodations. "What more do you want?"

"How about a place to take a dump without freezing my goddamned ass off?" Jeff said. He and everyone else except Evan laughed at that. For now, though, the men would have to make do with the primitive resources they had.

And make do they did.

After Jeff was settled and everyone was plying a drink, the men cobbled together a more than passable supper of hot dogs, baked beans, brown bread, and fresh salad, which Fred had brought. The only refrigeration they had was the coolers they brought, but as long as there was beer and wine…plenty of beer and wine…they'd be set. Mike had brought a box of twenty Cuban cigars just for the occasion, and everyone except Evan lit up after supper. Dense clouds of blue smoke rose into the darkness above them as they eased back and talked. After thirty-five years, there was plenty to catch up on.

Jeff already knew that Evan was married, had two kids, and lived in Medford, Mass., but he didn't learn a whole lot more about Evan's real estate development business. Truth was, he was grateful Evan didn't try any more hard sell on them, but he was sure the pitch to invest would come before the weekend was out. Evan had to be using this weekend as a tax write-off.

Jeff learned that Fred had been married and divorced twice and was no longer looking for a woman to be a part of his life. After Jeff dropping his standard line about how if he was ever going to remarry, he'd buy a woman he hated a house and car, he let Fred tell them about his job as manager of the water filtration plant in a small town in Vermont. Jeff noticed that Fred didn't talk much about his personal life, but that was fine with him. He remembered Fred as being, maybe not shy, but at least reluctant to talk about his feelings.

Mike let everyone know that he had never gotten married and was still single, living with his aging mother to help her out. After Tyler expressed surprise that Mike had never found the right person, Jeff was convinced that the suspicion he'd had about Mike back when they were campers might be correct. Mike was gay, and he was doing a damned good job of covering it up.

Of course a lot of the conversation centered on Tyler and the work he did in Hollywood, representing movie stars as well as producers and directors and some screenwriters. Although he professed not to have all that important a client list and that he really shouldn't even mention any of his clients because of confidentiality issues, he dropped a few names Jeff definitely had heard of. Frankly, he was impressed that one of their little group appeared to be quite successful in the world. He started thinking his job selling real estate in southern Maine wasn't all that much of an achievement.

"Ahh…It's nothing, really," Tyler said with a dismissive wave of the hand. "They're just people like you and me, you know?"

"People like you and me with a shit-load of money, you mean." Fred said, laughing before he tilted his head back and drained his fifth or sixth beer of the evening.

No wonder you've got a weight problem, Jeff thought…and maybe a drinking problem, too. Fred had been knocking them back hard ever since supper, and he didn't look like he was going to be slowing down any time soon.

Maybe he's got a good reason to drink.

"So tell us," Evan said, leaning forward with a lascivious leer. "You fucking any famous Hollywood stars?"

Jeff was taken aback that Evan would ask such a crude and personal question.

Maybe he wasn't used to drinking like this, and the few beers he'd had were going to his head faster than expected. Jeff remembered Evan as always being somewhat aloof…someone who didn't engage in the typical gross-out horseplay the others did, even as kids.

Maybe he said what he said so he could fit in a little better.

Or maybe he had a genuine prurient interested in Tyler's sex life.

In any event, Tyler smiled and shook his head as he glanced down at the floor, clasped his hands, and said, "Can't say that I have."

"Can't say is not the same as saying you never did," Evan said.

Tyler paused and took a sip of beer, then added, "Although I have to admit there are a few I wouldn't mind putting the ole' wood to, if you catch my drift."

"But you're married," Fred said.

"I am. And happily, believe it or not," Tyler said, but he made a poking motion with his fist that made everyone burst out in gales of laughter… everyone, that is, except Evan, who looked a little bit pissed because Tyler had made light of his question and not given him a straight answer.

"Hey you guys," Jeff said. "Remember those stories Mark used to tell us?" He was hoping to take the pressure off Tyler to reveal things he obviously didn't want to talk about.

"Don't get started about Hobomock," Fred said. He folded his arms across his chest and made an exaggerated motion like he was shivering. "Fuckin-A, those stories used to scare the *shit* out of me."

"Scarred him for life…as you can plainly see," Tyler said with a smirking grin.

"No. Seriously." Fred hunched forward and turned to face the fire. "There were times when we'd be out on an overnight camping trip or whatever, and Mark would tell us one of them stories just before we went to sleep, and I'd be up all night, worrying and waiting for some Indian demon or ghost or something to come and get me."

"Do you remember any of the stories?" Evan asked in a hushed voice.

He had been sitting off to one side, as far away from the cigar smoke as he could get. Even now that the cigars were finished, he kept his distance. The orange firelight under-lit his face at an oblique angle, making his cheekbones and brow ridge stand out in sharp relief. Jeff thought his eyes appeared sunken, more deeply set than they did in daylight, as if they were sinking into his face. For the first time, he realized just how old Evan really looked. Time and worry had aged him like anyone else in the room, and in a dimly lit room like this, it really showed on him now that he was relaxed.

Jeff wasn't the only one who had caught the odd note in Evan's voice. Tyler shot him a questioning look and then glanced at Fred, whose face held an expression of increasing discomfort and maybe even fear.

Before anyone could say anything, a sudden gust of wind slammed against the dining hall, rattling the shutters on the windows and making the roof timbers creak and groan. Fine grit filtered down from the rafters, sprinkling them like pepper.

"Wind's picking up," Mike said. The hollow tone of his voice perfectly suited the mood.

"I told you," Jeff said. "There's a storm coming. This must be the front moving through."

"Don't worry. We'll be safe and warm in here," Evan said. "A night like this is *perfect* for telling some of those old stories." For some reason, when he said this, he looked squarely at Jeff. "Don't you think?"

"I dunno." Fred's voice was low and tight. "I'm not sure I even want to remember any of them." He sniffed with false laughter and shook his head.

"Ah, come on," Evan said, leaning closer to Fred so the firelight bathed his face with a rich, orange glow. "You should remember them if they scared you so much."

Jeff shifted where he was sitting. He didn't like the direction this conversation was taking. It was one thing to get together after so long and catch up, but there was something almost mean about the way he was talking to Fred. It was like he wanted to find his weak spot and go straight for it.

What would he have against Fred? Jeff wondered, and one again, he questioned Evan's motives for getting all of them together out here.

Maybe it isn't to try to sell us on his development.

Maybe he has something else… something more sinister in mind.

He didn't know Evan or any of these guys. How could he know what any one of them was up to?

"I don't think so," Fred said, his voice strained and low. "All I remember is being scared shitless that there was something…this demon or evil spirit hiding in the woods who was gonna jump out and snatch me away."

"That's the whole point of telling ghost stories, for Christ's sake," Tyler said. "You're supposed to get scared."

"Yeah, but not so bad it scars you for life," Fred said. "A couple of years ago, I researched it and found out Hobomock really was a Native American demon. Mark wasn't making those stories up."

"And did Hobomock catch people and eat them?" Evan asked, arching his eyebrows.

He still had an odd expression that Jeff couldn't read, and he wondered what Evan was trying to accomplish here.

Was he trying to make himself feel better by finding and picking at Fred's obvious bad childhood memories?

Why do something like that?

Is it just to make himself feel more important?

Is this his way of establishing that he still is the one in charge…that he *had* been, and always *would* be, the Alpha male?

"I doubt it," Jeff said, hoping to diffuse the awkward situation, "but if we're gonna dredge up horrible memories, what say we raise a glass and toast the memory of Jimmy Foster?"

He had poured himself a tall glass of rum and raised it while lowering his gaze and saying, "To the memory of a good guy…Jimmy Foster…who should be here with us tonight."

"Amen," Mike said.

"Hear, hear," Tyler said, and everyone raised whatever glass or beer can they were holding, clinked them, and took a sip. Jeff noticed Evan's reluctance to join in, and he saw the cold, angry light that glowed in his eyes.

Jeff narrowed his eyes for a moment and let the rum burn its way down into his belly. Then he cleared his throat and said, "It's just so fucking weird to think how so much has happened since the last time we were all here together."

He didn't like to feel as though he was belaboring the obvious, but right now…at this particular moment in this particular place…he was almost overwhelmed by a sense of time past…of opportunities taken and lost…of lives that had intersected for one brief moment and then drifted apart for whatever reasons.

And now, here they all were, back together.

At least most of us, he thought, and in some strange way, it felt as though even Jimmy was sitting here with them.

Feeling the way he did, Jeff could just about convince himself nothing that had happened in any of their lives in the intervening years had meant anything. What difference had any of their lives made to the world? The darkness and the sound of the wind blowing against the old building and the faint, rhythmic sound of the waves against the shore all contributed to create a strange feeling of timelessness and how sad and pitiful and dispensable any one human life was.

Or maybe he felt this way because of the more than usual amount of rum he'd drunk tonight.

Whatever it was, he had a deep sense of contentment and well being, as though being here in this place with these people was where he really belonged.

"So…? No one remembers any of those stories Mark used to tell?" Mike asked.

Drawn from his reverie, Jeff opened his eyes and looked at his friend. His vision was blurry, but now that he thought about it, there was something about the expression on Evan's face that he found irksome. It struck him as odd that he would suddenly be filled with anger at Mike.

Did he feel protective of Fred, who had already made it clear that he wanted no part of telling any of the stories that had given him nightmares as a child?

Or was it much simpler than that?

Maybe there was something about Evan he just didn't like. Just because they'd been friends years ago didn't mean he had to like him or Mike or Tyler or anyone now.

"I remember one story," Evan said, "but it wasn't one about Hobomock. It was about the guy with the hook for a hand. Remember that one?"

Everyone except Jeff grunted and nodded. Jeff still eyed Mike in the flickering firelight, trying to figure out why he'd had such a sudden, violent reaction to what was, in truth, a fairly innocent suggestion. All they were doing was reminiscing, and the stories their counselor used to tell was just a part of it.

What the hell was the big deal?

"I remember that one," Fred said, his eyes glazing over as he stared at the flames. "They didn't scare me anywhere near the way the Hobomock stories did."

"So tell us that one if you remember it so well," Evan said.

Jeff noticed that Evan had moved a bit closer to Fred, and he felt protective of Fred. He tensed, wondering if Evan was suddenly going to attack Fred or something. He shouldn't purposely be poking and prodding him like this. No one should.

Wondering why he was getting so paranoid, Jeff heaved himself up from the floor, stretched, and rolled his head to loosen the stiffness in his neck.

Maybe he just needed to move around some.

He'd been sitting in the same position for a couple of hours now. At his age, the floor wasn't very comfortable.

"I'm glad you told me to bring one of them egg-shell sleeping pads," Jeff said to Evan.

There was still some undefined tension in the air, and Jeff decided even if he was just imagining in, he had to do *something* to shift gears.

"I gotta take a whiz," he said, shivering as he looked down the hallway that led to the side entrance they had never used as campers. They had always entered the dining hall using the lakeside door.

"Too bad the plumbing's not working in the old crapper," he said. "I'm not too keen about freezing my ass."

Evan gave him an irritated look as he shook his head. "Be thankful you don't have to shit in the woods like a bear."

"Or the Pope," Mike piped in, eliciting a few faint chuckles from the others.

"Help yourself to the rum while I'm gone," Jeff said as he placed the half-empty bottle on the floor within easy reach.

With a stirring of trepidation, he walked down the hallway to the exit. The screens in the door were long gone, but Evan, probably in the last few days when he was out here getting things ready for them, had nailed a thin sheet of plywood across the gaps. The spring that drew the door shut was rusted a rich brick red. It twanged loudly when Jeff pushed the door open and stepped out onto the small, covered porch.

"Watch your step out there," Evan called out. "The wood on the landing's getting kinda punky."

Kinda punky? Jeff thought as he walked carefully across the porch to the steps. The floorboards sank beneath his weight, and rusted nails made loud creaking sounds as they pulled from the rotting wood. The sound set his teeth on edge, and he felt much safer once he stepped down onto the ground. But as he looked around, a deeper chill grabbed him by the scruff of the neck.

Other than the faint glow of firelight coming from inside the dining room, there was absolutely no light anywhere. The smell of wood smoke drifted in the air and was pleasant enough. The sound of waves breaking on the shore was so familiar and comforting he loosened his shoulders and relaxed a bit. Still, there was an unaccountable tension twisting inside him.

He'd brought a flashlight with him for the weekend and wished he had thought to take it with him now. Looking around, he remembered how, when he was a camper, there had been a row of lights lining the campgrounds. Granted, there were a few places that weren't brightly lit, especially along some of the winding paths leading to the tents deep in the woods, but when he was a kid, he had never felt threatened or in any real danger when he walked around the camp at night. There might be skunks or raccoons in the woods, maybe even a deer or two that had swum out to the island or crossed over in winter when the lake was frozen. But there was nothing really *dangerous* out here.

Was there?

Nothing except for whoever or whatever killed Jimmy Foster.

A deeper shiver took hold of him and ran its cold hands over his body.

As he walked from the dining hall to the Port-a-Potty, the sounds of his friends, talking and laughing inside, grew steadily fainter until they all but faded away. He wound his way between the trees, glancing up at the night sky every now and then. Through the pines overhead, he could see the solid wall of dark sky with no stars. The clouds he had seen in the west on the boat ride over must have closed in while they were having supper and settling in.

Great… Just fucking great.

Things would only get worse if it rained later tonight. There'd be no way he'd be able to get comfortable and cozy curled up in a sleeping bag on a hardwood floor. He wasn't twelve years old any more, and he definitely had lost his sense of adventure.

And what if it snows?

Jeff shivered at the thought.

This much further north from Portland, it was possible that any precipitation would come as snow. The hunters would love once hunting season started because it would make tracking deer easier, but snow struck Jeff as just another inconvenience.

He wondered again why Evan had been so insistent about all of them coming out here now instead of waiting until spring. It just didn't make sense to be so cold and miserable, for what…?

Jeff decided not to use the Port-a-Potty. Instead, he stood close to one of the pine trees, unzipped his pants, and pissed against it. He listened to the steady splatter of piss on the ground and wondered how many times as a camper he had taken a leak in the woods like this instead of going to that latrine. A thrill of excitement mingled with rising fear took hold of him, and—just like he had when he was a kid—he imagined that somewhere, unseen in the woods, someone or some*thing* was watching him…ready to pounce.

If there was anything out here, it was probably just a raccoon or skunk waiting for him to go away so it could go back to checking out all of these new scents and maybe do a little exploring in the garbage cans.

But what if it is Fred's dreaded Hobomock?

What if a forest demon still lingers in these woods, a relic of a bygone age who guards his domain and is prepared to protect it from any and all intruders?

Jeff thought it was taking an unusually long time for him to empty his bladder. He'd noticed, as he got older, that the old water pressure wasn't what it used to be, but this was getting ridiculous. The stream of urine was steady and strong, splattering loudly on the ground. Chuckling to himself, he started swinging his penis back and forth, spraying the area just to have some variation in the sound his stream of urine made as it hit the ground.

When he glanced over his shoulder at the dining hall, he wondered if his friends were getting concerned because he was taking so long.

When would they start to worry that something might have happened to him?

How long should he stay out here?

Maybe he should wander off so he could have some time to himself.

Maybe he could find someplace comfortable to hunker down for the night and think things through.

After all, there was a lot to think about. There was a lot to process. Seeing these guys after all these years, while not really upsetting, was certainly confusing. He wasn't sure what he thought about any of them…especially Evan. Try as he might to think only good things, Jeff could tell that Evan had some kind of agenda. It might be as simple as setting them up to pitch them about investing in his resort development, but Jeff felt there was more involved.

"'N I'll figure it out, too, goddamnit," he whispered, surprised at the sudden sound of his own voice intruding on the silence of the night.

Another, stronger shiver ran through him. He finished pissing and, quickly zipping his pants back up, took another bracing breath of the cold night air, but he didn't turn to go directly back to the dining hall. Through the trees on his right, he could hear the waves as they lapped against the shore. His body was tensed as he started toward the lake. He soon realized just how bad his night vision had gotten over the years because he kept stumbling over roots and rocks and fallen branches as he made his way slowly through the darkness down to the lake.

He remembered how, when he was young, it had been so easy to move through the darkest woods at night. He recalled feeling as though he could glide along as silently as a shadow cast by the moonlight, but he knew he could easily be exaggerating his memories of how things were. It was all too likely that he was 'misremembering', as his son Matt used to say when he was little.

Pinecones and twigs snapped underfoot. They sounded like a small, crackling fire burning, unseen. As he got closer to the water, a faint rotting fish smell filled his nose and brought back even stronger memories. He had always associated that fishy smell with the lake. In fact, it had been one reason he was so reluctant to swim in the lake his first year here as a camper. He had always assumed the smell was a hot weather smell, and it surprised him how, even on a cold autumn night with a strong wind blowing, the smell was still there. He wondered if some dead fish had washed up onto the beach and were stinking up the place, but then another more frightening thought struck him with such power he drew to a halt and gasped out loud.

It's the smell of death!

Without consciously knowing it or choosing it, he realized he had walked down to the shore and was at the exact spot where, thirty-five years ago, he had watched in mute horror as the emergency medical team and the local firemen had taken Jimmy Foster's body away on a police boat.

Is that what I smell? Jimmy Foster's rotting corpse?

The thought was unnerving enough to make him whimper out loud.

The pathway leading down to the beach was overgrown more than it had been back then, and the docks and floats that enclosed the swimming area were long gone, but there was a frightening familiarity to the place, as if the scene had been seared into his brain.

And no wonder.

It had been a traumatic experience to see one of his friends dead.

Jeff was painfully aware how vulnerable he was, walking around down here alone like this. The feeling that someone was watching him from the darkness hadn't gone away. If anything, it was stronger and almost too intense to bear.

"Don't be a moron," he whispered, trying to convince himself there was nothing to be afraid of.

He licked his lips and tried to whistle a tune, if only to bolster his courage, but all that talk about Hobomock and remembering how their counselor used to enjoy scaring then with spooky stories had unnerved him more than he might have liked.

Jeff wound his way through the trees until he reached the margin of the beach. If the sky hadn't been overcast, he would have had a great view even if the moon hadn't been up. As it was, he gazed at the stretch of sand that

The Wildman

glowed eerily white in the darkness. The lake was lost in darkness. The sound of waves hissing on the beach and, a little further down, lapping against the rocky shore was soothing, but he couldn't stop thinking back to that horrible day when they pulled Jimmy Foster out of the water.

Once his parents had picked him up and brought him home, Jeff had been so scared he never wanted or dared to try to find out what had really happened. Night after night, he cried himself to sleep, trying to convince himself that he hadn't seen Jimmy Foster's throat cut. He had told the police what he had seen, but they hadn't taken him seriously. His mother and father told him time and again that he had been so frightened he had seen something that wasn't really there. Regardless, that was the last he ever heard about it and, over the years, he had never dug any deeper into what had happened to Jimmy.

But Evan obviously had.

His memories of summer camp seemed to be a lot sharper than Jeff's. Why else would he have taken the time to track down everyone from Tent 12?

Jeff felt bad about Ralph Curran, dying the way he had. It would have been great to see him again, too, to find out what kind of adult he had become. But all in all, it was…maybe not great, but certainly interesting to see how his childhood friends had turned out. He had to leave it at that and try to forget about the horrible thing he had witnessed.

But as he stared at the sandy beach and the churning, dark water beyond, Jeff was filled with an indescribable sadness. He couldn't help but feel how tragic it was that Jimmy never had a chance to grow up, never got to live his life…never even got laid.

And no matter how hard he tried, Jeff just couldn't help but feel as though there were still unresolved issues about his friend's death. He wished he could push such dour thoughts aside and go back to the dining hall and have a merry old time with his friends, but he told him that feeling sad for Jimmy Foster was just as necessary a part of being back at Camp Tapiola as goofing around with his friends.

"I miss yah, man," he whispered as he picked up a stone from the beach and threw it out into the lake. He waited to hear the distant *plunk* and then turned to go back to the dining hall. If nothing else, his friends might be starting to worry about how long it was taking to go to the bathroom.

As he turned to leave, though, off to his left he caught a hint of motion in the darkness.

It wasn't much.

Just a quick hint of...*something* darker than the night; moving—fast-between him and the dining hall. But it was enough to make Jeff freeze. It was gone in an instant, lost in the deep darkness of the woods, but he was convinced he had seen something.

It looked big enough to be a bear, but Jeff wasn't sure if bears were nocturnal or not. Skunks and raccoons definitely were. They'd knocked over his trashcans enough times for him to know that. But what he had seen was a lot bigger than any skunk or raccoon.

Jeff resisted the impulse to run as fast as he could back to the dining hall. Suddenly, all of those fears of the dark he'd had when he was a kid came rushing back. He thought again about the ghost stories Mark had told him and the other guys in the tent and how afraid he had been, like Fred, after lights out.

Don't be fucking ridiculous, he told himself, but that didn't stop a ripple of goose bumps from running up his arms and neck. His scalp tightened as he cocked his head to one side and listened for a sound, any sound, above the rushing sound of waves and the hiss of wind in the pines overhead.

"Jesus," he whispered. "You're acting like a goddamned baby."

His shoulders hunched and his hands clenched into fists as he started toward the dining hall. The surrounding shadows looked much darker and deeper than before. Every time he shifted his eyes to one side or the other, he was positive he saw more figures, moving silently beside and behind him, tracking him as they slowly closed the distance between him and them.

Jeff fought back the sudden urge to run. It'd be just his luck to slam into a tree or something, and knock himself silly.

"Christ on a cross," he whispered as his fear steadily mounted.

His feet scuffed the hard-packed ground. Up ahead, the dark bulk of the dining hall, a huge, black rectangle, loomed against the night sky. Faintly, he saw the orange glow of firelight inside the building. When he inhaled, the smell of wood smoke filled his nose, reassuring him that friendship was close by. But that didn't make the near blinding panic that had seized him subside. He imagined Hobomock or some other demon or ghost lurking in the darkness...tracking him down...to claim him.

And then an even worse thought occurred to him.

What if Jimmy had been murdered? And what if his killer's still out here... waiting for me... the only witness... so he can end it all?

Jeff told himself that was impossible, but he picked up his pace nonetheless.

Jeff wanted to believe that Jimmy *hadn't* been murdered, that he had been so upset about his performance in the softball game he'd gone down to the swimming area to be alone and then…somehow…he had fallen into the lake… maybe he'd even gone for a swim…and there wasn't a lifeguard on duty…and when he dove in, he had bumped his head on the dock…or a rock underwater…and if there really was a gash on his throat, it wasn't from a knife or whatever someone had used to cut his throat… maybe he'd scrapped on a rusty nail…or a piece of broken glass on the lake bottom because some jerk had thrown a soda bottle into the water, and it had broken…

Jeff was walking at a fast pace now, almost running. He weaved between the trees, trying not to trip or bump into anything. Again, he wished he'd brought his flashlight. He wanted to stop and turn around and face whatever he feared was behind him. Then he would see there was nothing there. All he was doing was letting his fears get the better of him, and maybe because of the rum he'd drunk, it was all spiraling out of control.

There's nothing there… no Hobomock… no ghosts… no demon… nothing… unless…

… unless it's Jimmy Foster!

The thought filled Jeff with blinding fear.

When he chanced a look back at the beach, now far behind him, he bumped into a tree hard enough to knock the wind out of him. Tiny white stars exploded across his vision, and he was lucky he didn't drop, unconscious.

Jeff gasped, staggered to a stop, and leaned forward with both hands on his knees. He shook his head to clear it.

Is that what I'm afraid of? he asked himself as panic coursed through him.

Am I afraid Jimmy Foster's ghost is still lingering where he died… that he's been waiting here all these years… waiting for someone… for me… to come back?

Come back and do what?

Help him?

Jeff wanted desperately to believe there was nothing more he could do, either then or now.

He was just a kid at the time. Even if something bad had happened to Jimmy, even if he had been murdered, what could he have done about it? The police, his parents… nobody believed him when he told them what he had seen. They said Jimmy's throat hadn't been cut. He had drowned, and that was the end of it.

If none of the adults, not even his parents or the police, believed him, there was nothing more he could do about it.

He was panting heavily. In spite of the cold night air, sweat bathed his face. Jeff scanned the beach and surrounding forest. It was hard not to imagine a lost, lonely spirit haunting the darkness, waiting…alone…for something or someone who never came and would never come.

Jeff took a breath that turned into a barking sob. He told himself he wasn't crying. As he wiped his tears on the sleeve of his jacket, he tried to convince himself that the cold wind blowing into his face was making his eyes water. Squaring his shoulders, he took another deep breath and told himself to stop acting like a scared little kid.

There's nothing out here… no ghosts… no demons… nothing!

And he almost believed himself, but as he walked the rest of the way back to the dining hall, a cold tingling sensation danced between his shoulder blades. As he stepped up onto the stairs, he was starting to feel a bit calmer… calm enough to face his friends, anyway, when a huge shape suddenly loomed out of the darkness and bumped into him.

The impact almost knocked him down. As it was, he staggered back a few steps, feeling the floorboards yield beneath his weight.

Jeff clenched his fists and ducked into a defensive crouch, but an instant later, someone shouted, "Jesus! I didn't hear you coming."

It was Evan.

Even though relief flooded Jeff, he was suddenly angry at his friend.

"What the *fuck* are you doing?"

"Same thing as you," Evan said. "I came out to take a piss."

"Off the edge of the porch?"

"What the fuck?" Evan said. "I own this property, don't I? So I can do whatever the hell I want."

Jeff's heart was still pounding heavily in his chest, but above it he could hear the sound of Evan's stream of piss as it splashed on the ground beside the porch.

"Hope I didn't ruin your aim," he said with a tight laugh.

Evan chuckled, but in the darkness, without being able to see his face, Jeff caught a dull hollow tone in his friend's laugher, as if he didn't really mean it.

"Well—ahh, look," Jeff said. "I, umm, feel kinda uncomfortable, talking to you knowing you have your dick in your hand." Jeff still couldn't see anything in the darkness under the porch roof. He raised his foot and placed it down carefully. The spongy wood sagged as he shifted his weight forward.

"See you inside then," Evan said as the sound of splashing urine continued unabated.

"Sure," Jeff said as he felt his way to the door, swung it open, and went inside. He couldn't believe the relief he felt when he saw the roaring

The Wildman

blaze in the fireplace and the smiling faces of his friends, who looked up as he approached.

"Took you long enough," Tyler said, but Jeff simply nodded as he settled back down on his sleeping pad, basking in the warmth of the fire.

Chapter Five

Late Night Stroll

SOMETIME BEFORE MIDNIGHT, the wind died down, and the clouds passed. Jeff was the first one to notice that the sky was clearing. A cold silvery glaze of moonlight lit the landscape like a coating of frosting. High-blown clouds racing across the face of the moon created a dizzying strobe-light effect. Every now and then, a strong gust of wind would slam against the old building, making the windows rattle and the wallboards and rafters creak. The fire was still roaring away, though, and the dining room was warm…almost cozy.

Almost…

Jeff and his friends had been talking and drinking for hours, their conversation punctuated every now and then when someone got up to get something to eat or, more likely, get another drink. Although he'd been looking forward to getting loaded this weekend with these guys, Jeff had eased off the rum and was sipping a Sam Adams lager Tyler had given him.

Try as he might, he couldn't stop thinking about what, if anything, he had seen outside. He wanted to believe he'd been jumping at shadows, seeing things that weren't really there and scaring himself…just like he had when he was a kid. But no matter how hard he tried to convince himself he was just spooking himself, he couldn't stop thinking there *was* something seriously wrong about this weekend. Something wasn't adding up. He just couldn't quite put his finger on it.

"How 'bout you, Jeff?" Tyler asked, leaning forward and looking at him with arched eyebrows.

"Huh?"

Jeff realized he'd been lost in thought, not paying the least bit of attention to what his friends had been talking about.

"I missed that."

Tyler sighed and shook his head. Everyone was looking at him like he'd lost it or something. A flush of heat warmed his cheeks and the back of his neck.

"We were talking about how it might be cool if we, all of us, maybe buy into Evan's development here," Mike said.

"You mean like a joint venture?"

"Yeah. We could form an association and get a time share on a single unit." Mike said.

"We could each have a couple of weeks every summer on the lake," Fred added. "Just like old times."

"It would definitely not be like old times," Jeff said.

"Yeah," Mike said, "but we could have a reunion one weekend a year."

"Without wives and kids," Tyler said, and Mike quickly added, "—or significant others."

Jeff gave it hardly a thought before he shrugged and, looking at the group, said, "Sure. Might not be a bad idea."

All he was thinking was, *First we have to get through this weekend and see what we think of each other.*

They hardly knew each other, and here they were, casually talking about a substantial commitment of time and money when they didn't even know if one or more of them were complete assholes. Hoping to play it off, Jeff stretched out his arm and glanced at his wristwatch.

"Christ! It's almost two in the morning." He stifled a yawn behind the back of his hand. "What say we grab a little shut-eye."

"You always were a pussy," Tyler said. A wide grin split his face.

"Not really." Jeff smiled back at him. "I was just always the sensible one. Unlike *you*, over the years I've learned to pace myself. I'm thinking about getting up early and taking a hike around the campgrounds."

Even before he finished the sentence, a shiver took hold of him because he knew that the first place he'd go would be down to the shore where the docks had been…where he had last seen Jimmy Foster dead on a stretcher.

"There's not much left of things," Evan said. "Everything's so grown up. I could hardly figure out where the ball field was."

"How 'bout one more beer," Mike said, and before anyone could respond, he started digging into his cooler.

"Can I snag one, too?" Fred asked. Without a word, Mike tossed a bottle of beer over to him.

"Anyone else?" Mike asked.

"You guys can stay up as late as you want," Jeff said. "I'm a heavy sleeper. Your yakking won't bother me."

The Wildman

That was a total lie, but he wasn't about to get between them and their fun. Truth was, especially since Susan left, he was lucky to get five hours of sleep a night.

Turning his back to the fireplace, he adjusted his sleeping pad and fluffed up his sleeping bag and pillow. He was positioned off to one side, wanting to keep as close to the fire as he could in case it got really cold during the night. He remembered nights when they were campers when the temperature dropped down close to freezing. And *that* had been in *July*. He couldn't imagine what an October night would be like, but he was about to find out.

Since there was no running water, he couldn't wash up or brush his teeth…not unless he went down to the lake, and he wasn't about to do *that*. Maybe in the morning he'd give it a try. After stripping down to his boxer shorts and t-shirt, he slipped into the sleeping bag, shivering from the cool touch of the fabric. He put his head inside the sleeping bag and blew out several puffs of hot air, hoping to warm up quickly.

Once he was settled, though, Jeff wasn't the least bit sleepy. He lay with his back to the fire and listened as his friends talked on into the night. The conversation wandered all over the place as they talked about their lives, their jobs, the people in their lives—wives, ex-wives, and kids—as well as sports and finances, where they went to college, and generally how they saw their lives going.

Jeff found it soothing to listen to them without having to participate, and he started dozing off as their voices rose and feel as regularly as the waves, washing against the sandy beach outside.

Eventually, their voices toned down and faded. Jeff wasn't sure if he was falling asleep or if his friends were finally succumbing to sleep. Everybody had their limits.

❧ ❧ ❧

Sometime later, Jeff awoke with a start.

It was still dark, but he heard…something out of the ordinary that had set off an alarm inside his head.

Holding his breath, he sat up and looked around.

The fire had burned down low, and the dining hall was much darker than it had been throughout the evening. It felt a lot colder, too. Shadows in the rafters looked thicker and seemed to be closer. Grunting softly, Jeff turned and looked at the fire. It was just a pile of glowing coals that cast a warm, vermilion glow. He looked at the mounded humps of his friends as they slept in their sleeping bags. They were arranged on the floor like the spokes of a wheel with the fire as the hub. One of them, he was sure it was Mike, was snoring with a series of loud, blubbering snorts.

But that wasn't what had torn him from sleep.

He considered getting up and putting a few more logs on the fire, but he was nice and toasty where he was. He wished he could lay back down and go back to sleep, but he was still bothered by whatever had awakened him. After another moment or two, he realized what it was.

There were only three people asleep on the floor.

Someone was missing.

Jeff's teeth started chattering as he sat up and, leaning forward, tried to figure out who was missing. It didn't take him long.

It was Evan.

Evan wasn't there.

He scanned the shadows that filled the dining room, realizing now that the sound that had disturbed his sleep had been the creaking of floorboards…

As if someone had gotten up and was sneaking around.

A stronger, deeper chill took hold of Jeff, shaking his shoulders as he looked down the short, dark hallway to the door that led out onto the porch.

Had he also heard the faint twanging sound of the spring as the door opened and Evan went outside?

It was too dark to see anything in the hallway except the faint, gray smudge of night beyond the screen door. For all he knew, Evan was standing right outside the door. Jeff wouldn't be able to see him.

What business of his was it, anyway, what Evan did?

They were adults now, not campers who had to sneak around. Besides, Evan owned the island and everything on it. It was his property. He could do whatever he wanted.

But he couldn't get rid of the thought that it hadn't been a noise Evan had made that had awaked him. He tried not to imagine the restless ghost of Jimmy Foster lurking in the night outside the dining hall, a pale, tattered remnant in the patchy moonlight.

"Screw it," Jeff whispered.

He wanted to go back to sleep and forget all about it, but now that he was awake, he had to find out what was going on. His teeth were chattering as he slipped out of the sleeping bag and scrambled to put on his clothes before he got too cold. He cast a wary eye at his three sleeping friends, expecting one of them to sit up and ask what the hell was going on.

The truth was, he had no idea what was going on, but he was determined to find out.

The Wildman

Even if it was as innocent as Evan getting up to take a piss, Jeff wanted to figure out what had awakened him…he wasn't going to be able to get back to sleep until he did.

After getting his pants on, he put on the socks he had worn yesterday and his sneakers. His legs were stiff from the cold, and his hip ached from sleeping on the floor. His knees popped when he stood up, and he had to rotate his arms to get the circulation going. He was still shaking from the cold when he tiptoed across the floor and down the hallway to the side door.

He almost laughed out loud as he wondered why he was sneaking around like this.

It would be hilarious if he ended up scaring the be-jezus out of Evan, who in all likelihood really had just gotten up to use the Port-a-Potty. After all the rum and beer he'd consumed earlier, Jeff was surprised his bladder wasn't screaming for relief, too.

The floorboards creaked with every step he took. The sounds made him cringe, but he realized this sound was *exactly* what had broken into his sleep.

When he got to the door, he looked outside. The ground was bright with splashes of moonlight that filtered through the pines. The black shadows of tree trunks stood out in harsh relief against the moonlit glow. As his eyes adjusted to the dark, Jeff realized that Evan wasn't standing on the porch.

Jeff paused and listened. The only sound was the crackling of the fire and the heavy breath of his sleeping friends in the dining hall.

So what's he doing… where'd he go?

Jeff placed his fingertips on the screen door and started to push it open. The twanging sound the spring made as it stretched open made him cringe. The sound seemed loud enough to wake the sleepers, but Jeff glanced back and saw that no one had stirred.

Except for Evan… For some reason, Evan's up and about at this hour… Doesn't he ever sleep?

Jeff wondered why he was so mistrustful of Evan. As far as he could see, Evan hadn't said or done anything so far this weekend that wasn't completely above board; but a couple of times something he said or the way he reacted to something gave Jeff pause. He couldn't help but wonder if Evan was up to something. And no matter how much he tried to stop his thoughts from going in a particular direction, he couldn't help but think it had something to do with what had happened to Jimmy Foster.

Or it all could be because of his own lingering guilt he'd dredged up since coming back to Camp Tapiola, or what was left of it?

When the screen door was open just enough for him to slip outside, he stepped out onto the porch and eased the door quietly closed behind him. His vision had adjusted to the darkness inside the dining hall, so the bright moonlight bathing the campgrounds was enough to hurt his eyes.

Off to the right, he heard the steady sound of small waves, lapping against the shore. Overhead, the wind, whenever it gusted, whistled in the pines. The sound was faint and lonely, like someone hissing a warning for him to be quiet. The resinous scent of pine filled his nose, but beneath that, he caught a hint of something else…something with a dead, rotting taste.

Under the shadow of the porch roof, Jeff walked over to the steps. With every step, the floorboards sagged from his weight. As he looked all around, trying to see where Evan had gone, he felt predatory…like one of those spiders he knew was lurking in the darkness above the rafters of the dining hall. He wasn't out here taking a piss off the side of the porch, but maybe he was using the Port-a-Potty. Jeff strained to hear but didn't catch any sounds coming from that direction.

So if Evan isn't out here, where the hell is he?

Jeff hesitated to step out into the direct moonlight. If Evan saw him and confronted him, he could always say he'd come outside to go to the bathroom, but he was determined to know what Evan was up to.

Maybe if he found out, it would reconcile the unsettling feelings he had about this whole reunion weekend.

After taking a breath and letting it out slowly between his teeth, Jeff walked down the steps to the ground. He was shivering from the cold, but there was also something bracing…almost magical…about the night. Inky shadows of the pines shifted from side to side as the wind gusted, and clouds raced across the face of the moon. The effect was dizzying, making Jeff feel drunker than he knew he was as he started away from the porch. He kept looking for any sign of Evan, and was about to conclude that he was nowhere around when he saw a black silhouette shift against the backdrop of the trees. It disappeared from sight in an instant, but Jeff knew it was on the path leading into the woods.

Was that him?

A bone-deep shiver gripped him.

Or is that Jimmy's ghost… or maybe our old friend Hobomock?

As Jeff headed in the same direction, walking away from the lake, he told himself it was ridiculous to let his imagination get carried away like this. It couldn't be anyone *except* Evan, but Jeff was determined to make sure. He had to find out where he was going this late and what he was up to.

The Wildman

Make it a game, Jeff told himself. *Pretend you're twelve and sneaking around, spying on people.*

Chances were Evan wasn't up to anything bad. Jeff sniffed with laughter at how foolish he would feel if he started along the path where it would be much darker in the woods, and stumbled over Evan.

The sensible thing, he knew, would be to go back inside, throw some logs on the fire, and get back into his sleeping bag so he could warm up and sleep. Evan can do whatever he wants to do out there. He obviously was going far enough away from the dining hall so he could have some privacy. How awkward would it be if he found him jerking off out there or something?

What business was it of his, anyway?

He shouldn't be following Evan around like this.

Still, Jeff had to know. When he stepped out from beneath the trees, the harsh glare of moonlight made him feel vulnerable, as if he had just stepped into a spotlight, and danger was all around him.

He hunched his shoulders protectively as he looked left and right. He felt certain Evan knew he was following him. He probably was already hiding somewhere nearby, watching his every move.

Jeff crossed the open space where the snack bar used to stand. All that remained was a slight depression in the ground and one or two old cement support posts that stuck up from the ground.

Behind that was the forest.

Jeff sucked in a quick breath and held it a long time before he stepped out of the moonlight and into the deep shadows of the trees. His heart was racing in his neck as he strained every sense to figure out where Evan had gone.

There were or, at least, had been well-worn trails winding all through these woods connecting different parts of the camp. The vast network of trails led from the tents to the latrine and dining hall, the meeting hall and the campfire site, the swimming area and the softball and soccer fields. Back when Jeff was a camper, this complicated maze of trails had been as familiar as the streets and shortcuts back home. He and his friends used to run along them day or night without the least concern. Besides, they were on an island, so it was impossible to get lost for very long before you made it to the shore and could follow it back to camp.

But now, for some reason, the forest and what might be left of the trails projected nothing but menace. As Jeff started along the trail—surprised that it was still discernable after more than thirty years—he tensed, ready for something…for *anything*…to leap out at him from the darkness.

He couldn't stop wondering why he was so worked up, but he couldn't deny that there was something about Evan that raised his suspicion. Sneaking off into the woods like this was just one more thing that made Jeff wonder what his old friend was up to.

Slanting bars of silvery moonlight lanced through the pine trees, lighting Jeff's way with bright splotches of pale light that only made the shadows under the trees that much darker. He paused every now and then and listened for any indication that Evan was somewhere up ahead. The only sound was the hissing of the wind in the pines. It was too late in the year for crickets or frogs. The soft thud of his feet on the ground seemed strangely amplified in the surrounding darkness.

Jeff made his way along a trail that, he recalled, led out to the tent site where he and his friends used to bunk. He wondered if the latrine was still there. If it was, maybe Evan had come out here to use it instead of the Port-a-Potty.

As he navigated the narrow trail, Jeff started to get disoriented. Even though there was no way he could really get lost, it would be embarrassing as hell if he went too far into the woods and couldn't find his way back. For all he knew, Evan had already done whatever he had come out here to do and returned. Maybe he'd doubled back on another trail and was already back at the dining hall, wondering where the hell Jeff was off to.

When Jeff reached a fork in the trails, he paused and looked down first one trail, then the other. The one to his right, he knew, led out to the ball fields. The one to his left went past the latrine and then swung around past the old infirmary and finally back to the old tent site.

He doubted the old tent platforms would still be there. Any ropes or canvas that had been left behind when the camp closed would have rotted away long ago. Jeff wondered if Evan was feeling as nostalgic as he was, and had come out here simply to have a look around and reminisce about the old days. He had just decided to head out to the ball fields and see what was out there when a flicker of motion off to his left drew his attention.

Jeff dropped into a crouch and stared to his left, trying to discern what had caught his attention.

The woods got eerily quiet. The trees, swaying in the breeze, made the shadows flicker and wave with a peculiar underwater feeling.

Is that all I saw? Jeff wondered as tension wound up his back. *Was it a tree shadow… or maybe a passing cloud?*

He hoped so because who knew what had happened on this island in the thirty-five years since there was a camp here?

The Wildman

There could be deer or bear out her, or maybe even someone living out here, camping out illegally.

Before long, Jeff's knees started to ache, so he straightened up, wincing as his legs extended and his knees popped. The tension in his neck and shoulders was sharp. He knew he should turn around right now and take the quickest path back to the dining hall.

But something urged him on.

He decided to go left and walk past where the latrines and tent areas used to be. This would also take him past the infirmary. He doubted that old building was still standing, either, but he smiled at a memory. One summer, he must have been nine or ten, he had gotten a bad case of poison ivy…so bad he spent the last three days of that camping season in the infirmary where the camp nurse, Mrs. Stott, practically bathed him in Calamine Lotion. The worst thing was that he'd gotten some on his crotch, and his tent buddies, especially Evan, had teased him unmercifully, asking him how he'd gotten it down *there*.

Jeff wished he could enjoy the peace and quiet of his late-night walk. He took several deep breaths and looked around, wondering why he couldn't relax and appreciate the natural beauty that surrounded him. Living in a suburb of Portland, he hadn't realized how out of touch with nature he'd become. Throughout his life, he had felt as though he had a deep connection with the natural world; but now—actually being in it—he felt differently. All he was aware of was the sense of danger…of something threatening.

The winding path looped around for half a mile. Jeff never saw the old latrine and assumed it, like the old snack bar, had rotted away long gone. Some time years ago someone must have demolished the old buildings and hauled away the lumber because Jeff hadn't even noticed a depression in the ground. Now he figured he must have already passed it.

It was sad to consider that entire buildings, everything he knew and loved about this place, had rotted away in such a relatively short time. He assumed the infirmary would be gone, too, so he was surprised when he rounded a bend in the trail and saw the old building up ahead.

At a distance, it looked smaller than he remembered, but that had been a typical reaction this weekend. Moonlight edged the sloped roof with fine lines of silver that cast the front of the building into deep shadow. The small roofless porch out front remained, but Jeff couldn't see if the front door was there or not. There was a large, black rectangle that certainly looked as if the door had been torn off.

Jeff slowly approached the building, trying to take in the flood of memories. It was as though he was moving in slow motion, in a dream. The moonlight cast sharp-edged shadows that rippled across the uneven ground. No matter how hard he tried to imagine it, Jeff just couldn't accept that this was the same place he remembered from his youth. He wondered if Mrs. Stott was still alive. She must have been in her forties back then, so she would be in her seventies or eighties now. It was very likely she had died years ago, and he had never heard about it. He wished now he had thought to Google her before coming to the reunion, and he made a mental note to do just that when he got home.

Jeff had been taking short, shallow breaths, and he forced himself to breathe evenly and deeply as he moved closer to the building. When he was only a few feet from the door, he saw that it was still there, intact. It had been painted bright green back when he was a camper. Maybe because it was protected from the elements, the paint hadn't faded as much as he thought it would have, or maybe in the intervening years someone had repainted it or replaced it. The front steps leading up to the small front porch, he noticed, were missing.

Jeff's heart was racing as he stepped up onto the porch, reached out into the darkness, and tried the door handle. It clicked, but when he pushed against the door, it didn't open.

No surprise there.

Feeling around in the darkness, he found a lock and hasp just above the door handle. It struck him as odd that the building would be locked up like this.

Was there something of value still inside?

Jeff felt the lock more carefully, surprised that he didn't feel a coating of corrosion on it. Was it new?

Perhaps Evan or some of the construction or surveying crew had been out here and left some equipment behind until next spring. That made sense, but why not use the dining hall? It was definitely more secure. Besides, in an isolated place like this, anyone who wanted to break in could make as much noise as they liked without disturbing any neighbors, who were a mile or more across the lake.

Jeff gave the lock one last, frustrated tug and then slammed it against the door. Almost immediately, from inside the building, there came a soft thump.

The sound startled Jeff. He froze where he was, thinking there had to be a raccoon or skunk or something inside the building. Probably a big rat. There had been a recent outbreak of rabies in the area among the raccoon population, so Jeff was ready to run if he heard or saw anything else.

But after that first thump, the silence of the night remained unbroken. The sound wasn't repeated, and no animal came charging around the side of the building to attack. After a while, Jeff realized he'd been holding his breath, so he let it out slowly. Then he turned and walked away.

He followed the trail back to the open area of the campgrounds, feeling a surprising measure of relief when he saw the faint glow of firelight in the windows of the dining hall. He quickened his pace, covering the distance to the building and was practically running by the time he leaped onto the porch and shouldered the door open, unmindful of any noise he was making.

"*Christ!*" someone shouted. "'S almost four o'clock."

Jeff drew up short. Someone had gotten up while he was gone and placed more wood on the fire. The high blaze was warm and cheery, but as he looked at the sleeping shapes of his friends, no one was stirring. Then he saw that Evan's sleeping bag was still unoccupied. He jumped when Evan stepped out from the shadowed doorway that led into what used to be the kitchen.

"Where've you been?" Evan asked, eyeing Jeff narrowly.

Jeff couldn't miss the hint of challenge in his voice. He shrugged and rubbed his hands together. "Just out…for a walk." It took effort to keep his voice from trembling. "It's a beautiful moonlit night, in case you hadn't noticed. I woke up and, when I didn't see you, I went out and strolled around the grounds a bit."

"See anything interesting?" Evan asked.

There was still a slight threatening tone in his voice, but when he stepped out from the shadows of the doorway, Jeff caught the tight smile that lit his face.

"Nah," Jeff said with a dismissive wave of his hand. "Same old place, far as I can tell."

He knew he shouldn't say what he wanted to say next, but no matter how hard he tried to hold it back, it came out anyway.

"So where were you going?"

Evan lowered his gaze and sniffed with laughter as he shook his head and rubbed his nose with the back of his hand.

"Like you," he said simply. "Just out walking. Enjoying the natural beauty."

"Until your crew comes and tears it all down."

Evan shrugged as he took a few steps closer to Jeff. Although he had a warm, welcoming expression on his face, Jeff couldn't help but feel threatened somehow.

Why had Evan been hiding in the shadows like that?

It was almost like he'd been caught doing something he didn't want Jeff or anyone to see.

"It won't be as bad as you think," Evan said. "They—I plan on working around the natural landscape so we can retain as much of the woodsy feel as we can, you know? It doesn't make much sense to move out to the country and then destroy what you came here for, right?"

"Pave paradise and put up a parking lot," Jeff said under his breath.

Evan chuckled. "Joni Mitchell had it right, didn't she?" He yawned as he looked past Jeff. When Jeff turned and looked out the window, he could see the faintest hint of gray streaks of dawn in the east.

"Morning's coming, and here we are pulling an all-nighter like a couple of idiots." Jeff yawned and then looked at their three friends, all sound asleep on the floor in front of the fire. "Lucky bastards," he said. "Sleeping like little babies."

"Think we ought to grab an hour or two of shuteye?" Evan asked.

Jeff nodded, but he noticed the odd expression etched on Evan's features. It didn't dispel any of the doubts he'd been having about what his childhood friend's real motives were for having them out here for the weekend. The sudden paranoid thought crossed his mind that it might not be safe for him to fall asleep, but he pushed it aside as he walked over to his sleeping bag and started taking his clothes off. The air in the dining hall had warmed up from the re-stoked blaze, but his teeth were chattering as he ran the zipper of the sleeping bag down and slipped into it.

"Have a good snooze," Evan said. "I'll rouse you around six or seven. I have a fantastic breakfast planned."

"I'll bet," Jeff said as he lay down and rolled over so his back was to Evan. His eyes were grainy with sleeplessness, and his body felt wrung out, but he thought there was no way he'd be able to fall asleep…not as long as he knew Evan was still awake, watching him.

For the next two hours, he lay there with his eyes wide open as he watched the sky to the east gradually brighten. Red and orange streaks flared across the sky like angry welts, and all Jeff could think of was the old sailor's saying: "Red sky in morning, sailors take warning."

Chapter Six

Morning Walk

JEFF DIDN'T FEEL very rested. An angled beam of sunlight shot across the dining hall floor, casting long, blue shadows over the worn wood and shining directly into Jeff's face.

He might have nodded off a little, but he never fell into a deep sleep. Images from his moonlight walk around the campground mixed with other, more unsettling images that had something to do with the Indian demon Hobomock and the lonely ghost of Jimmy Foster. All of this left Jeff feeling sad and lonely and maybe a little bit frightened as he began to stir.

But Evan hadn't lied about one thing. He *did* have a fantastic breakfast planned. The sounds and smells of frying eggs and bacon got him and everyone else stirring just as the sun was rising.

"Up 'n at 'em, boys and girls," Evan called out when the other guys started to shift about on the floor, moaning and grunting. Mike let a loud, sputtering fart that got everyone laughing.

"You know, I learned something," Fred said.

"What's that?" Mike asked.

"That sleeping on the floor just ain't what it used to be." He groaned as he sat up with his legs splayed out in front of him, and, leaning back, drove a knuckled fist into the small of his back and rubbed. "I didn't sleep for shit."

"Like hell you didn't," Tyler said, scowling at him. "You were snoring louder than a goddamned chain saw."

"No way."

"Way. You kept me awake practically the whole night."

Jeff smiled at the bickering, thinking it was exactly how they sounded in Tent 12 thirty-five years ago. He sighed and shook his head.

"All three of you were sleeping like little babies," he said. "And Tyler—

you shouldn't be accusing anyone of snoring…not the way you were sawing wood last night."

"Bullshit! I don't snore."

Evan caught Jeff's eye and smiled, then turned back to his cooking. He slid a pile of bacon onto a platter lined with paper towels and then started cooking another batch. Three wire racks leaned against the inner wall of the fireplace above the coals, each with six pieces of bread in them, toasting. They were already a nice golden brown.

It was Tyler's idea to go down to the lake and wash up before breakfast. Everyone except Jeff and Evan went. Ten minutes later, they came back, their feet covered with sand, their hair stringy and dripping, and their teeth chattering like machines.

"Fuckin' *invigorating* is what *that* is," Mike said, shivering as he danced up and down on his toes and hurriedly pulled on a bulky sweatshirt. The logo read: SOME DAYS IT'S NOT EVEN WORTH CHEWING THROUGH THE RESTRAINTS. It made Jeff chuckle.

In the brightening light of day, so much of what Jeff had been thinking and worrying about last night now seemed totally irrelevant. He could almost convince himself he had been asleep and dreamt his moonlit walk around the campgrounds. It was already fading into a distant memory. Still, he was left with a vague sense of disquiet, and he wished he could pinpoint what was causing it. He vowed to try not to think too much about it today. They were here to have fun, not mope about and get suspicious about everyone and their motives.

Typically, Evan took charge of all the cooking and refused any offers of help until it was time to set everything out. He cooked the eggs sunny-side up in a huge cast iron skillet that Jeff thought must have been left behind when the camp closed. It certainly looked like something old Herbie and Ben-the camp cooks—would have used. As soon as the first bunch of eggs was done, Evan started another while urging the guys to dig in.

"You gonna eat, too?" Jeff asked Evan. He never ate much for breakfast and was waiting for the second round, thinking there would be less bacon grease than in the first batch. He had to watch his cholesterol these days.

"I'm the host," Evan said with a wide smile. His eyes shined like quicksilver in the early morning light. "I won't eat until all of my guests are satisfied."

Tyler, Fred, and Mike apparently had no qualms about digging in without him. Muttering approval, they sat down cross-legged on the floor and ate and drank with gusto. In the corner by the kitchen door was a huge aluminum industrial urn filled with steaming coffee. Jeff was surprised he hadn't noticed the smell of it brewing when he had been lying there awake.

Maybe he had slept a little. He still didn't feel rested.

"So," Tyler said as he tore off a piece of toast and mopped up egg yolk from his plate. "What's on tap for today?"

"Whatever we want," Evan said with a shrug. He turned his attention to the sizzling eggs and flipped them over.

"How about first we take a tour of the old camp grounds?" Fred asked.

"Gonna have to, to work off these calories," Mike said before stuffing some more bacon into his mouth. "I haven't eaten like this in…years."

"Gotta watch that cholesterol," Tyler said.

"Fuck cholesterol. I gotta die of something."

Jeff caught the quick glance Evan shot at him and wondered if there was any meaning behind it.

"No, seriously," Fred said after swallowing what was in his mouth.

Tyler chuckled and said, "My wife's got me on this low fat diet. She's got me eating so much goddamned fiber I practically shit sawdust."

Jeff didn't eat until Evan did. They shared the last batch of bacon, eggs, toast, orange juice, and coffee while the other guys lazed around, slurping their second cups of coffee. Fred slipped outside to have a cigarette on the front steps even though Evan and everyone else said it was okay if he wanted to smoke in the building. Fred said he was used to being ostracized and went outside anyway.

Once everyone was finished with the meal, they carried their plates and utensils down to the lakeside to wash them. Jeff volunteered to clean the frying pan, which was a big, black, heavy piece of cast iron. He dipped it into the water a few times, watching a rainbow swirl of grease fan out across the surface. Then he took a handful of sand and started scrubbing it.

"Make sure you dry that, too," Evan said, watching him carefully as though the frying pan was a prized possession. "That's cast iron. It'll rust if you don't dry it completely."

Jeff was tempted to tell him he already knew that, but he let it drop. He didn't like the way he still bristled at Evan, resentful at feeling as though he was bossing him around like he had when they were little. Kneeling beside the water's edge with tiny waves lapping the sandy shore, he stared over to the far shore of the mainland as he scrubbed. The sun had long since cleared the horizon. The sky was a deep, rich blue that hurt his eyes to look at. Out on the lake, the water was gray and riffled by the wind. It looked like corrugated steel. The camp was in a sheltered cove, so they were protected from the westerly wind.

"Gonna be a chilly day," Mike said as he placed his hands on his hips and surveyed the expanse of water. "Glad it never got this cold when we were campers."

Tyler sniffed. "Oh, I remember nearly freezing my ass off some nights."

"I never got cold," Mike said.

"That's because you used to take the extra blankets off everyone's bunks and use them," Fred said.

Mike ignored him as he looked up and down the beach. There was a curious look on his face, almost as if he was expecting to see someone else.

"So the docks and swimming area were over there, right?" He pointed to the stretch of sand about a hundred yards down the beach from the dining hall. He sighed and shook his head. "It's funny how it still looks exactly the same, isn't it?"

"But smaller," Tyler said. "Everything looks a lot closer than I remember."

"Maybe, but I mean—all the trees, even the underbrush looks exactly like it did back then. I wouldn't be surprised to see kids running around, jumping into the water."

"Not in this weather," Jeff said. "You couldn't pay me enough to go swimming."

Evan snorted. "You would if you had to."

Still lazily scrubbing the pan, Jeff turned and eyed his friend. Once again, he had a little twinge of suspicion about Evan. He wished he would stop feeling this way.

"Well," Jeff said with a smile, "I'm just glad I don't have to."

"I wish we'd thought to bring canoes or kayaks," Fred said. "It'd be cool to paddle out around the island and check it out."

"We can use the motor boat," Tyler suggested. He turned to Evan. "What do you say we take a little cruise later today and check things out? After all, you *are* trying to get us to buy into your development, aren't you?"

For an instant, Evan looked at them with a strange, distracted expression on his face as if he didn't quite understand the question. Then he smiled and said, "Of course I am, but this isn't a sales weekend. We're just here to have fun."

"Yeah…right," Mike said with a sniffing laugh.

"No. Seriously." Evan looked like he was getting angry. "I mean, once the project gets going and all—sure, if any of you guys want to buy in, I'd be more than happy to work something out, but that's not the point of us being here this weekend."

"It's not?" Jeff said. "Then what *is* the point?"

His voice cut the morning stillness like the crack of a whip, making all of his friends turn and look at him as if he'd said the exact wrong thing. Feeling suddenly self-conscious, he wished he could think of some witty rejoinder, but everyone seemed to have caught the sharp note of accusation in his voice.

"The point...?" Evan echoed, rubbing his chin as he looked first at Jeff and then shifted his gaze out over the water. "The point is to reconnect with old friends. To think about the summers we spent here. For me, at least, they were probably the best times of my life."

"Amen to that," Mike said.

"I've always felt a special attachment to this place. That's why, when it came up on the market, I snapped it up as soon as I could."

"For old time's sake?" Tyler said, sounding a bit doubtful himself.

"Yeah. For old time's sake." Evan turned and eyed them, one by one. "And that's the *only* reason I dragged your sorry asses out here. So we could remember the fun times we had as kids."

There was a chorus of murmured agreement, but Jeff couldn't ignore the irksome feeling inside him, telling him no matter *what* Evan did or said, there was something else…some other motive just below the surface. He stood up, the heavy frying pan in his hand, weighing down one side of his body.

Jesus… forget about it… will you? he told himself. *Relax and enjoy the weekend.*

※ ※ ※

They spent the rest of the morning wandering around the campgrounds as a group, reminiscing about which buildings were where, where the tents had been pitched, and all the things they had done as campers. Jeff was surprised by some of the memories the others had. Evan didn't say much, but some events that were significant to Tyler or Mike or Fred were things Jeff barely remembered at all.

When they approached the old baseball field, which was now choked with underbrush and scrawny swamp maples, Mike couldn't stop exclaiming about how small the area looked to him now. The maples had already lost their leaves, so they had a fairly good view of the expanse of the field.

"Come on," he said, looking around in utter amazement with his mouth hanging open. "This *can't* possibly be it. It was so much bigger."

"No," Jeff said. "You were a lot smaller."

"I know that," Mike said, rubbing the sagging bulge of his belly, "but, come on. Look at this! The service road's still over there." He pointed to the remains of an old road that wound through the woods toward where their tents used to be. "And you can still see the path going down to the beach. It went by sheds where we kept the sports equipment. And there's the brook out in center field. It's still there." He sighed and shook his head as though deeply saddened. "But how the *hell* did we ever play baseball on such a tiny field?"

"Like I said…you…we all were a lot smaller back then." Jeff was suddenly convinced Mike's weight was an issue for him. He didn't want to say anything that might hurt his feelings, so he quickly tried to change the subject. "Remember how you used to belt the ball into the woods just about every time you were at bat?"

"I can't remember how many times I played centerfield and would have to fish the ball out of the brook," Fred said.

"I did have a pretty good swing, didn't I?" Mike smiled, looking satisfied with the memory.

But it wasn't all good memories.

When they started down the old dirt road, heading toward the tent sites, Fred started bitching about how they used to have "quiet time" where they spent the hour after lunch in their tent before they could go swimming or out to play ball. This was when they were supposed to take naps or write letters home or read quietly. Jeff used to read *Mad* magazine during rest hour. One thing they all agreed on was that rest hour was the most boring part of their day.

"That whole thing about waiting an hour before swimming. That's bullshit, you know," Mike said. "The counselors just did that so they could have some free time instead of watching us."

"Can't say as I blame them?" Tyler said. "I mean, think about it. We must have been one helluva handful for them. None of them were much older than us. How old do you think Mark was?"

"I did the math when I read his obituary," Evan said with a curiously flat tone in his voice. "When he died, the newspaper said he was twenty-nine years old, so he would have been nineteen years old the last summer we were here."

"Twenty-nine." Mike whistled as he lowered his head and shook it. "Jesus, man. It's just so weird to think a guy as cool as Mark is dead."

"He died so young," Fred said.

"We always looked up to him," Tyler added.

"I sure as hell didn't," Evan said. There was a sudden sharp bitterness in his voice that gave everyone pause. He bent down and picked up a dead branch and, gripping it tightly, swatted at the branches that lined the road. "I always thought he was kind of an asshole."

"No way," Jeff said, and simultaneously Tyler said, "Really?"

"Yeah. Really," Evan swatted dead leaves off a nearby branch. "Especially after my...after Jimmy died. I thought he—"

Before he went on, he caught himself and, taking a breath, looked back and forth at his friends while shaking his head. He was biting down on his lower lip as though struggling to stop himself from saying more.

"What the hell did Mark have to do with Jimmy dying?" Tyler asked, obviously not wanting to let it drop. "He was just as freaked out as the rest of us."

When Evan turned his head quickly and glared at Tyler, Jeff caught the flash of rage in his eyes. For a split second, he was afraid Evan was going to whack Tyler with his stick.

"I dunno," Evan finally said. He sounded calmer, but Jeff had the impression it was forced. "I mean, he was our goddamned counselor, wasn't he? That means Jimmy and all of us were *his* responsibility. Right?"

"Well...yeah. Sure," Tyler said with a shrug. "But I don't see where—"

"But *nothing!*" Evan's anger boiled up, making his face flush so he looked like he had a sunburn. He gripped the branch he was holding so tightly his knuckles turned bone-white, and his arm started to tremble.

Evan took a quick, noisy breath and, obviously aware that his outburst had surprised his friends, tried to get control of himself. "I...my whole life, I've blamed him for what happened," he said. "That...that's all."

"Not directly, I hope," Mike said.

The road narrowed until it was just a path, and they started walking in single file with Mike in the lead. He had to turn and look back at Evan, who was walking between Fred and Tyler with Jeff bringing up the rear.

Evan started to say something else, but whatever it was, he couldn't get it out. The only sounds were the snap of branches underfoot and, off in the distance, the solitary cry of a blue jay. Finally, Evan said, "Okay. Maybe not *directly.* But *someone* sure killed him."

Fred stopped short in his tracks, turned, and faced Evan, openly sneering now as he shook his head.

"There's no way," he said. "No one *killed* Jimmy. 'Least not the way I heard it. My parents said Jimmy drowned."

Everyone else had stopped, and Evan regarded Fred with a long, cold, unnerving stare.

"Then what was all this stuff about his throat being slit?" Evan turned to face Jeff. In a flash, he pointed his stick at Jeff and said, "You saw it, Jeff. Right?" His voice was low, and it quavered.

Flummoxed by the sudden accusation, all Jeff could do was shrug.

Why was Evan getting so upset about what had happened to Jimmy?

Jeff wished again that he had declined Evan's invitation to come out here this weekend. Digging up old shit like this just wasn't healthy for any of them.

"Well...?" Evan said, all but leering at Jeff. He was still pointing the branch at him, and when he took a few steps closer, Jeff cringed, convinced he was going to whack him with it.

"To tell the God's honest truth," Jeff finally said, his voice quavering, "I have no idea *what* I saw. All I know is, I was scared out of my goddamned mind."

"But you said—" Evan's voice cracked with barely repressed rage. "You said in the tent that night his throat was cut right across the windpipe."

"I said that?"

Jeff squinted and shook his head as though he was having trouble remembering. He wished the conversation hadn't taken this turn, but somehow it seemed inevitable, as if this was what the whole weekend was really all about.

"You know, I honestly don't remember telling anyone that."

"I don't see how you could remember anything," Tyler said. "You were probably traumatized, seeing one of your friends dead. Did you ever have to see a shrink about it?"

Jeff regarded him steadily for a second or two and then shook his head, grateful to see a trace of sympathy in Tyler's expression.

"No," he finally said, "but I was freaked out. It was the first time I ever saw a dead person." As the image rose in his mind, it took a great effort to keep his voice from cracking. "I was pretty scared."

"But that...that's not the fucking point," Evan said in a low, trembling voice. Jeff shied away from him, still wondering if he was going to take a whack at him with the stick. "The point is, Jimmy died, and *someone* had to be responsible for it." He took a sharp, whistling breath. "All I'm saying is, I still blame Mark Bloomberg for what happened."

"Well...I dunno," Tyler said, pursing his lips like he was about to whistle. "Maybe it was, you know, like everyone said, just an accident."

Tiny flecks of foam dotted Evan's lips, and his eyes were wide and bloodshot. Sunlight coming through bare branches overhead cast stripes of light and shadow across his face. Veins pulsed in his neck, and Jeff was suddenly worried that his friend might be having a seizure or stroke or something. The last thing he wanted was to have to make an emergency trip to the mainland to the emergency room. He wished they could just continue their walk and be quiet for a while, but when he looked down the trail and saw the old infirmary, the memory of his late night walk out here last night only ratcheted up the tension inside him. He wished they would turn around and go back the way they came, but Mike, still in the lead, was already walking straight toward the infirmary.

"Holy shit! I can't believe this!" he called out as he broke into a run, heading toward the building.

Jeff and Evan exchanged glances, and Jeff couldn't help but wonder if it had been Evan he had seen out here last night. If it was, he wanted to know what he had been doing out here.

The others followed Mike, approaching the infirmary from the back. There were three windows on the back, but all of them were boarded over. The shingles on the roof, facing north, were curled up and carpeted with moss. The eaves were lined with numerous old mud wasp nests. The day was chilly, but two or three wasps were outside one of the nests, buzzing as they moved their wings to warm themselves.

As they got closer to the infirmary, Jeff noticed something else he hadn't noticed last night. A powerful stench of sewage hung in the air. Maybe the wind had been strong enough to blow it away from him last night and they were downwind now, but as he came close to the building, the smell was so strong it gagged him.

"Jesus! Did something crawl under there and die?" he asked as he waved his hand in front of his face.

"Yeah," Evan said, wrinkling his nose. "Let's steer clear of this place. It smells like the cesspool backed up."

"Hold on," Mike said as he went around to the front of the building with the others following. "I wanna take a look inside."

"Remember Mrs. Stott?" Fred said. He smirked as he held his hands up to his chest like he was cupping two large grapefruits. "Man, she had the rack, didn't she?"

Mike turned to him with a frown. "You know, you're one sick son of a bitch. She was how old?"

"No. Seriously," Fred said. Jeff thought this was the first time all weekend Fred had shown even the least bit of animation. "Don't tell me you don't remember how big her tits were."

"Hell, no," Mike said, still scowling. "She was an old lady back then. Probably old enough to be your goddamned grandmother."

"Yeah," Jeff added. "And she's probably dead by now, rest in peace."

Fred shrugged, looking suddenly nervous, like he'd said or done something wrong. "I was...I'm just saying..."

Without another word, Mike approached the small porch with the missing steps. The others were a few steps behind. Mike stopped short when he looked up and saw the padlock on the door. Jeff saw that, as he had suspected last night, the lock looked brand new. Mike pulled on it, slammed it against the door in frustration.

"Shit! Why would anyone lock this?" He turned to Evan. "You own this place. Did you lock this?"

"Huh…? No, I…ah…I don't know anything about this," Evan said.

Jeff had the distinct impression he was lying.

"Maybe, you know, the surveyors who were out here last summer to start locating the house sites left some equipment in there and locked it," Evan said. "To tell you the truth, I don't think we should be messing around out here."

"Maybe I can see in one of the windows," Mike said, ignoring what Evan had said. "I just wanna have a look inside." He glanced at Jeff and said, "Remember that time you got poison ivy on your balls?"

"I didn't get it on my *balls*," Jeff said.

"The hell you didn't. You were scratching your balls something fierce."

"Maybe in your dreams," Jeff said. He cringed the instant he said it because it was obvious, to him, at least, that Mike was gay. He didn't want to say or do anything to hurt his feelings or piss him off. "I *never* had poison ivy on my *balls*," he added weakly.

"No. Just in your crotch," Tyler said, obviously trying to lighten the mood, but Mike scowled at Jeff for a moment until he finally shook his head as if it wasn't worth the effort to argue any more.

After inspecting the locked door again, he jumped down off the porch and walked over to the boarded up windows to the right of the front door. Standing on tiptoes, he peered between the cracks. Obviously frustrated, he wedged his fingers under the edge of one of the boards nailed over the window and tried to pry it back. In spite of the years, the planks were nailed down tightly, and they didn't yield. Jeff walked up closer to the building and noticed that the nails in the wood, like the lock on the front door, looked new. They certainly hadn't been out here rusting away for the last thirty-five years.

"You haven't even checked out what's in here?" Jeff asked, turning to Evan.

Evan shook his head sharply as he stood back, keeping his distance from the building. His face was pinched as if he smelled or tasted something nauseating.

"What's the point?" he said feebly. "It's all coming down in the spring, anyway."

Jeff shrugged as if he could just about care, but there was something about this place that bothered him. Something strange was going on here that he just couldn't figure out. Not knowing what it was irritated him no end, and he was more determined than ever to find out.

"How 'bout we take that boat ride now?" Evan said, his voice sounding suddenly bright and chipper. Jeff had the distinct impression he was trying to distract them in order to draw them away from the infirmary.

"Is this where we get the sales pitch?" Tyler asked.

Evan shook his head in vigorous denial.

"Absolutely not," he said. "I promise not to mention the development at all. We'll just cruise around a bit. I wish I told you guys to bring your fishing gear. Do any of you fish?"

"My wife and I have a camp up in the Sierras," Tyler said. "I drown a few worms now and again. I thought of bringing my gear but decided not to hassle with it on the plane."

Looking like he was barely paying attention to any of them, Evan turned and started walking down the path that led to the dining hall. Tyler, Fred and Mike followed a few steps behind him, but Jeff, still unsatisfied, lagged behind. He wasn't looking forward to the prospect of going out onto the lake…at least not now. The day was colder than he liked, and if the wind picked up once they were out of the shelter of the island, they'd freeze their butts off.

Besides, he had to find out what was going on in the old infirmary that *someone* felt needed to be locked up.

Was it just his imagination, or could Evan be hiding something out here? He obviously didn't want anyone to hang around out here.

And what was with that smell?

In front of the building, he could no longer smell it, but out back, for a second or two the stench of raw sewage had been almost too much to handle.

"Hey! You coming?" Evan called out. He and the others were waiting at a bend in the trail.

Jeff considered for a moment, wishing he could lag behind a little longer, but if Evan was hiding something out here, he wouldn't let him dally. He'd find some way to drag him away. With a sigh, Jeff started out after them, but when he was a few feet from the building, he heard something—a sound from inside.

It wasn't much.

Just a single, loud thump like what he heard last night, and it had definitely come from inside the building.

He stopped in his tracks and, turning, looked back at the old building. He was poised, waiting for the sound to be repeated, but all he could hear was the light breeze blowing through the pines around the building. Then Evan, now out of sight around the bend in the trail, called out.

"Come on! Boat's leaving with or without you."

"How about without me," Jeff whispered, but he knew Evan wouldn't leave without him. The one thing his friend didn't want was to leave him here alone to his own devices.

He waited a few more seconds to see if the sound came again, but it didn't. He didn't know what might have caused it, but he was determined, one way or another, to find out.

Jeff looked longingly down the trail. His friends were long out of sight. He knew he wasn't obligated to go wherever they went. He could take time for himself if he wanted. That was at least part of the point of being here. Let them take their damned boat ride. Once they were out on the water and out of sight, he wanted to come back and take a more careful look around.

Clenching his fists, he started jogging down the trail after his friends. The sun was warm on his face, and the cold air was bracing as it washed into and out of his lungs. As he ran, he thought about all the times when he was a kid and had run along this same trail. It was weird how familiar and yet so foreign it all felt.

Without his friends around, he played a game in his mind and, for a short while at least, he was a little boy once again, playing in the woods. He imagined he was a wild man—like Tarzan or an Indian brave—running through the primeval forest, tracking food…or enemies. A powerful feeling of primitive energy infused him, and he was disappointed when he rounded a turn in the trail and saw his friends up ahead. In an instant, the illusion of being someone he knew he wasn't evaporated.

No, he thought, holding onto the image of a younger, stronger, more primitive version of himself. *These are enemies who have invaded my sacred land… and they must be stopped… They must die…*

Jeff was amused to realize how, just below the surface, there was still a little boy inside him, but then he wondered—

Is it a little boy… or is it something else… Is it something more primal?

Once again, he found himself thinking about the stories Mark used to tell them about Hobomock, the Indian demon who tricked enemies and friends alike, and caused their destruction. As he ran to catch up with Evan and the others, he wondered if that might not be what was happening here.

He felt protective of this island and this camp and the memories of what it used to be.

The Wildman

Maybe the hostility or edge of agitation he was feeling about Evan was simply because he didn't like what was going to happen out here.

Maybe he didn't want civilization in the form of Evan's development to come here and destroy the forest and beach and camp the way he remembered them.

Jeff was more winded than he thought he should be when he finally caught up with his friends. He signaled for them to stop, leaning forward with both hands on his knees as he tried to catch his breath.

"What took you so long?" Tyler asked.

"Stop to take a crap in the woods?" Fred said.

Mike sniffed and, under his breath, said, "Hope you didn't get poison ivy on your balls again."

But Evan regarded Jeff with a long, steady stare that Jeff found bothersome…so much so he couldn't look his friend in the eyes for long. It wasn't that he was afraid of what he might see inside Evan; he didn't want Evan to see what was inside of him.

"No…I—ah…" It irritated him that he was still panting so heavily. "I thought I…heard something…in the infirmary, and…was just…checking it out."

He looked up as he said this to see if he could read Evan's reaction, but Evan regarded him steadily with a blank expression.

"Probably a raccoon or skunk knocking around in there," Evan said. "Haven't you noticed? They're all over the place."

"Yeah," Jeff said. "Probably." He hawked up a wad of mucous and spit into the dust at his feet.

Evan stretched out his left arm and glanced at his wristwatch.

"It's already almost noon. What say we rustle up some lunch before we take our boat ride?"

"Sounds like a plan," Tyler said.

"Yeah. I could use a cold one," Mike said.

Everyone else nodded their agreement…everyone, that is, except Jeff, who was still wondering how he was going to get away from everyone else so he could go back to the infirmary and check it out.

There was something inside there, and he wasn't going to rest until he found out what it was.

Chapter Seven

Cruisin'

LUNCH CONSISTED OF cold roast beef sandwiches, potato chips, pickles, and beer—lots of beer. After lunch, Jeff was feeling so bloated all he could think about was how nice it would be to take a short nap…especially after not sleeping much last night. He never saw an opportunity to tell Evan that he didn't want to go for the boat ride, so the five of them headed down to the beach where the boat was moored. They were all wearing winter coats, hats, and gloves, but the cold wind cut like a knife into Jeff's face. At the risk of being called a pussy, he suggested it was too cold, at least for him, and he'd just as soon sit this one out, but Evan and the others pressured him to go.

Throughout lunch, he'd kept watching Evan carefully, looking for some hint that he knew Jeff suspected he was up to something, but Jeff had no idea what he was suspicious of. He couldn't very well confront him and say he had a "bad feeling." He wanted to figure it out, to get a handle on what was bothering him.

He needed something tangible.

Still, he couldn't stop wondering why he was so suspicious. He told himself he should just relax and enjoy this time catching up with old friends. At the very least, he should try to get through the weekend with minimal upset. Come Sunday, they'd all go their separate ways, and if Evan or anyone else attempted to stay in touch, he could let e-mails and phone calls go unanswered until they finally stopped trying. Soon enough, he'd be back into his routine, and this weekend—like his time here as a camper—would be a fading memory.

As they walked down to the boat, Tyler was yammering on about how he'd read an article in some magazine or newspaper about how it wasn't really necessary to wait an hour after eating before going swimming. The whole justification for "quiet hour" in the tent, he said, was bullshit.

"So if one of us falls in and has to swim," Mike said, "he won't get cramps?"

"You would," Fred said at the same time Tyler said, "Absolutely."

Jeff was only half-listening to them, treating their banter like a conversation going on in another room with thin walls. He was unengaged and felt more than a little alienated. For him, this whole "reminiscing thing" had run its course. It bothered him that none of his old friends seemed to want to, or seemed able to, discuss their current lives and what concerned them *now*.

Maybe, he thought, *just below the surface they're just as miserable as I am… or maybe they see what a pathetic loser I am and don't want to rub it in.*

Maybe that's it… our lives have become so boring… so empty and meaningless, all we can do is carry on about shit that happened thirty-five years ago.

If that was all he was going to get out of this weekend, he wished all the more he'd stayed home. If he wanted some time off, he would have been better off driving out to Ithaca for the weekend and seeing how Matt was doing.

When they got to the boat, Jeff acknowledged that something else was bothering him more than he wanted it to and certainly more than he cared to admit.

No matter what he did, no matter where he went or what he said, he couldn't stop thinking about Jimmy Foster.

A sour churning filled the pit of his stomach when he saw that the boat was tied up close to where the old swimming docks had been…close to where they had pulled Jimmy's body out of the water. As they got the boat ready, Jeff's teeth were chattering, and he knew it wasn't just from the cold as he looked up and down the deserted beach.

The wind was blowing hard, and far out on the water, gray waves were laced with whitecaps. Jeff's memory of the lake was of warm, inviting blue water with a trace of algae bloom that turned it green in the sheltered cove. Even on rainy days, the lake water was always "piss warm," as they used to say out of earshot of their counselor.

With winter fast approaching, the lake had changed. It looked cold and dangerous. Jeff shivered as a mental image rose up of Jimmy's ghost, haunting the beach as ice sheathed the lake, and snow blew in blinding gusts across the land.

"You even listening?" Tyler said so suddenly it snapped Jeff back to attention like the crack of a bullwhip.

Jeff shook his head, dazed. "Huh?"

The Wildman

"I asked if you brought a bottle of rum along. It might be a nice warm-up once we're out on the water."

It still took a moment for Tyler's question to sink in. Then Jeff shook his head and said, "Ahh—no. I didn't think to." He looked back at the dining hall. "Want me to go get some?"

"Well, duh," Tyler said.

Evan and Tyler exchanged looks of amusement or thinly veiled irritation that made Jeff think they were up to something. If this had been thirty-five years ago, he would suspect they were going to ditch him and take off in the boat by themselves.

But what sense would that make now?

Truth was, it would work in Jeff's favor, because all he could think about was going back to the infirmary and checking it out to see what, if anything was going on out there.

"Sounds like a good idea to me," Evan said as he slapping his arms to ward off the cold. "It's a bit nippier than I expected."

"I told you we should have waited 'till spring," Jeff said through chattering teeth.

This was his chance to back out, but if he did, probably some or all of them would think better of it, too. That would defeat what he wanted to do, so he was going to have to figure out a way to take off by himself without anyone else knowing where he was going or what he was up to. It was beginning to look like that opportunity wouldn't come until later...maybe not until tonight, once the rest of them were asleep.

Leaving the others to monkey around getting the boat ready, Jeff dashed back up the beach to the dining hall. It wasn't far, but by the time he got there, he was more winded than he thought he should be. Sweat was running down the inside of his shirt, and he was sure that would make him more uncomfortable out on the water.

Inside the dining hall, out of the wind, Jeff felt somewhat relieved. He inhaled the smell of wood smoke and looked at the inviting fire, which was blazing away on the hearth. But being alone in the dining hall jacked up his nerves, and he had a weird feeling that someone was nearby, watching him.

Stop being so goddamned paranoid, he told himself.

But he couldn't stop the feeling as he walked over to his supplies, fished around in one of the bags, and grabbed an unopened bottle of Myers. Gripping it tightly with his gloved hand, he turned to leave, but he suddenly froze. The feeling of being watched was even stronger. He shivered at the thought that somehow...as crazy and impossible as it seemed...Jimmy Foster was close by, keeping a watchful eye on him and everyone else on the island.

Maybe he's like Hobomock, Jeff thought with a deep shiver, and he wondered if, when Evan's development was finished and people were living out here, anyone would sense Jimmy's…or *something's*…presence.

Was the island really haunted by something more than their memories of summers past?

Jeff was still bundled up against the cold and, not wanting to get too warm, he left the dining hall and started back to the beach, moving at a much slower pace. When he was about halfway there, a loud sputtering sound came from the beach as Evan started up the engine. It took a few tries, but as Jeff walked down onto the sand, the engine caught. A huge blue cloud of exhaust billowed out across the water and was swept away by the wind.

"A little sluggish from being so cold overnight," Evan said as Jeff joined the other guys at the water's edge.

All of them watched as Evan gunned the engine a few times and then cast off. Once out on the open water, he gunned the engine a few times before taking off. The boat bounced and skipped over the choppy gray waves, leaving a wide wake before finally leveling out. A huge fan of spray rose from the side of the boat as Evan steered a wide, sweeping arc. His expression was rigid…grim. He looked like he was terrified, not enjoying himself at all.

"Is he gonna come back for us?" Mike asked as the motor roared, and the boat skipped across the choppy water.

"He's just blowing off the stink," Fred said.

After swerving around a bit, Evan guided the boat back to the shore. Cutting the engine, he rode it up onto the sandy beach where the hull crunched on the sand.

"That can't be good for the boat," Fred said.

"Someone's gonna get wet shoving us off," Evan called out. His face was pale with bright red splotches on the cheeks. As he shivered against the cold, Jeff questioned the wisdom of taking a boat ride today, but he smiled with contentment and patted the bottle of rum in his jacket pocket. He'd be fine, he told himself.

"I got it," Tyler said as he grabbed the rope Evan tossed to him. He stood back and let the others scramble on board. The boat was barely big enough to hold all of them, and Jeff worried that, with the water as rough as it was, they might not be safe.

Talk about taking a swim just after eating.

Now—if ever—it was time to back out, but he knew Evan and the others would insist he come with them, so he clambered aboard with the others and settled on one of the hard, wooden seats.

The Wildman

Once everyone else was settled, Tyler pushed the boat away from the shore. The engine was still chugging away, sending up a thinner cloud of exhaust that smelled like the fuel mixture was too rich. Ignoring the cold, Tyler waded out into the lake until the keel was free of the sand and then heaved himself up over the gunwales. He was wet halfway up to his knees, and his teeth were chattering as he settled on the seat next to Jeff.

"I'll take a slug of that rum now," he said, leaning close to Jeff.

Before Jeff did anything, Evan gunned the engine, starting out maybe a bit too fast. Tyler almost fell over backwards, and whatever he said was lost beneath the roar of the engine. Jeff was sure he read Tyler's lips correctly. Once he was seated securely, Tyler turned to Jeff and held his hand out to him.

"Rum…Now!"

Jeff handed him the bottle and watched as he twisted off the plastic cap, breaking the seal. The skin on Tyler's hands was so pale it was almost translucent as he toasted Jeff before tilting his head back and taking a huge, gulp.

"Save some for the rest of us," Fred said with a tight smile. He was hugging his arms to himself and shivering as Evan steered the boat out of the small cove and onto the open water.

Once they were out of the shelter of the cove, it was much colder than Jeff had expected. Within seconds, his face went numb, and the inside of his nose started stinging. The speed of the boat heading into the wind made the wind chill feel like it was twenty below.

Spray rose from the bow as the boat bounced across the choppy water. Every now and then, a particularly strong gust of wind would blow whitewater over the passengers, drenching them. Seated in the bow, Mike and Fred looked positively miserable, but Tyler was smiling. Maybe it was the rum. In the stern, Evan was grinning like an idiot when he got Jeff's attention and said something. Whatever he said, it was lost beneath the wind and the roar of the engine. Jeff shrugged and pointed to his ears, indicating he couldn't hear a damned thing, so Evan concentrated on piloting the boat.

In spite of the cold, Jeff had to admit that the island and lake had a certain raw beauty, in a Northern kind of way. Dark green slashes of pine swayed against the sky. Off to the west, a line of dark clouds was building up, promising more bad weather.

There weren't many camps along the shore, and Jeff tried to imagine how, over the next several years, this whole area would be utterly transformed. It wouldn't be long before it was unrecognizable.

Once again, a sad nostalgia for everything swept over him, and he mourned for what was going to be lost in the name of progress. Men and machines would chop down trees and rip up and remold the earth, bringing "civilization" and destroying the wild forest forever.

It didn't seem right, but what could he or anyone else do to stop it?

It wasn't his business, anyway. Evan and anyone else with enough money could come out here and do whatever the hell they wanted. Just because he'd spent a couple of summers here as a kid, that didn't give him any special privilege or claim to the place.

Moving carefully and steadying himself against the pounding the boat took from the waves, Tyler got up and made his way back to Evan. They leaned their heads close together so they could talk. Jeff glanced at them and wondered what they were talking about, but then shifted his gaze, content to look at the wilderness in respectful silence.

When he was a camper, Jeff had taken a canoe out for a paddle every now and then. He and his friends, usually Evan, would pretend they were Indians, scouting the shoreline for enemies. But other than the boat ride to and from the island with his luggage each summer, he had never been far out on the lake like this. With the icy wind biting his face and working its frigid fingers inside his collar, he was sure it was an experience he wasn't going to repeat in the near future.

Evan took the boat around the north end of Sheep's Head Island. Once they were in the lee of the island with the wind blocked, the air felt almost pleasant. The engine was running smoothly, and the cloud of exhaust was gone.

Jeff watched as they came closer to the shoreline. Savoring the moment, he took the bottle of rum from his pocket and took a long pull. When he was finished, he tapped Fred on the shoulder and passed it to him. Fred smiled widely as he took a drink before passing it along to Mike who handed it to Tyler and then to Evan.

As the bottle made the rounds, with the rum burning like a warm coal in the pit of his stomach, Jeff felt a moment of contentment. His eyes were watering from the cold wind, but he wiped his tears away with his jacket sleeve. In spite of the natural beauty surrounding them, though, all he could think about was getting back to the dining hall so he could warm up.

"Hey!" Mike called out, giving Jeff a nudge on the shoulder. "There's the Pulpit."

"The *what?*" Jeff shouted so he could be heard above the roar of the engine.

"The Pulpit! Don't tell me you don't remember the Pulpit."

Jeff thought about it and then shook his head. As far as he could remember, he had never heard about such a place.

"We used to come down here and fish," Mike said. There was a distant, wistful look in his eyes as he stared at the chunk of gray granite that stood out on the end of the island. It was angled over the water and was squared off at the top. Jeff could see how it had come to be called "The Pulpit," but he had never been fishing out here so far from camp. He and his friends used to catch "sunnies" and the occasional baby bass off the dock, but that was about it.

"When'd you ever come down here?" Fred asked, leaning close so he could be heard. He held his hand out to Jeff for the rum bottle. When Jeff gave it to him, he took a quick sip and passed it to Mike.

"Mark and I used to come out here," Mike said.

A disturbing thought occurred to Jeff, but he didn't voice it. In all his years at Camp Tapiola, he had never heard about going fishing at "The Pulpit." It struck him as a bit odd that their counselor or any other staff member would take one of the campers out here…alone and unsupervised so far from the campgrounds. Jeff wondered if, even back then, Mike knew he was gay, but had Mark been gay, too?

Had coming out here been Mike's initiation?

Was that why he remembered the place so fondly?

Jeff pushed such thoughts away, not wanting to speculate about anyone else's personal life.

"Gonna be bitchly cold once we come around the point," Fred said, nodding to where the waves were smashing against "The Pulpit." The water was much rougher on the windward side of the island. Jeff was tempted to suggest they turn back, but he knew Evan well enough to know he would never turn back. It wasn't his style. So Jeff tightened his collar around his neck and shrank into himself, bracing for the blast of cold that would hit once they got out of the shelter of the island.

But as they passed within fifty feet of "The Pulpit," the engine made a funny clunking sound. It kicked once so hard it made the boat shiver and then sputtered.

"*Fuck!*" Evan shouted, loud enough to be heard by everyone. He revved the engine, but the sputtering only got worse. The engine chugged, and the boat lurched so hard everyone was knocked off balance. Jeff would have fallen overboard if he hadn't been clinging to the gunwales.

"Shit! What's the matter?" Fred shouted, but Evan ignored him as he worked the controls. The chugging sound got steadily louder and then, with one last, loud *thunk*, the engine seized up and died. There was the sound of metal grinding against metal as a huge cloud of thick, black smoke shot out

The Wildman

from under the engine cowling. Then all was silent except for the shrill wind and the steady slapping of waves against the side of the boat.

"What the *fuck?*" Mike said with a scowl.

Evan looked at them with a tight, worried expression. His lips were nearly bloodless, and his eyes were glistening and wide.

"Please don't tell me the engine just died," Tyler said, leaning close to Jeff.

"'Fraid so," Jeff said. "I thought the way it was smoking the mix was off."

His grip on the rum bottle tightened, and he watched as the boat, carried by the current, started drifting away from the island. Once it was back in the wind, it came around so the bow was heading into the wind.

"What the fuck are we gonna do?" Mike asked, sounding angry, but Evan ignored him as he flipped the ignition switch on the engine several times. The only result was a steady *click-click-click* that lasted as long as he held the ignition on.

"Are we fucked or what?" Fred asked as he looked at the shoreline, which was rapidly receding as the wind carried the boat further out onto the water. The frightened note in his voice made it easy for Jeff to imagine Fred had reverted to a terrified twelve year old boy.

Jeff took a quick glance over his shoulder at where they were headed. The mainland looked like it was at least two miles away in the direction they were going. To port and starboard, the shore was much closer, but it didn't do them much good without an engine.

"Break out the oars," Evan said simply.

Jeff noticed the oarlocks on the sides of the boat and the two oars, gray and splintered with age, on the floor underneath their seats. Without a word, he handed the rum to Mike and positioned himself on the center seat. Leaning down, he grabbed the oars and pulled them out. After fumbling the oarlocks into place, he positioned the oars and, gripping them tightly, bent his back and started rowing.

"You want me to take one of those?" Tyler said, tapping Jeff on the shoulder.

"I think I...got it," Jeff said.

It had been a long time since he had rowed a boat, and he was finding it difficult to get a steady rhythm going. With just about every other stroke, one or the other oar would pop out of the oarlock and clatter against the gunwales.

The wind was blowing so hard and steady at his back that it felt like someone was behind him, pushing him with steadily increasing pressure. He didn't want to look over his shoulder at the island to see how close it was. He knew he'd get discouraged when he saw how far he had to row. The wind was picking up strength, and the clouds were closed in. It wasn't long before Jeff was tired and started thinking about letting someone else take over, but he doubted even two of them rowing together could make much headway.

"Think we should…head to…the mainland…and see…if we can find…someone with a…motorboat who can…bring us…back to the island?" Jeff asked, grunting with every stroke.

"I doubt anyone's around this late in the year," Evan said, shading his eyes with his hand as he scanned the distant shoreline. After a moment, he came forward and pushed Jeff to one side and sat down next to him. Without a word, he took the oar on the starboard side from Jeff, and the two started rowing, synchronizing their strokes. Before long, they developed a steady rhythm.

"Just like the old days…in the whaling boats…huh?" Evan said, smiling a wide, toothy grin. The wind tousled his hair, and his eyes held a wild, almost crazy light. He looked like he was actually having fun, but Jeff was sure there was no way he could be *enjoying* this.

"More like…galley slaves…in *Ben Hur*," Jeff replied, bending with each stroke.

"You know…the Romans…never…used slaves to…row their…galleys."

"Really? I'll keep that in mind…next time I'm on *Jeopardy*."

Jeff was smiling, but not as much as Evan. The truth was, he scolded himself for not seeing this coming. He'd had a bad feeling about this weekend, and now here they were, adrift on the lake in near-freezing conditions with rain or snow threatening, and no help in sight.

Yeah… Some fun!

But in a way, Jeff felt like a little kid again, too. He and his best friend from summer camp were doing something together that was fun and adventuresome and dangerous and—yes, maybe even a little crazy, but wasn't that part of the fun? It was the kind of thing they would laugh their asses off about once it was over.

But it wasn't over yet.

Before Jeff allowed himself to enjoy it too much, something else occurred to him that deflated any sense of fun or adventure.

What about tomorrow… when we're all packed up and ready to leave? How are we gonna get off the island if the goddamned motorboat's defunct?

In spite of the cold wind, sweat ringed his neck and shoulders, tickling as it ran down his sides from his armpits. His shoulders and arms were going to be screaming with pain once this was over, but—just like when they were kids—he and Evan were the leaders of the group. They were the ones everyone depended on. He may not see it in their eyes now, but he knew Tyler, Fred, and Mike were counting on them to bring them safely to shore.

"Man! This is a bitch!" Evan shouted as he leaned into it, grunting with each stroke. His good humor was replaced by grimness as the seriousness of their situation sank in.

"Piece of…cake," Jeff said, but he was also beginning to lose hope.

How humiliating was this going to be if they had to put in to shore and then walk however far to find someone who could help them get back out to the island?

"How we…doing?" Evan asked, not looking up as he rowed.

From the bow of the boat, Tyler shouted, "You're doing great. We're gaining on it."

What do you mean 'we,' Kimosabe? Jeff thought.

Evan shot Jeff a look he found impossible to read. His eyes still held a glow of childlike amusement, but his mouth was set in one of the grimmest smiles Jeff had ever seen. He tried not to think about what Evan might be thinking as he put all his strength into rowing.

"If the water was any warmer, I'd dive in and pull the boat in," Mike said, but Jeff scowled and shook his head. There was no way even someone as strong as Mike would be able to challenge this headwind.

"Fuck it!" Jeff suddenly shouted when his oar popped out of the oarlock and clattered against the side of the boat. He was pulling back hard and ended up punching himself in the gut hard enough to knock the wind out of him. As he was repositioning the oar, he saw the watery swelling on the palm of his hand—the beginnings of a blister that would probably be the least of what he would suffer from this.

If only he had stayed back at the camp and let everyone else go for their little ride.

Maybe the extra weight of so many people on the boat had strained the motor and made it conk out.

But this was no time for recriminations or to stew about what he should or shouldn't have done. He had to bend his back into the rowing and get himself and his friends out of this jam. Then he could deal with blisters and aching bones and muscles.

"Wanna 'nother swig?" Mike asked as he held the rum bottle out to Jeff.

Jeff nodded, and Mike shifted forward so he was kneeling in front of Jeff where he could hold the bottle up to his mouth and pour some in.

Jeff's eyes started watering all the more as the rum exploded in his mouth, warming his throat and belly. *That* was something they wouldn't have had if this had happened when they were kids. With the alcohol warming him, he redoubled his efforts. He purposely didn't pay any attention to how close they were to the island. He just kept rowing as if it was the only thing he knew. By now he and Evan had developed a steady rhythm. The boat cut through the water almost as swiftly as if it had a motor.

Without warning, the wind blowing at Jeff's back cut off so abruptly it was as if someone had turned off a huge fan that was blowing across the lake. In the sudden calm, Jeff knew they had to be close to shore. He hadn't realized how fast they had been rowing, but he didn't break the pace he and Evan had developed.

"We're in the…lee of…the island," Evan said, grunting with each stroke. Whatever anger or concern had clouded his face before, it was gone now, replaced by that sappy grin of his as he glanced at Jeff.

Without speaking a word, they let up and rowed easily. The boat skimmed across the unruffled surface of the water where long, wavering reflections of dark pines rippled on the surface like huge spikes. Jeff sighed with relief when he looked over the side and saw the rocky lake bottom.

I can't fucking believe we made it, he thought, and with that thought came the deep muscle aches he knew would come. He stopped rowing and got up from the seat, letting the oar clatter onto the floor. Keeping one hand on the gunwales, he made his way to the stern of the boat and sat down.

"Someone else can row," he said as he took the rum bottle from Mike and took a huge gulp. The alcohol hadn't started to affect him yet, but this swig sent his head reeling.

Evan stopped rowing shortly after Jeff did and, leaning back, groaned.

"Mother *fucker* that was a bitch!" he said as he held his hand out to Jeff for the bottle.

Mike and Tyler took their places at the oars and began rowing. It took them a while to develop any kind of rhythm. In spite of himself, Jeff couldn't help but feel resentful that they got to row on the calmer part of the lake, once they were safely out of the wind.

They passed "The Pulpit" and, hugging close to shore, made their way back to the beach in front of the dining hall. By the time the keel hissed up onto the sand, Jeff's muscles were screaming with agony. He glanced at his watch and saw that it was almost two o'clock. After not sleeping much last night, he was going to need a nap.

And that, he thought, might work in his favor because even after the boat ride, he was determined to find a way to get away from everyone else and investigate the old infirmary.

If only the plumbing was working and he could take a long, hot shower. That would minimize the pains he was going to feel from such unaccustomed

The Wildman

exercise. He noticed that the rum bottle was empty and threw it into the woods, where it frightened a squirrel that scampered away with a shrill warning cry.

He had things to do, but first…first, he needed some rest.

Chapter Eight

Idle Chatter

WHEN JEFF AWOKE a few hours later, he didn't feel much better, but he was surprised that his shoulders and back hadn't cramped up. A slight jab of pain tightened the base of his neck, but it wasn't nearly as bad as he'd expected. His head was still a little buzzed from the rum.

It was dark outside, and a huge fire was roaring in the fireplace. All four of his friends were sitting in a semi-circle around the hearth. Flashes of bright firelight flickered across their faces and cast huge shadows on the wall.

Everyone looked cozy and peaceful as they talked softly to one another. Jeff hesitated to break the tranquility. He rolled over and, for a long while, lay there with his back to the fire and stared out the dining hall windows. It took him a few moments to realize that it was raining. Silvery rivulets of water were running down the window, and every now and then a gust of wind would rattle the panes of glass.

"Shit," he muttered.

"You're awake," Tyler called out.

Jeff raised a hand and waved languidly, but that tiny motion sent a jolt of pain shooting between his shoulders.

"You alive over there?" Evan asked.

"Barely," Jeff replied, groaning loudly when he tried to sit up. The muscles between his shoulders were like knotted ropes, and he collapsed back down. Rolling his head back and forth, he listened to the faint crackling sounds his neck made before giving it another try. This time he made it, and he forced himself to smile at his friends.

"Not used to working so hard, I guess," he said as he placed his right hand on the back of his neck and rubbed.

"You want a massage?" Mike asked, starting to stand up and come over to him.

Jeff waved him off with a quick, "No thanks. I'll be all right." He sighed. "Just give me a second or two."

"We were waiting for you to wake up before we started supper," Evan said. He stood up without any difficulty, making Jeff think he must be in a lot better shape. He walked over to the stack of supplies he'd brought and, opening the lid of the large cooler, fumbled around inside for a few seconds. Then he raised his head and looked at them.

"Okay, looks like we have a choice of hamburgers…hamburgers…or…ahh…yeah, hamburgers."

"As long as there's beer involved, I'm good with 'burgers," Mike said as he grabbed a bottle of Sam Adams from his cooler. "Anyone else?"

Fred and Tyler each nodded and took a beer from him, but Jeff waved him off. Jeff wasn't surprised he had conked out like he had, probably as much from the rum as the exertion, but he was grateful he'd gotten a short nap because…who knew how late he'd be up tonight?

He still was suspicious of Evan's motives. Something was going on here that he still hadn't figured out. No matter how much he wanted to believe it was just because he felt uncomfortable with these people who were really strangers, he had an undeniable feeling that *something* wasn't quite right.

"Yeah. I guess I'll go with a hamburger," Fred said.

"You need help cooking?" Tyler asked, but Evan waved him off and said, "I got it covered."

Jeff kept stretching, trying to work out some of the kinks in his shoulders and back before he tried to stand up. With his back to the fire, he luxuriated in the steady warmth, but he shivered when he looked at the rain-streaked windows.

He sure as hell didn't feel like snooping around out there in the rain. Maybe this was just a shower, and it would pass. He knew the damp chill would only make his aches and pains worse.

"Anyone got some Tylenol or something?" he asked.

Without a word, Evan opened one of his bags, fished around in it for a second, and then tossed a small plastic bottle to him. It rattled when he caught it.

"Thanks," Jeff said even though the motion of catching it hurt. He flipped off the cap, shook out three tablets, and swallowed them dry. The thought of washing them down with rum or beer made his stomach clench.

Moving stiffly, Jeff got up and started walking back and forth in front of the fireplace, all the while rotating his shoulders and twisting his neck from side to side.

"This getting old shit really *sucks*," Fred said with an expression of genuine sympathy. Jeff nodded but wasn't sure what to say in return.

"We owe you, both you and Evan, for getting us out of that jam today," Tyler said.

"Amen, brother," Mike said.

"Hell, it wasn't that bad," Evan said with a sniff and a wave of the hand.

Jeff shrugged in spite of the pain and said, "Ahh…it was nothing."

"Yeah," Mike said. "Nothing…except you can barely move."

"Like Fred said…this getting old shit is for the birds."

"Beats the hell out of the alternative," Evan said tonelessly. He had an armful of meat packages, which he set down on the floor close to the fire. Then he got the frying pan he had used for eggs and bacon this morning and set to work, positioning it on the grate over the coals.

"Anyone wants their buns toasted, they can do it themselves," he said.

Jeff had caught the slight grimace Evan made when he lifted the heavy frying pan, so he knew rowing had taken its toll on him, too. But as always, Evan wasn't going to let anyone catch him in a moment of weakness.

"I dunno," Fred said. "Hey, Mike. You want your buns toasted?"

The way he said it, everyone else caught what seemed like veiled innuendo. Jeff felt a surge of anger at Fred and thought it was uncharacteristic of him to tease or bait Mike like that, but Mike was the first to smile.

"I dunno," he said, lowering his voice and batting his eyelids. "But I'll be only too *glad* to toast *yours*."

That flustered Fred, and he looked as if he thought Mike was seriously propositioning him.

Was he so naïve he didn't realize Mike was gay?

Fred smiled and, lowering his gaze, said mildly, "Thanks, ahh—but no."

Evan was smiling as if enjoying a private joke as he broke the burgers out of the packages and slapped a few into the pan. As the sound and smell of sizzling meat filled the dining hall, the friends' conversation ranged over a variety of topics—their work, their kids, where they went to college, what they planned for the future. In all of this, Jeff noticed that—like last night—Evan remained relatively aloof. It could be that he was preoccupied with preparing supper, but Jeff was thinking now was a good time for Evan to pitch his development-if that was his plan-but he worked silently.

When Tyler and Mike got into a heated discussion about how the Red Sox had choked again this year, Jeff started to feel alienated again. Excusing himself, he stepped outside, thinking he'd try to call Matt at college to see how he was doing. It would be nice just to hear a friendly voice.

When he first stepped out onto the porch, it appeared that the rain had let up. Huge drops still fell from the trees and plopped on the porch roof. When he looked at his phone, he saw only one signal bar, but when he stepped off the porch and moved away from the building, a second bar appeared. Heartened, he pressed the speed dial for Matt's phone and held the cell to his ear. After the phone rang once, a loud beep sounded. He took the phone away from his ear and looked at the message on display.

NETWORK NOT AVAILABLE.

"No shit, Dick Tracy," he muttered as he walked out from under the pines toward the beach. Maybe the signal would be better there.

The rain had, indeed, let up, and he wandered further away from the dining hall. Still, the signal bars never rose above two.

He figured the mountains were blocking the signal, or else there simply was no signal available out here.

With no cell service, what would they do if there was an emergency and they had to call for help?

One of the other guy's phones might use a different service and pick up a better signal, but what if all of their cells were useless?

Had Evan planned ahead? Did he have a radio or a landline to call for help if they needed it?

The wind was picking up, and the moon had cleared the clouds; but off to the west, a thick bank of dark clouds was closing in, moving fast across the night sky. Leaving the shelter of the trees, Jeff walked along the shore, all too aware that—once again—he was heading toward where they had pulled Jimmy Foster out of the lake.

He hesitated and was about to turn around, but for some reason, he couldn't change direction. He was still convinced something wasn't quite right about this weekend, and he didn't want to believe it had anything to do with what had happened back then. In spite of his overactive imagination, he didn't *really* think Jimmy Foster's ghost haunted the beach where he had died.

No…it was something else…something he was either not seeing…or was forgetting.

Regardless, he was still convinced his friend hadn't drowned.

He had been murdered.

That thought kept gnawing at Jeff's mind and wouldn't let go.

So if Jimmy was killed, who did it?

And why?

Why hadn't anyone been arrested and convicted?
Has someone gotten away with murder and—even more frightening—might they still be alive?
And then a terrible thought occurred to him.
What if it's one of the men in the dining room?
What if Evan or Tyler or Mike or Fred knows more about what had happened that day than they've admitted?
Is this why Evan seems to be acting so strange?
And what's the deal with Fred?
He sure seems uptight about something.
Or what if Mike or Tyler know more than they're letting on? What if their gregarious natures are a front to hide the terrible truth they know?
What if one of them knows exactly what had happened?
Even if they aren't the killer, what if they saw or heard something and never told anyone?

Jeff glanced at the cell phone in his hand. The signal bar was back to one, but he tried Matt's number anyway simply because he was desperate to hear a friendly voice.

It would help reassure him.

But the call failed again, and Jeff kept walking, his feet dragging in the wet sand, leaving long, scalloped tracks behind him. When he reached the end of the beach, he turned to start back. The stretch of beach before him was all but lost in the darkness. The white sand at his feet glowed with an eerie luminescence that looked like thick ground fog, not sand. Dark water lapped against the shore, sounding like a thirsty animal, drinking. Feeling the cold and knowing more rain or snow was on the way, Jeff started back, picking up his pace.

He was halfway to the dining hall when a thought hit him so hard it staggered him.

"Holy shit," he whispered.

His voice was whisked away by the wind. He imagined it was twisting and turning like ribbons as it was carried away on the breeze.

What if I know?

His throat was raw and burning as he swallowed and looked around frantically at the night as it pressed in close around him.

What if I saw something… and I've blocked it out all this time?
Is that possible?

The idea unnerved him so much his body began to tremble. The ache in his shoulders got worse. The cold, sour nausea in his stomach was a memory of how he had felt that day when he had seen Jimmy's pale white body lying on the stretcher.

He was paralyzed by terror, realizing the pitifully small body was one of his friends…someone he had known for the last three or four summers…someone he had played baseball with and gone swimming with and goofed around in the tent with, and now he was dead and was never, *never* coming back again.

Jeff couldn't be sure Jimmy had been murdered, but he was suddenly confronted by the thought that maybe he had seen it happen and had been so traumatized he had blocked it out of his mind entirely.

And then another even more frightening thought occurred to him. He let out a gasp loud enough to fill the night.

What if I did it?

A chill took hold of him and shook him.

"No…no," Jeff muttered in a low, strangled voice as he staggered a few steps backwards. Raising his arms to protect himself, he shook his head violently back and forth in adamant denial.

No… This is insane, he told himself and wanted to believe.

If he started thinking like this, he should be writing horror novels instead of selling real estate. He had no reason to hurt, much less *kill*, Jimmy Foster.

If anything, over the years he felt guilty that he had never found out what really happened.

How was it possible, in a summer camp full of campers and staff, for a boy to wander down to the swimming area alone, dive into the water, hit his head on something underwater, and drown?

How come not a single person had seen him and wondered where he was going, wandering away from the baseball game?

Someone must have seen *something*.

Someone must know more than they've told.

And what if… what if that someone is the one who cut Jimmy's throat and threw him into the lake to make it look like an accident?

Jeff had been told by the authorities that the cut on Jimmy's throat hadn't been what killed him, but he never believed it.

It was a knife wound!

Jeff couldn't stop trembling as he looked out at the dark water and, narrowing his eyes, tried to imagine what had happened here thirty-five years ago.

"Come on, Jimmy," he whispered. "If you're still here, tell me…tell me how you died."

He jumped and let out a shrill squeal that hurt his throat when a hand clamped down on his shoulder from behind.

"*Jesus!*" Evan shouted, stepping back quickly as Jeff wheeled around with his clenched fists raised.

"Fuck *you!*" Jeff yelled. "What the *fuck* are you *doing,* sneaking up on me like that?"

Evan shrugged innocently as he waved his hands in front of himself.

"I was—shit! I was looking for you," he said in a high, tight voice. "I was gonna tell you the burger's are getting cold."

Jeff's pulse was pounding so fast the steady *thump-thump-thump* made his neck and wrists ache. It took him a long time to catch his breath, but even then, chills raced up and down his back.

"What are you doing out here, anyway?" Evan asked. "It sounded like you were talking to someone. Did you actually get a cell phone signal?"

"No, I—ah, I…" Jeff let his voice drift off as he raised his hand so Evan could see his cell phone. "There's no signal out here."

"I didn't think so," Evan said. "You'd better come back before you food's ice cold…or before Mike gobbles it all."

"He'd do that, wouldn't he?" Jeff said, trying to inject a note of humor into the situation if only to dispel the nervousness winding inside him.

Before Evan turned to leave, though, he caught Jeff by the elbow.

"You were thinking about Jimmy, weren't you?" he said.

Jeff's throat closed off, and he couldn't say a word, but he nodded.

"I know." Evan said. "It's a real bummer what happened, isn't it?"

He shivered, and Jeff had the impression it wasn't just from the cold. Still, all he could do was nod.

"Cell phone service is real spotty out here," Evan said, sounding as if he was purposely changing the subject to something more pleasant. "It works better in the day time, for some reason."

Jeff nodded and then managed to say, "So when all these people you're selling houses to are living out here, are they going to have service?"

"We're trying to get the phone companies to put a relay tower close to the lake," Evan said. "The nearest one is more than fifty mile south of here." He laughed lightly. "Can't very well get people to move out here unless we provide all the benefits of modern civilization—cell phones, satellite TV, shopping malls."

Jeff could tell Evan was trying to make light of the situation, as if talking about Jimmy had upset him, too. But they had more immediate concerns, like what would they do if they couldn't get the boat started in the morning?

Besides basics like food, shelter, and water, Jeff, for one, had a job to go back to. He couldn't very well not show up for work, and the other guys had obligations and responsibilities.

Evan turned and started walking toward the dining hall, but Jeff stayed where he was for a while longer, staring out at the lake. He was embarrassed that Evan had been able to sneak up on him from behind like that without him catching even a hint he was there until he tapped him on the shoulder. And he couldn't help but wonder if Evan had done it on purpose to scare him.

Does he have some reason he doesn't want me wandering around here alone?

The wind was whistling in the trees overhead, and the lake was so churned up whitecaps appeared on the waves close to shore. It seemed like a hell of a storm was coming, and Jeff wondered if they'd get off the island tomorrow even if the motorboat *was* working. He chuckled, thinking how it was going to be a long, long time before civilization ever came to Sheep's Head Island.

As he followed Evan back to the dining hall, Jeff could imagine all too easily that the Indian demon their counselor had told them about might still lurk out here in the forest.

Maybe, he thought, *that's what I should be afraid of.*

※ ※ ※

The rain picked up again shortly after Jeff got inside and was sitting down to a meal of cold hamburgers, potato chips, pickles, and beer. At least the beer was cold, but Jeff wished someone had thought to bring some wine or cider to mull over the fire.

Now *that* would drive away the cold.

As rain pelted the windows, a high-pitched, whistling wind blew through cracks in the window frames, sounding like someone playing the flute. The rest of the guys were filling the time after the meal gabbing about things that didn't hold Jeff's interest for long. After a while, he moved closer to Evan and, whispering to him, said, "So, what are we gonna do?"

Evan arched his eyebrows and said, "Do about what?"

"The boat. The engine's dead, right?" Jeff rubbed his hands nervously together. "The way it conked out, it sounded to me like it might have given up the ghost for good."

"Given up the ghost," Evan repeated with a sly smile. "Now *there's* an expression I haven't heard in a while."

"I'm serious, man." Jeff turned to face him directly and nailed him with a harsh stare. "How much of this did you think through? Do you have a backup plan for if the engine's fucked? Did you make arrangements for someone to maybe check on us to make sure we're all right out here?"

Evan stared back in silence at him for a long time. He was sitting at an angle to the fire, and the harsh firelight lit up one side of his face and cast the other side into shadow that highlighted the lines on his face, especially around his eyes.

"Don't worry," he said at last. "We'll be all right. Even if we have to row the fucker over and back a few times. Christ, if we have to, we could swim back to the mainland."

"In this weather? I doubt it." Jeff anger flared, and he pointed at Evan, jabbing his forefinger into his chest as he said, "*You're* responsible here. Are you saying you don't have a backup?"

Evan scowled as he swatted Jeff's hand away from him. Clenching his fist, he was ready to throw a punch if Jeff pressed him much more.

"I said don't fucking worry about it." His voice was low and even with just a hint of a tremor. "I've got it covered. You don't have to worry about how we're going to get off the island, okay?"

"So you have a spare boat somewhere, or what?"

Evan visibly relaxed as he leaned forward and, placing his hand on Jeff's shoulder, pulled him close.

"Just relax. We're here to have a good time. Don't fuck it up. We'll deal with all that shit in the morning."

Jeff still wasn't satisfied, but he knew he wasn't going to get anywhere with Evan right now, so he backed off and rejoined his friends around the fire. It took him a while to calm down, and he kept casting wary glances at Evan, but before long, Jeff relaxed enough to join in with the conversation.

"How about you?" Tyler asked, turning to Jeff with a look of hopeful expectation on his face.

Jeff shrugged and said, "What about me? What are you talking about?"

"The question under discussion is-what's the worst thing you've ever done in your life?" Tyler said.

Jeff was taken aback by that, and he looked from face to face.

"Ole' Mike, here, says probably the worst thing he ever did was not come out of the closet sooner, right Mike?"

"Especially to my parents." Mike said, nodding. He looked like he was blushing, or maybe it was from the glow of the firelight. "Abso-fuckin'-lutely. Even back when we were campers here, I knew or at least was pretty sure I was different. I wasn't interested in girls the way the rest of you were. And my life overall would have been a helluva lot better, things would have gone a lot smoother, if I'd had the courage to let everyone know who I was…who I *am*."

"Hear, hear," Tyler said, raising his beer bottle. "I'll drink to that."

They all clinked bottles and took long gulps.

"Yeah," Jeff said. "I agree, but seriously, even when we were kids, you knew?"

Mike was still slugging down beer, but he nodded.

Fred cleared his throat and said, "Well…you know I'm not anti-gay or anything. Honest, I'm not. But you, like, you didn't have the hots for any of us, did you?"

Mike hesitated for a moment, then leaned close to Fred and ran the back of his fingers across Fred's cheek. "Only for you, Freddie boy," he said in a low, lascivious voice, "and I've been hoping and praying all weekend I'd be able to get into your pants."

"Cut the shit," Fred said as he batted Mike's hand away. Smiling weakly, he looked at the other guys for support.

"I'm just screwing with you," Mike said. "I've been with my boyfriend for over ten years, now, and we couldn't be happier."

"I'm glad for you," Jeff said, and he meant it. He had been so miserable following his divorce that he was glad to hear about any couple, straight or gay, dedicated to each other and happy together.

"How about you, Jeff?" Tyler said, turning to him and leaning forward. "What's the worst thing you've ever done?"

"You mean besides cheat on my taxes and beat up Girl Scouts when I see them out and about, delivering their cookies?"

That didn't get the laugh he expected, and he realized that while he'd been talking to Evan, the others had been having a rather serious discussion. He took another swig of beer so he could compose himself.

"Well," he said thoughtfully, "probably the worst thing I did was cheat on my wife."

"Come on. You gotta do better than that," Tyler said. "I mean—any of us who are married, we've all been tempted, right?"

"Tempted, sure," Mike said. "But there's a big step between *thinking* about doing something and actually *doing* it."

"Plus," Fred said, "You told us you couldn't say if you had screwed any of your Hollywood starlet clients."

"What's a lawyer do if not screw people?" Tyler said.

"Sure." Jeff nodded his agreement. "Everyone's probably been *tempted*, but this was right after our son was born, and…I dunno…I just always felt guilty about doing it. That's all."

The Wildman

Jeff noticed that everyone, even Evan, seemed engaged in the discussion now…everyone, that was, except Fred. He was leaning back with a beer in one hand and staring at some hazy, middle distance. A curious expression of worry and maybe trepidation was frozen on his face. The corners of his mouth were twisted downward as though he wanted to say something but was struggling to hold it back.

What if he saw what happened to Jimmy? Is that's what bugging him?

The thought sprang into Jeff's mind unbidden but strong enough to make him jump. Once the idea was planted, it quickly took hold.

Is that possible? Where was Fred during the baseball game? Had he ever told them?

Now that he thought about it, he didn't remember seeing Fred at the game. He'd always assumed he was, but Fred was such a lousy player no one ever wanted him on their team. Whenever they played one tent against another, Jeff's tent lost sometimes, even with Mike on their team, and it was usually because of something Fred did or didn't do.

What if on that particular day they had made it clear to Fred that he wasn't wanted or needed on the ball field? What if he had wandered away from the game? What if he ended up down by the lake when Jimmy was there?

Jeff's reading of Fred this weekend was that he was a mild mannered, withdrawn person. He might even consider him uptight, and it certainly was possible he was holding something back. All weekend, Fred hadn't said much about anything of real substance, as if he wanted to keep things on a superficial level. And he definitely was keeping his thoughts and feelings to himself. It seemed unlikely he would have had anything to do with Jimmy's death, but he might have *seen* something.

Studying him now and trying to guess what he was thinking, Jeff thought he sure looked like he had something important to say but just couldn't bring himself to say it.

Jeff wondered if anyone else was picking up on Fred's obvious nervousness, or was he jumping to wrong conclusions again because of things he'd been thinking about earlier.

"How 'bout you, Fred?" Jeff said.

He didn't miss Fred's reaction. His left leg twitched, and his eyes widened as though he'd gotten a mild electrical shock. In the glow of the firelight, the skin on his face looked almost translucent.

"What? What about me?" Fred's voice sounded tight and higher than normal.

Jeff shrugged, trying to look totally casual about the discussion, but he was suddenly convinced Fred had something really important on his mind.

He didn't know the guy, so he didn't know if he would have to coax it out of him or if he would have to pressure him to confess whatever he was hiding. He knew he should let Fred keep whatever it was to himself, but Jeff didn't want to do that…especially if it had anything to do with Jimmy's death.

"You sure look like you got something on your mind," Jeff said. "Is there anything you want to tell us?"

Fred bit down on his lower lip until it went bloodless as he shook his head vigorously. The tightness around his mouth and eyes indicated something definitely was bothering him. His hand started shaking as he raised his beer to take a sip. When he swallowed, his throat made a loud gulping sound.

"Come on," Evan said. "Tell us." He seemed not to have noticed Fred's reaction and was just playing along with the discussion. "What's the worst thing you ever did?"

"Could we talk about something else?" Fred asked. His voice wavered, and he had trouble looking directly at any one of them for more than a second or two. A hint of frantic desperation lit his eyes. Jeff caught it even if no one else did.

"Why's that?" Evan asked.

There was no way Jeff could miss the sudden shift in Evan's tone of voice as he leaned forward, practically glaring at Fred, who withered visibly under his intense stare.

"No…no reason," Fred said. "I just think after…after all these years, maybe there's something a bit more—you know-more interesting to talk about."

"By the expression on your face," Evan said, now leering at him, "I'd say you've got some serious shit you're holding back."

"No…no way," Fred said. His voice was high and strained as he looked at the floor and shook his head in vigorous denial.

"Come on," Tyler said, bristling at Evan. "Back off, will you? He obviously doesn't want to talk about it."

"Yeah," Mike piped in. "Let's change the subject."

Evan turned on both of them with an angry fire in his eyes.

"No," he said coldly. "I'm interested. And I think it would be good for ole' Freddie-boy here to talk about whatever's bugging him. That's what we're all about here, aren't we?" He looked from person to person as though soliciting support he knew he wasn't going to find. "We trust each other one hundred percent, don't we? Well? Don't we?"

For a long, uncomfortable moment, no one said a word. The logs in the fire blazed and crackled.

"Sure we can," Jeff finally said. He was feeling sorry about starting it all by pressing Fred the way he had. If Fred or anyone else didn't want to talk about something, they didn't have the right to force it out of them. "I'm just saying…if he doesn't want to—"

"Aww, come on. What is it?" Evan said, cutting Jeff off and turning to Fred. "Did you kill someone or something? Is that it?"

Jeff didn't like where this was going. It was just like when they were kids and, without ever talking about it or agreeing on it, somehow they all picked the one kid in the tent to heap their abuse on—the scapegoat. Usually it was someone who was new that year, but was that what Fred was now…their scapegoat? For what?

Jeff's anger flared at Evan when he saw the wounded expression on Fred's face. Before, he had been looking tense and worried, but now he looked like he was so scared he was about to burst into tears. His eyes glistened in the firelight, and the lines on his face deepened into shadow that looked like thin ink lines.

"Stop picking on him, will you?" Jeff said. "For Christ's sake."

But Evan ignored him as he stared at Fred, still pressuring him. Jeff wanted to tell Evan that he was acting like a bastard, that he shouldn't be picking on Fred or anyone else like this. Why was he being so pushy about it? They should all act like adults here, not turn it into some kind of *Lord of the Flies* thing.

After another short, tense silence, Fred took a deep breath and let it out in a long puff as he turned to look at Evan with a steady, empty stare.

"You really want to know? The worst thing I ever did?" His voice was low and shaky. "I'll tell you, and you're gonna wish to God you'd never asked."

"No. Wait," Jeff said, waving his hands impatiently. "You don't have to tell us anything, Fred." He looked at the others. "This isn't fair."

But Jeff could see that something inside Fred had snapped. Any second now he was going to flip out and let them all have it. Jeff wished he could scream at both Evan and Fred to just shut the fuck up, but he fell silent as he waited for the explosion.

"I…I killed one of my kids," Fred finally said, breaking the silence that had settled over them. He heaved a phlegmy sigh that rattled in his throat.

The confession hit them all like an exploding bomb. For a long time, no one said a word as Fred and Evan stared at each other. Fred had a blank stare, and his lower lip was trembling. Evan looked like—for once-he had no idea what to say.

"There! You happy?" Tears filled Fred's eyes and ran in glistening streaks down his cheeks.

"Aww...shit, man," Evan said, looking absolutely crest-fallen. "I didn't mean to— Jesus, I'm sorry."

"Shut up for once, will you just shut the fuck up?" Fred shouted. There was pain and rage on his face, and Jeff realized he had never seen Fred like this, either as a kid or as an adult.

"How...how'd it happen?" Tyler asked, his voice laced with sympathy. "I mean...if you don't want to talk about it, I understand."

"Jesus, man," Mike said as he reached out and placed a hand on Fred's knee. Fred flinched at the touch and drew back.

"That's gotta be..." Tyler said, but then his voice faltered because he obviously didn't know what else to say.

Fred sniffed loudly and wiped his eyes with the palms of his hands. Jeff thought he looked diminished, somehow, so sad and vulnerable. He wondered how Evan was taking this, but the truth was—he didn't care.

Fuck Evan! He thought. *If he feels like shit now—good! He deserves it.*

"It was our second child...our first son. We named him Alex."

Fred's voice hitched and closed off with a loud click. This was obviously taking a great deal of effort, but Jeff had the feeling, as tough as it was to talk about, this might be exactly what Fred needed...especially since he obviously had been bottling it inside for so long.

"He...he was born with a...a brain defect." He narrowed his eyes as though in pain and clenched his hands into fists. "I don't want to go into all the medical bullshit, but I lived with it for so long...so goddamned long. The bottom line was, the doctors all said Alex would be severely retarded all his life, and there was no hope of a cure, so one night—one night—"

Again, his voice closed off as more tears flowed from his eyes. He leaned forward, cupping his face in his hands and resting his elbows on his knees as he sobbed. Mike moved his hand to Fred's shoulder and patted him, but Fred gave no evidence that he noticed the touch.

"Take it easy there, buddy," Mike cooed softly.

With his face still buried in his hands, his voice muffled, Fred continued.

"We already had a child—a girl, Lara, and she was—she is the brightest little thing you'd ever want to meet, thank God. She's fourteen now, and she's not giving us any trouble like you hear about from teenagers these days. But Alex...he...I just...I couldn't face it, you know?"

Mike kept patting him on the back, and everyone—even Evan—made soft murmurs of agreement.

"So one night...when he was asleep, I...Oh, sweet Jesus in Heaven, I'm so sorry, but I..."

The Wildman

He let out a barking cry that sounded like an animal that had been hit by a car. He slammed his beer bottle onto the floor, shattering it into dozens of amber shards. His shoulders were shaking violently as he leaned forward and crumpled in on himself.

"You don't have to talk about it," Tyler said softly. "I…I'm sorry we brought this whole thing up."

Jeff wanted to say it was his fault, but he was still angry with Evan for pressing Fred the way he had. It had been obvious he didn't want to talk about this, and here they were, practically strangers to one another, talking about something as private and horrible as the murder of a child. There was no excuse for making anyone admit to something like that.

"I *had* to do it. Don't you see?" Fred took his hands away from his face and looked at them with absolute anguish and despair etched on his face. "I smothered him in his crib with a stuffed toy—a goddamned Winnie the Pooh bear— so I…so *we* wouldn't have to live with…so *he* wouldn't have to live his life with something like that."

"Oh, man. I understand completely," Jeff whispered. "Who can blame you?"

"I…the medical examiner determined it was SIDS, you know? Sudden Infant Death Syndrome. But I'm pretty sure—I'm positive he knew I'd done it."

"And I'll bet he understood, too," Tyler said. "That's probably why, if he *did* suspect what really happened, he didn't make anything of it, you know?"

Fred's face was contorted with agony as he looked at Tyler, but a distant coldness filled his eyes…a coldness that made it all too clear to Jeff, at least, how absolutely alone he felt. No one here could possibly begin to understand what he had been through.

How could they?

How could *anyone* understand the torment being so bad that you were forced to suffocate your own child?

Jeff was ashamed of himself. All along, he had been thinking Fred had been holding back something about what had happened to Jimmy Foster. He wished there was something he could do or say to make Fred feel even a little bit better.

"So—" Fred said, sniffing back his tears and looking at them. "Does that constitute the worst fucking thing any of us has ever done? Does it?"

Moving slowly, he got to his feet and stood there for a long time, silently staring at the broken beer bottle on the floor. The flickering firelight shot amber rays of light through the glass and onto the worn wooden floor. After a moment, Fred hitched his pants and said, "I think I'll take a little walk."

"It's gonna start raining again," Jeff said. He didn't like that anyone would feel uncomfortable enough to be driven out on a night like this.

Moving as if he hadn't even heard him, Fred bent down and grabbed his raincoat from the pile of clothes on the floor. His face held a curious, blank expression as he pulled his raincoat on and zipped it up to his chin. When he pulled the hood over his head and tugged the drawstrings, his face was lost in shadow.

"I just need some time to clear my head," he said in a distant, hollow voice. "Don't let me bum you guys out."

With that, he walked to the side door and went outside. The screen door banged shut behind him loud enough to make Jeff jump. For a long time, everyone in the dining hall remained perfectly silent until, finally, Tyler let out a loud breath and said, "Christ on a cross."

"Who'd a thunk it?" Mike said with a shrug.

"You had to push him, didn't you?" Jeff said, turning to Evan. "You didn't see how much this was bothering him?"

"How was I supposed to know? I had no fucking idea," Evan said, shrugging as though absolutely helpless. "Honest to Christ. If I had known…"

"Yeah, well you might want to think before you open your goddamned mouth next time," Jeff said with a snarl.

The words were out of his mouth before he could stop them. He knew he would regret them later—just as Evan seemed to regret what he had just done. But it was too late. For either of them. The anguish and pain Jeff had seen on Fred's face and in his demeanor made him furious at Evan, and he had no doubt this would cause a rift between him and Evan for the rest of their lives.

But what did it matter?

He hadn't had a *real* friendship with Evan for over thirty-five years.

Why should he give two shits what he thought now?

"I said I was sorry." Evan cast a sullen look at Jeff. "What more do you want?"

"You can start by apologizing to Fred when he gets back," Jeff said.

"I already apologized. I don't think I have to—"

"Oh yes you do. Apologize again, and make goddamned sure he knows you mean it."

Evan started to reply but stopped before he dug himself in any deeper. Lowering his gaze, he nodded his agreement. Only the crackling of the fire and the hissing sound of wind-blown rain, beating against the windows, broke the silence of the room.

"Uhh...yeah...all right, then," Tyler said as he rubbed his hands together. "Look, guys, we can't let something like this ruin the whole weekend. Can we?"

Jeff glared at him, genuinely confused what to say or do. Once again, he cursed himself for agreeing to come out here in the first place. He should have left well enough alone. He had all the good memories he needed about being a kid here, and that's where it should have stopped. He and Evan and the rest of them were fools to think they could recapture any of the innocence and freedom they had felt back then.

All of that was over...done...dead.

As dead as Jimmy Foster.

"I didn't mean to upset him," Evan said. "I didn't know." He moved over to the cooler and grabbed a beer. Before opening it, he glanced around at the others and said weakly, "Anyone want one?"

After a moment, Mike raised his hand and said, "Sure. Why not?"

Jeff couldn't see how they could ignore what had just happened. Then again, they shouldn't let Fred's problems—as bad as they were—ruin their time here. Without saying anything, he stood up and pulled on his raincoat.

"Where are you going?" Evan asked.

"For a walk," he said as he grabbed his small flashlight and slipped it into his pocket. "I need some fresh air."

He started for the door, knowing what everyone else was thinking. All of them, maybe even Evan, assumed he intended to find Fred and talk to him to calm him down. And he knew they'd be content, at least for a while, to leave them alone.

He shivered as he opened the screen door and stepped out onto the porch. He clicked on his flashlight and stared at the cold lines of falling rain. He was content to let them all think whatever they wanted to because he had other plans.

He was going to use this distraction to go out to the old infirmary and have another look around.

Of course, what had happened with Fred still bothered him, but he had his own things to deal with. All evening, the feeling that something was wrong had gotten steadily worse, and now he was going to do something about it.

Chapter **Nine** ———————————

Grim Discovery

ROILING CLOUDS WHISKED by overhead, casting wavering shadows across the land with a disorienting strobe light effect. The rain had stopped, at least for the time being, but Jeff could tell by how fast the weather front was moving that there was more—and probably worse weather—on the way. As he made his way along the winding path leading out to the old infirmary, he had his flashlight in hand, but he kept it turned off. He didn't want anyone, especially Evan, to know where he was headed.

The going was sloppy. There were puddles everywhere, and much of the trail had turned to mud. He made his way around or through ankle-deep streams of runoff. Thick mud clung like paste to his sneakers, threatening to pull them off his feet with every few steps. It wasn't long before Jeff's pants were saturated from the knees down. Water clinging to the overhanging branches dropped, snapping and popping on his hood like tiny bullets.

As he made his way deeper into the woods, Jeff felt tension rising inside him. Overhead, the pine trees swayed in the wind, their branches clacking like old bones with every powerful gust. An ozone-tinged freshness filled in the night, making him feel heady, like he'd had more than a few shots of rum.

This is absolutely crazy, he told himself time and again.

He had no business snooping around like this. It didn't matter what kind of creepy feelings he got about Evan or anyone else. If he had any smarts, he'd turn back now and get back inside where he could have a shot or two of rum, warm up, and dry off.

Why was he chasing around in the woods at night like this?

He had no idea, but something was spurring him on. Even if it was just to satisfy his curiosity, he had to do this. He couldn't deny there had been something strange about Evan's reactions when they were out here earlier today.

And that sound from inside the building—twice. He'd heard the same sound twice.

Things simply didn't add up.

Besides, what harm would there be in having one last look around before they all left on Sunday?

When the clouds obscured the moon, the woods got so dark Jeff was concerned he might lose his way, so once he was out of sight of the dining hall, he snapped on his flashlight. The tiny oval of light wasn't much help, darting and weaving back and forth as he looked for the driest parts of the trail.

There weren't many.

He wasn't worried, though. Even after all these years, the campgrounds felt so familiar to him he was sure he could find his way around blindfolded. Following instinct as much as the indistinct trail, he moved quickly until, up ahead, he saw the hulking shape of the infirmary. It loomed in the night.

"Okay…Now what?" he whispered as he shined his flashlight onto the closed and locked door. Shivering, he blew on his hands for warmth. He wished he'd brought some rum with him as a warmer.

Of course, he didn't have the key for the lock, and he was sure it wouldn't have been smart to ask Evan for it. That left him no choice but to do a little B&E.

Bending low, he swept the ground with his flashlight beam, looking a rock or something big enough to break the padlock. It wasn't the brightest idea, smashing someone's brand new lock, but if Evan was telling the truth and had no idea what was in the building, he wouldn't even notice the vandalism before they left the island tomorrow. And if he *did* know what was in there… well then, it would be better if Jeff knew what it was, too.

After a bit of a search, Jeff found a fist-shaped rock that would do. It was slippery in his grip, but he squeezed it tightly in his right hand while positioning the padlock so he would have a good clean shot at it. When he was ready, he trained the flashlight on the lock with his left hand and swung the rock with all his might.

The first hit rang out like a shotgun blast in the night, rattling the door. Jeff hoped the wind would mask any noise he made from the people in the dining hall. Still, he cringed.

What if someone isn't back at the dining hall?
What if someone followed me out here?

The blow left a long scratch on the shiny metal hasp and put a good-sized ding in the rotting wood, but the lock held. The hinges were probably rotted, and it would no doubt be easier to kick the door in, he thought, but talk about vandalism.

Gritting his teeth to stop them from chattering, Jeff gripped the rock tightly and gave the lock half a dozen quick, solid blows. Each hit rang out, but when he stepped back and looked at his progress—or lack thereof—he was filled with frustration. Other than a few more dings and divots in the wood, the lock looked like it had barely been touched.

"*Son* of a fucking *bitch*," Jeff muttered as he turned the lock over and gave it another six or seven sharp blows on the backside.

Still nothing.

Sniffing with grim laughter, Jeff wondered why breaking into someplace always looked so easy in the movies. Locks always gave after only one or two quick hits. He was about to give it a few more whacks when, from inside the building, he heard a faint sound.

A *thump*.

He was so nerved up he couldn't tell if it was the same sound he had heard before. Turning to one side, he pressed his ear against the cold door and listened, but raindrops dripping from the trees onto the roof created a steady pattering sound that drowned out anything else he might have heard.

"Come *on* you *lousy* son of a *bitch!*" he whispered heatedly as he pounded the rock repeatedly on the door hard enough to make his teeth ache. He was making so much noise he was sure everyone back at the dining hall could hear, but he no longer cared. Hell, they could probably hear him a mile away on the mainland.

Frustration and rage filled Jeff as he slammed the rock repeatedly against the lock. It jangled and bounced, and Jeff was so caught up in his fury that he barely noticed when the hasp finally popped. He continued to rain half a dozen more blows against it. Finally, though, he saw that he had succeeded.

Inhaling sharply, he straightened up so he could catch his breath. He let the rock drop from his hand, and it landed in a puddle close to the infirmary's foundation. Sweat mingled with rainwater ran down his face. A rising surge of apprehension filled him when he pushed the door open slowly and directed his flashlight beam inside.

The place obviously had not been used in a long time. The nurse's desk, exam table, file cabinets, and all of the paper-thin partitions and small, metal-framed beds had been removed. As he swept the perimeter of the room with his flashlight beam, he saw definite signs that animals had been nesting in here. Shredded leaves and paper were piled up in the corners, and overhead in the rafters, black clots of cobwebs swirled in the breeze.

Jeff cringed as he took a few steps into the building. The rotten stench he'd smelled outside earlier was stronger in here…so strong it made his eyes start to water.

"All right…all right," he whispered to bolster his courage. He should be satisfied. He could see that there was nothing untoward here. The interior was in such disrepair it didn't match up with his memory of what it had been like years ago. Like the rest of the campground, it appeared so much smaller than he remembered. A thick layer of dust and dirt mixed with what looked like bird and animal feces coated the floor. At the back of the building was the door to a supply closet, but he hesitated to walk over to it. If any critters were nesting in here for the winter, that's probably where they'd be.

He was about to leave when the heavy thump he'd heard before sounded again. And this time, he had no doubt where it was coming from.

The supply closet.

Jeff gasped as a tingle of excitement ran through him. He trained his flashlight on the door, his heart beating so fast it made a clicking sound in his throat.

Something's in there… maybe it's trapped it there.

Again, the thought that a raccoon or skunk was nesting in the closet urged him to back out of the infirmary now and leave well enough alone. It was foolish to intrude on the wild like this, but he couldn't help himself. Without thinking it through, he stomped down hard on the floorboards and shouted, "*Hey!*"

The floor shook, and for a second or two, the only sound was the splattering of rain on the roof and his own labored breathing, but then, faintly, the thump sounded again.

"Go on!" Jeff shouted, clapping his hands loudly. "Get the hell out of here!"

He took a few steps closer to the storage room door, bringing his feet down heavily with each step. He paused and cast a quick glance over his shoulder to make sure no one, especially Evan, had realized what he was up to and come out here to stop him, but the doorway was empty. He was alone.

After waiting in silence for a count of ten, trying hard to convince himself there was nothing to this, he was about to leave when the thump sounded again.

This time there was no doubt.

The sound had come from behind the storage closet door. If it was an animal, it should have been scared off by now…unless it was trapped in there…but the sound seemed to be a response to the noise he was making.

Tension took hold of Jeff like cold hands wrapped around his throat as he moved slowly, cautiously toward the closet door. His hand holding the flashlight

The Wildman

was shaking, making the light jiggle around. He sucked in his breath and held it once he was close enough to touch the doorknob. A chill raced through him as he held the cold metal doorknob, preparing to turn it. He was coiled up, ready to react if, when he opened it, a raccoon or something leaped out at him.

So… don't open it, a rational-sounding voice in his head said.

But he knew he was going to.

How could he not?

His fingers tightened around the doorknob, squeezing until his knuckles throbbed. He was still holding his breath, and he listened to the rapid thunder of his pulse in his ears. When he yanked the door open, he was prepared to step behind it, using it as a shield if something charged him.

"Okay…okay," he whispered to keep his courage from flagging. And then, with a sudden, savage grunt, he twisted the doorknob and flung the door open.

Nothing came rushing out at him.

Jeff's body was trembling almost out of control as he shined his flashlight into the tiny closet, but no matter how much he had prepared himself for something terrible, he wasn't ready for what he saw.

The beam of light reflected from a pair of wide-open eyes that glistened as they stared up at him from down on the floor.

It took Jeff several heartbeats to realize he was staring at a person's face.

❉ ❉ ❉

A sudden gust of wind slammed the infirmary door shut with a bang that split the night like a gunshot.

"*Jesus!*" Jeff shouted as he jumped and turned around. He almost dropped his flashlight as he swung it around and trained it on the door, fully expecting to see Evan standing there with a gun aimed at him.

Another gust of wind slammed into the side of the building, and something that sounded like hail splattered against the roof. Jeff's pulse was racing so fast it almost choked him as he turned back to the person—

It really is a person!

—lying on the floor of the storage closet.

Jeff could see it was a man, even though his face was covered with sweat-streaked grime. His light-colored hair was matted in thick, greasy clumps against his forehead. A strip of duct tape covered his mouth, and his fear-widened, bloodshot eyes stared into the glare of the flashlight with utter hopelessness. Snot that glistened like slug trails ran from his nose across the strip of duct tape.

"What the hell?" Jeff muttered as he stared in utter amazement at the man.

For a moment or two, he thought he was imagining this, but then the man blinked and made a muffled gagging sound behind the duct tape. When he jerked his legs, his feet made the same hollow thump Jeff had heard before.

"Jesus Christ on a cross," Jeff said.

Snapping to, he knelt down and, pinning his flashlight between his body and his arm, reached out to peel away the duct tape. It had been wrapped a few times around the man's lower face. He uttered a pained grunt when Jeff pulled off a loop that also yanked out a clump of hair. He kept staring up at Jeff with pure terror lighting his eyes, and Jeff wondered if the man had gone insane. It was obvious the man had no idea who he was and must think he'd come here to hurt him or kill him.

"Take it easy buddy," he said softly. "I'm gonna— Ahh! Shit! Sorry 'bout that." Jeff knew he was causing the man pain as he removed the tape, but there was nothing he could do about that. "Just be another second or two."

He gave the strip of tape one last quick tug, and the man's mouth was free. His head fell backwards, clunking against the wall, and he inhaled with a raw, watery gasp that blended into a heart-wrenching sob.

"Just hang on. Relax," Jeff said as he placed a reassuring hand on the man's shoulder.

The man flinched at his touch, shying away as if expecting Jeff to hit him. Once it was obvious Jeff didn't intend to hurt him, the man visibly relaxed and let his breath out in a long, anguished sigh that shook his body. Tears glistened as they spilled from his eyes.

"What the fuck's going on here? Who are you?" Jeff asked as he stared in disbelief at the man. "How'd you get here?"

The man licked his lips before he tried to speak, but his throat made a funny rattling sound, and he doubled over in a fit of coughing. Before the coughing subsided, the man made a deep grunting noise as his stomach convulsed. Leaning forward, he puked onto his lap. The stench of sour vomit filled the closet, almost making Jeff throw up as well. He forced himself to ignore the stench as he pulled the man forward and started working to release the ropes binding his hands and feet.

"Take your time," Jeff said. "Just relax." His fingers fumbled with the knots in the rope. "Shit! Wish I'd brought a knife."

The man tried to say something again and ended up coughing.

"I know. You need something to drink."

The Wildman

Jeff glanced over his shoulder at the infirmary door again when it suddenly blew open. Outside, the rain running off the roof looked like silvery threads against the backdrop of the night.

"A sip of rain water will do."

The man stared at him wordlessly and then nodded eagerly, still looking like he'd lost his mind. His eyes glowed with a sparkling gleam that looked positively crazed.

"Hold on," Jeff said.

He stood up and rushed to the door and then, reaching outside, let the water running off the roof fill his cupped hands. Walking back carefully, he held his hands up to the man's mouth so he could take a sip.

There wasn't much water, but the man gulped greedily and then sighed as though he'd drunk ambrosia. He smacked his lips, which were cracked and peeling, and then the faint trace of a smile appeared.

"There. That better?" Jeff asked.

The man stared at him and nodded. He looked as though he barely understood what Jeff was saying. Did he even know English?

Jeff went back to the door, filled his cupped hands again with water, and returned to give the man another small drink. It apparently did the trick because, for the first time, Jeff saw a tiny spark of rationality return to the man's eyes.

Reaching behind the man again, Jeff continued to work to loosen the ropes. The bitter smell of feces and urine mixed with the fresher stench of vomit made Jeff's stomach lurch, but he held it down as he worked to free the man. It seemed to take forever, but—finally—the knots loosened, and the rope fell away in coils onto the floor.

"So who the hell are you?" Jeff asked, sitting back on his heels. "How'd you end up out here?"

"Evan—" the man said, but his voice cut off with an audible click, and he had to swallow and lick his lips before he could continue.

"Evan did this to you?" Somehow, Jeff wasn't surprised. So much for the innocent act. "I *knew* it! That mother-fucker!"

Still barely able to speak, the man shook his head from side to side. When Jeff repositioned him so he could start working on the knots binding the man's legs, he let out a low, pained groan that sounded like it might be the last sound he would ever make.

"How long have you been here?" Jeff asked as he worked. It was obvious from the stench that the man had been in the closet for quite a while. The stench of raw sewage hung in the air.

"Evan...Pike..." the man said in a voice that sounded like tearing paper. "Me...I'm...Evan...Pike."

"What the—?"

Jeff wasn't sure he'd heard him correctly. He shined his flashlight into the man's face. The man winced and shielded his eyes as Jeff stared at him.

"Did you say...?"

The man nodded, still keeping his eyes averted to avoid the bright glare of the flashlight. Then he took a deep breath and repeated what he had said, this time more emphatically.

"Yes. *I'm* Evan Pike."

"But Evan is—" Jeff hitched his thumb in the general direction of the dining hall. "If you're Evan, then who the hell is the guy who brought us out here?"

The man let out a long, shuddering moan as he shook his head from side to side. The motion made him wince. It was obvious it still hurt his throat to speak, and his voice was just barely above a raw whisper.

"That's Ben...Ben Foster."

"Ben Foster? Who the fuck is Ben—"

A cold, creeping feeling slithered up Jeff's back as what the man said slowly sank in. The rain splattering on the roof and the wind whistling through cracks in the building set his nerves on edge.

"He's Jimmy...Jimmy Foster's...brother," Evan said with great effort.

Unable or unwilling to believe this was really happening, Jeff narrowed his eyes and shook his head in denial. Bones in his neck made faint crackling sounds that he could barely hear above the wind and rain. He wished he could convince himself this was all a terribly elaborate nightmare...that he would wake up now and it would all be over, but what Evan said made sense. It confirmed the doubts and suspicions Jeff had been having all weekend.

"Jimmy Foster's brother," Jeff repeated as the realization sank in deeper.

Evan nodded even though it was obvious the motion caused him great pain.

"So how did he...? Whose idea was it to have us all come out here this weekend?"

A trace of a smile touched Evan's lips as he lowered his head.

"It was my idea," he said softly. "I just never thought he would...do what he did."

"Why did he tie you up and hide you out here?"

"Because he was through with me," Evan said with a trace of sadness in his voice. "I was no longer useful to him." He sounded somewhat better. "Once I got all of you out here, he was finished with me—"

The Wildman

Before he could say more, his voice choked off, and he leaned forward and started coughing again.

"You want another drink?" Jeff asked, not knowing what else to do.

"Please."

"I wish I had something to put it in." Shining the flashlight around the infirmary, he looked around but didn't expect to find anything useful. The place had been stripped clean long ago, so he went back to the open door and filled his cupped hands again so Evan could drink.

"It'd be best not to drink too much at first," he said as he poured the rainwater into Evan's open mouth. He reminded him of a fledgling bird being fed by its mother.

"How long have you been out here?"

Evan squinted and shook his head, looking confused.

"I have no idea. What day is it?"

"It's Saturday…Saturday night," Jeff said even though it felt as though he had been stuck on this island a lot longer.

"Jesus…Saturday night." Evan was still shaking his head from side to side. "That means he…I've been out here four days."

"Four days! Jesus Christ!"

"I came out to the island on Wednesday to get things ready for the reunion. They delivered the Port-a-Potty, and I was hoping to get a generator hooked up and running so we'd have electricity."

Jeff was still working to loosen the rope that bound Evan's legs. There were a lot of knots, and they had been pulled tight, maybe from Evan's efforts to free himself.

"How'd he trick you into this?" Jeff asked. "I don't get it. And why would he? What's he after?"

Evan sniffed with dry laughter and looked at Jeff with glistening eyes.

"Isn't it obvious? He wants to kill us."

"Kill us?"

Jeff wished he could stop sounding like Evan's echo, but this was too much to absorb.

"He wants to kill everyone from Tent Twelve."

"But why would he—"

Before he could finish his question, Jeff already knew the answer.

"Because of what happened to his brother," Evan said.

His voice sounded so distant Jeff could easily imagine it was his own thoughts. The chill of the night suddenly cut deeper into him, freezing his bones with an icy touch.

"He blames *us?*" Jeff asked.

He closed his eyes for a moment and saw a mental image of Jimmy Foster the way he remembered him when he was twelve years old. Jimmy was smiling his big bucktoothed grin that wrinkled his freckled cheeks and made his blue eyes gleam. But Jimmy's grin instantly melted into a frightening scowl, and both sides of Jimmy's mouth drooped down as if his face was made of melting wax. His lips peeled back, exposing wide, flat, white teeth that were clenched to hold back a scream. The light in his eyes was snuffed out, and for a terrifying timeless moment, Jeff could see that his friend was terrified as he stared into the bottomless depths of eternity.

"He blames us for Jimmy's death," Jeff said, his voice so soft he could barely hear it above the sound of the wind outside.

"He totally set me up," Evan said weakly. "He set us all up."

"How do you know this?" Jeff asked, suddenly growing suspicious. He stopped working on the knots and sat back when a sudden paranoid thought came over him.

Maybe this is part of the plan, too.

How could he believe this was really Evan Pike?

Maybe it was some elaborate setup to torment Jeff and his other friends, to torture them with guilt about what had happened.

"He told me, for Christ's sake," Evan said.

Looking at him, Jeff was convinced that no one would go to such extremes, sitting out here in their own shit, piss, and vomit in order to entrap someone. This *had* to be the real Evan, and he must be telling the truth.

"He was convinced Mark did it," Evan said.

"Did what? You mean killed Jimmy?"

Evan winced as he nodded.

"He's convinced Mark killed his brother and threw him into the lake to make it look like he fell in and drowned."

"But that…that doesn't make sense." Jeff was still finding it all but impossible to process any of this.

"Tell *him* that," Evan said with a sinister chuckle. "He tracked Mark down and was planning on killing him, but then Mark died before he got to him."

Jeff nodded numbly. "I know. Mark supposedly had a heart attack."

"Huh. I heard it was a drug overdose. That's what Ben told me, anyway. The point is, Ben blamed Mark for his brother's death."

"Yeah, but even if that's true, what's it got to do with any of us?"

Evan smiled thinly and sniffed with laughter.

The Wildman

"He's convinced we all knew about it, and none of us ever spoke up because we wanted to protect him."

"You mean Mark? You've got to be kidding me."

Jeff was dumbfounded. It was one thing to mistrust Evan or Ben or whoever he was, but he had never struck him as *that* crazy.

"He told me all of this once he had me safely tied up and gagged. The other night, it must have been Thursday, just before you guys arrived, he was ranting and raving like a freaking lunatic."

Jeff saw such fear and trepidation in Evan's eyes he *had* to believe him.

"He's been tracking us, all of us, for years. With the Internet and all, it's a lot easier than before. When he found out I'd bought the island and camp and was planning the development out here, he came to me, posing as an interested buyer."

"This is just—" Jeff shook his head, finding it impossible to think it all through clearly. "It's totally insane."

"Tell me about it," Evan said. "Look, would you please finish untying me? I'm sure Ben's wondering where you are, and we have to figure out what we're gonna do to get out of here alive."

Jeff realized he'd been away from the dining hall much longer than necessary. It would only be natural for Ben or whoever he was to start worrying that Jeff had found the real Evan. He could barely feel his fingers as he redoubled his efforts to free Evan. After a long struggle, the last ropes fell free. Evan sighed as he stretched out his arms and rubbed his shoulders to relieve the pain.

"Do you think you can stand up?" Jeff cast a worried look at the door, expecting any second now to see Ben standing there. "We've got to get you out of here."

"How are you gonna do that with Ben still here?" There was a look of apprehension mixed with pain in Evan's eyes, and his voice sounded absolutely hopeless. Jeff couldn't help but wonder if his mind had snapped while he was a prisoner out here.

"Well we'll think of something," Jeff muttered as much to himself as Evan. "We *have* to."

He stood up and then bent down to help Evan to his feet. Evan cried out in pain as his knees popped and his back snapped when he straightened up. He was much too unsteady on his feet after being tied up and stuffed into this closet for so long. He wobbled from side to side and finally had to brace himself against the closet wall so he wouldn't fall down.

"Has he been feeding you?" Jeff asked.

Evan grimaced and shook his head. "Just some stale bread and water once or twice. I don't know." He winced as he shook hands wildly in front of him. "Jesus, they tingle from not having any circulation."

"I don't see how you could stand it."

"It hasn't been easy. I was sure he was going to leave me here to die. I...I can't believe you found me."

Jeff shrugged.

"I can't either, but Evan—I mean *Ben* has been acting strange all weekend. There were several times where he just...I don't know. I couldn't put my finger on it, but now it makes sense. He didn't seem to know quite what was going on with the development. He couldn't answer some fairly basic questions about what he—what *you* planned out here, and he came across as a bit distracted a lot of the time."

"Yeah," Evan said. "He'd come out here at night and pump me for information. He tortured me by withholding food if I didn't tell him what he wanted to know. I was sure he was going to kill me, anyway, so I lied about a few little things, hoping it'd trip him up, and one of you would be smart enough to figure out something was wrong." He chuckled softly to himself. "Figures it'd be you."

"Yeah. Well, I always was the smart one," Jeff said with a grin.

"Yeah...after me."

Jeff was about to laugh and say something about how, if Evan was so damned smart, he let himself get tricked like this, but this was no laughing matter. They were in some deep shit here, and it was going to take some doing if they were going to get out of here alive.

"You think you can walk yet?" Jeff leaned forward to help support Evan if he needed it.

"I dunno. I can hardly feel my legs. Let's give it a try."

Evan sucked in a breath and held it as he slid one foot forward and shifted his weight onto it. His leg began to shake, and he lunged forward and grabbed Evan to keep from falling.

"Jesus. I guess I don't have the strength yet," he said with a fearful tremor in his voice. Jeff could imagine how he must be wondering if he'd ever be able to walk again. "So how are we gonna get—"

"Don't worry about it," Jeff said quickly. He had his own fears but didn't want to express them. Not now. "Don't worry. We'll think of something."

"We always did, didn't we?" Evan said.

But the truth was, Jeff was concerned that Ben would know why he'd been gone so long. If it wasn't such a crappy night, he could have sauntered back to the dining hall and told everyone he'd been for a long late-night stroll, but who was going to believe him on a night like this?

Certainly not Ben.

"We gotta get you someplace where you can hide…someplace dry."

"Other than the dining hall and here, you mean."

Jeff nodded.

"There aren't any other camp buildings left," Evan said. "And what if Ben comes out here and finds me gone? He'll know it's because you found me."

Frustrated, Jeff clenched his fist and smacked it against the wall hard enough to hurt. Shining the flashlight up at the rafters, he wondered if he could rig up a platform so Evan could hide up there, but he didn't have the necessary wood or tools. He certainly couldn't bring Evan back to the dining hall and confront Ben. Chances were he was armed. The only thing they had going for them was that now they could define the situation. They would have the advantage if they could throw Ben off whatever plans he had.

"I've been away too long," Jeff said. "Ben's gonna know something's up. You need something to protect yourself in case he comes out here."

He looked around but didn't see anything useful.

"How 'bout some rocks," he said.

"They're better than nothing."

Evan gritted his teeth as he tried to take a few more steps. His feet made loud scuffing sounds as they dragged across the bare wooden floor. After only two steps, he let out a sigh and collapsed against the wall. He was trembling all over.

"Are you sure you feel safe, hiding out here until I get back?"

"What choice do I have?"

Jeff bit down on his lower lip as he considered and then shook his head.

"None unless we can get you to the boat. Problem is, the motor's broken."

"That's not good. What happened?"

"It burned out when we were taking a cruise around the island." He took a deep breath, frustrated because he couldn't think of any alternatives. "Look. You just have to hang tight, okay? Use the time to get your strength back so you can walk."

Jeff started for the door.

"I'll get you some rocks, and if that son of a bitch comes out here before I get back, bash his fucking head in, okay?"

"With pleasure," Evan said with a grim chuckle.

Snuggling into his raincoat, Jeff went back outside. A low-lying mist wafted through the surrounding forest, looking like a dense layer of smoke.

Rivulets of muddy water gurgled as they ran down the slope toward the lake. The night air was filled with the damp, mulchy smell of the forest floor.

Jeff scrambled around until he found five fist sized rocks, which he brought them back to Evan who was sitting in the middle of the floor.

"You're looking good," Jeff said, surprised to see he had made it all the way from the closet on his own power.

"It knocked the shit out of me."

"That's understandable. Let's get you over by the door here." Jeff came around behind Evan and lifted him. Evan was still unsteady on his feet, but with Jeff's help he made it to the wall beside the door.

"I gotta get back there," Jeff said, "but I'll be back for you. Trust me."

"How long, do you think?"

"I have no idea, but believe me, I'm not going to let that son of a bitch get away with anything."

"He plans to kill us all, you know," Evan said in a flat voice heavy with resignation. "That's been his plan all along."

Jeff nodded grimly and said, "I know. But he hasn't done it yet."

Even as he said it, the fear that it was just a matter of time before Ben got them-all of them-picking them off one by one, sliced into him with the cold chill of a razorblade.

Chapter Ten

Drowning

JEFF WAS FILLED with trepidation when he closed the infirmary door and stepped out into the night. The lock and latch were smashed beyond repair, so if Ben came out here now, he'd know right away that Evan had help escaping. And it wouldn't take him long to figure out who had done it since Jeff was the only one who had left the dining hall alone.

As he started back to the beach, he shined his flashlight into the woods along the trail, looking for something—a stick or anything—he could use as a weapon. He found a broken birch branch that wasn't too rotten, but he knew it wouldn't be enough…not if Ben had a gun.

And he had no doubt Ben had a gun.

From what Evan had told him, he obviously had the whole thing planned out. Jeff wondered if, even now, he was playing into Ben's hands. Maybe Ben had anticipated that he would find Evan, and he couldn't help but wonder why Ben hadn't killed all of them already, the first night they were here.

He remembered how on edge he had felt all last night and hadn't gotten much sleep. Sleep deprivation and raw nerves plus exposure to the rain and cold were starting to take their toll. He was wrung out and weakening; he jumped at the slightest sound. He doubted he'd have the necessary endurance to do what he had to do tonight.

When he rounded a turn in the trail and saw the dining hall, he turned off his flashlight. Gripping the birch stick tightly, he slowed down, moving slowly and ready to react the instant he sensed danger. The overcast looked deeper, and he was afraid it might start raining again soon. He was sure the worst of the storm hadn't passed.

He wondered how he was going to warn the others about what was going on without alerting Ben.

What if, while he was gone, Ben had already killed the others? What if they were dead, and Ben was sitting there, waiting for him to come back?

Or what if—even now—Ben was standing unseen behind him, drawing a bead on him and was about to shoot him without warning?

Jeff shivered as he looked around. Moisture from the trees fell on his face. The visibility wasn't good, but as he moved forward, getting closer to the dining hall, he saw a faint glow of light far down on the beach.

Something was happening, but he held back, staying out of sight until he figured out what it was. For all he knew, Fred might still be wandering around, stewing about the confession he'd made to them.

Jeff found it easy to imagine he was twelve years old again, playing hide-'n-seek as he hunkered down in the wet brush. Then, as quietly as possible, he started moving from tree to tree, always keeping cover. He watched both the dining hall and the ever-increasing glow of light on the beach, and when he was about a hundred yards from the beach, he saw a second flashlight beam. They wavered back and forth in the night, sweeping the beach and lake. As he came closer, the sound of voices came to him, but the gusting wind carried away whatever was said.

One of the beams of light came to rest, fixed on one spot. Two figures were standing there, hunkered over a dark shape lying on the sand. Jeff's throat closed off when he realized it was a body—a human body.

He had an immediate flashback to that summer long ago when, from almost the exact same spot he was standing now, he watched the emergency workers carry the body of Jimmy Foster out to the waiting warden service boat. For a terrifying moment, he imagined he was seeing that horrible scene reenacted by the ghosts of the people who had been there. It was all too plausible that an event so horrible could leave a psychic echo, and someone sensitive enough to it could pick up.

Still keeping to darkness under the trees, Jeff moved even closer, straining to hear who was talking and what they were saying. There was a frantic edge in one of the voices, and Jeff realized it was Tyler. Someone else was standing off to one side with his hand to his ear. Judging by the bulk, Jeff guessed it was Mike. He looked like he was trying to make a call on his cell phone. So that left either Ben of Fred, who was leaning over the figure on the ground. Jeff was suddenly sure it was Fred, lying there.

"Jesus," he whispered, his breath coming out a gray mist that swirled away on the wind. A cold tingling tightened the skin of his face.

"We have to try!" Tyler shouted in a strained voice.

The figure kneeling down looked up at Tyler. The harsh glare of the flashlight lit his face. Ben shook his head.

He said, "It's too late."

Still gripping the birch stick, Jeff stepped forward to find out what was going on. He moved silently, and Mike was the first to realize he was there. He jumped and let out a squeal as he wheeled around.

"Take it easy," Jeff called out. "It's just me." He waved the hand holding the walking stick. "What's going on?"

"It's Fred," Tyler's voice was low and shattered. "We starting getting worried about him, about both of you, and when we came out looking for you. Evan found him in the water."

"Either he fell in and drown, or else he did it on purpose," the man posing as Evan said.

Jeff wanted to confront Ben then and there and say that there was another option, someone had killed him, but Ben was still trying to or pretending to resuscitate Fred, who was lying on his back on the sand. His head was cocked to one side as Ben administered artificial respiration.

"It's no good," Ben said after another few tries. He turned and looked up at Tyler. "He's gone."

"Oh, Jesus…Oh, sweet Jesus," Mike muttered, and he began pacing back and forth while pounding his fists against his thighs. His feet kicked up sprays of wet sand.

"You get a signal on your cell yet?" Tyler asked.

Mike shook his head and muttered a curse.

"It doesn't matter," Ben said. "It won't do any good."

Jeff eyed him intently, amazed that, even in an emergency like this, he could keep up the façade so well.

But then again, he thought, *that's exactly what he wants, isn't it? For all of us to trust him so we drop our guard, and he can kill us?*

"He's not breathing," Ben said. He reached down and placed his fingertips on Fred's neck. "And I don't feel a pulse. Even if we got him to the hospital, I don't think there's anything they could do for him. He's dead or will be before we got off this fucking island."

He sat back on his heels and, clenching his fists, pounded the sand in frustration. Jeff was impressed by his acting skills because he knew that's all this was—an act.

"Christ!" Mike shouted, still pacing back and forth as he repeatedly punched his leg. "*Christ* all-*fucking*-mighty! What are we gonna do? What are we gonna do?"

"There's nothing we can do," Ben said softly.

Moving stiffly, his face framed by ringlets of wet hair, Ben stood up slowly.

When Tyler trained his light onto Fred's face, Jeff recoiled in horror. The dead man's tongue was hanging from his opened mouth, looking like something he'd tried to swallow and choked on. He eyes were wide and staring, and they held a silvery gleam that looked like mercury.

"Who…who found him?" Jeff asked as he moved closer.

"I did," Ben said without any hesitation.

Jeff immediately thought that, by admitting it right up front, Ben could deflect any suspicion he'd had anything to do with it. And how did Jeff know he had? Maybe Fred really had been so despondent he killed himself.

Ben picked up his flashlight from the sand and swung the beam onto Jeff, who shielded his eyes against the glare.

"So where the hell were *you*?" he asked, his voice a mixture of exhaustion and impatience.

Jeff shrugged and, shaking his head, indicated the woods behind him with a feeble wave of his hand.

"Just out walking…I needed some time to think."

"Really?" Ben said.

Something in his tone of voice made Jeff bristle. He knew Ben was trying to raise at least a hint of suspicion that Jeff might have had more to do with Fred's drowning than he was letting on.

Nice move, Jeff thought. *Put suspicion on me when you no doubt did it.*

"Yeah…I…so what the hell happened?" Jeff asked.

"Who the fuck knows?" Ben bent down and brushed wet sand from his knees. Jeff saw that he was wet up to the waist.

"He was acting suicidal earlier," Mike said in a low, tremulous voice. "We all saw it, but what if—you know, what if the stuff we were talking about drove him to it?"

"What the fuck are you talking about?" Tyler snapped. "We didn't make him do anything."

"But we were pushing him real hard," Mike said. His lower lip was bloodless and trembling. Jeff had a strong suspicion he was afraid they might be held responsible for Fred's death. "We didn't…we didn't realize how much this was affecting him until it was too late, but all that stuff about killing his kid…Jesus! How could anyone live with something like that?"

"We didn't force him to kill himself," Ben said with just a touch of disingenuousness in his voice. "He snapped. That's all there is to it, and there's nothing any of us could have done to stop him. He'd been living with that guilt for so long that facing it probably drove him over the edge. No one drowned him except himself."

Jeff caught the reference to drowning and wondered if Ben was using it intentionally to remind him of what had happened to Jimmy.

"Yeah," Mike finally said, gasping, "But *we* were the ones who pushed him. He wouldn't have done this…he wouldn't have killed himself if we hadn't badgered him the way we did."

Jeff wanted to point at Ben and say: "The way *you* did," but he turned to Mike and said, "That's bullshit, and I want you to cut it out. We didn't force him to do anything. If he was going to kill himself, he was going to do it sooner or later." He grabbed Mike by the arms and shook him.

"Think about it. Think about how down he's been acting all weekend."

"He didn't seem all that down to me," Tyler said. "No more than when he was a kid, anyway."

Mike apparently wasn't convinced, either, and he stared long and hard at them. Jeff had the feeling he half suspected Ben might have had more to do with this than he was letting on.

Good work, Ben, Jeff thought. *Plant a seed of suspicion and watch it grow.*

"We have to get the goddamned boat working so we can bring him to the mainland tonight," Tyler said, struggling to remain calm. "We have to report this right away."

He sounded like the most reasonable one here, but Jeff could tell by the way his eyes shifted that he, too, wasn't far from losing his composure. For some reason, he wondered if this was the first time Tyler had ever seen a dead body. He sure was acting like it was. And once again, the mental image of Jimmy Foster, lying on the stretcher with his throat sliced open rose in Jeff's mind.

I know what I saw!

Now that Jeff knew what was really going on here, when he looked at Ben, he was ashamed at himself for not figuring it out sooner. Ben looked a lot like a grown-up version of his brother, Jimmy. Jeff acknowledged that he probably had caught the family resemblance, at least subconsciously. That's why he'd been feeling so uncomfortable all weekend about the man he knew was posing as Evan Pike.

It wasn't memories of Jimmy's death or childhood fears about the ghost stories their counselor told them in the tent or stupid fears that an Indian spirit named Hobomock actually haunted this island.

There was a killer in their midst, and Jeff was sure he still intended to kill all of them before the night was through.

He'd already gotten Fred.

Jeff wanted to ask Ben why his pants were so wet. Had he struggled with Fred and forced him into the water where he drowned him?

But this wasn't the time. He had to make sure he had the advantage.

"We've gotta cover him up or something and get him off the beach… at least until morning," Jeff said. He hoped everyone—especially Ben—would take the tremor in his voice as an expression of how nervous he was about what had happened, but when Ben glanced at him, he saw a flicker of suspicion—*or was it knowledge?*—in his eyes.

"Give me a hand," Ben said. "We'll carry him up onto the porch."

Jeff and Tyler each took one of Fred's legs while Mike and Ben each took an arm. The mist rolling in from the lake made everything wet, and they kept losing their grip. They almost dropped Fred a couple of times, and it took them a while to get into sync. Eventually they got Fred under the shelter of the porch roof. All of them were panting from the exertion.

"Does anyone's cell work?" Jeff asked, panting as he leaned against the porch railing. Now was a good time to overpower Ben, but he was beat from the exertion.

They all took out their cell phones, but after checking for service, they shook their heads in disappointment.

"What d'yah expect?" Mike said. "We're out in the goddamned willy-whacks here."

Jeff turned to Ben, watching him closely, studying him and trying to read his reaction, but in the darkness under the porch, he couldn't see Ben's expression.

"This is so fucked," Ben said, lowering his gaze and shaking his head.

Jeff was absolutely convinced Ben had something to do with Fred's death. It couldn't have been an accident or suicide. If he was perturbed now, it was only because he hadn't been able to exact his revenge on all of them yet. Maybe he was getting nerved up to finish the job. If he planned to kill them, as Evan said, would he make his move now? Or was he confident enough to toy with them first?

"So what the hell do we do?" Mike asked, his voice shaking as much from the cold as fear. "We can't just leave him out here all night. Jesus! The animals will get him."

Jeff was angry at Mike for not holding it together better. He'd always been the tough guy of the group, and here he was, falling apart like a little kid. If Ben really intended to get revenge for his brother's death, Jeff wanted to be able to count on Mike and Tyler to hold their shit together.

"I'm freezing my ass off," Tyler finally said. "And it sure as hell won't do Fred any good if we stay out here in the fucking cold and die of hypothermia. Let's put him in the entryway."

With that, he opened the door and bent to lift Fred. The others joined in, and before long Fred was lying on the floor just inside the building.

Jeff looked at the warm glow of the fire inside. It was so inviting he wished he could forget about what was happening and not have to deal with this stuff, but he had to find some way to get Mike or Tyler alone and tell them what was really going on.

Tyler went inside, but the others stayed outside on the porch, not saying a word. The wind had died down a bit, and when Jeff looked up, he thought the overcast looked like it was breaking up. Maybe the worst of the storm was past.

"How 'bout you?" Ben asked Jeff.

"What about me?"

"We could all use a knock of rum to drive out the cold, don't you think?"

Jeff grunted but made no move toward the door. He was hoping Ben would lead the way inside so he could grab Mike and tell him what he had found out. But Ben lagged behind, leaning against the side of the building, his arms folded across his chest as though challenging Jeff to make the first move.

Is this what it's gonna be? He thought. *A duel of nerves? All right, then… I'm up for it.*

"I think I might grab a smoke first," Jeff said as he fished into his shirt pocket inside his raincoat. He was sure his cigarettes were ruined from the dampness.

"I didn't know you smoked," Ben said.

"Oh, there's a lot about me you don't know," Jeff replied. Even in the darkness, he didn't miss Ben's reaction. He narrowed his eyes and practically glared at Jeff as if to say—*All right, asshole, I know you know, but I'm gonna get you, don't you doubt it.*

"Mind if I join you?" Ben said.

Jeff hesitated a moment, then shrugged.

"I'd rather be alone, if you don't mind," he said. "I need some time to think things through."

He wished Ben would get the hint and go inside so he could be alone with Mike, and he knew if he went inside now and tried to corner Tyler, Ben would be right there with him. Mike apparently caught the tension and, without another word, went inside, leaving Jeff and Ben on the porch.

Okay… This is it, Jeff thought.

He could easily confront Ben right now. Put him on the spot. Ask him to explain himself. If it came to a fight, unless Ben had a gun with him, Jeff was confident he could take him. He was bigger than Ben, but then again, Ben looked to be in pretty good shape. In any confrontation, it'd be best to have Mike and Tyler for backup. Then, if it came down to a fight, it would be three against one.

But Jeff was sure Ben had a gun. If he was going to kill them because of what he thought they did—or didn't do— to protect his brother, he would have everything planned so he could isolate each of them and take them one by one.

Fred was the first casualty.

The way Jeff figured it, Ben must have gone out pretending to look for him. When he found him down by the lake, after a brief struggle, he had held him under until he drowned.

So that was his plan. To get them one at a time. Maybe toy with them before he killed them.

The coward's way, Jeff thought.

Otherwise, while they were sitting around the fire, all cozy and warm, drinking and shooting the breeze, he easily could have pulled a gun and accused them all of being responsible for Jimmy's death. He could have gotten them all at once.

Or why hadn't he waited until they were asleep and quietly slit their throats?

Jeff shivered, thinking it was a damned good thing he hadn't slept last night. The lack of sleep might be getting to him now, but he would be sure not to let himself fall sleep tonight. He had to stay alert, ready for anything.

It bothered him that he couldn't figure out Ben's game plan, and he wondered if perhaps this guy he assumed was Ben Foster really was innocent.

What if the man he'd found in the infirmary was really Ben Foster…or someone else…and he was setting them up for…something?

Maybe he was using Jeff to kill Ben or whoever this guy was.

That didn't seem very likely, but how could Jeff know? Evan, or whoever that was out there, certainly looked and smelled like he'd been a prisoner for more than a few days. It would be one hell of an elaborate scheme, but what if *he* was the real Ben Foster, and this guy Evan was really innocent?

What if he was playing Jeff so he'd do the killing for him?

All of these paranoid thoughts rushed through Jeff's mind as he stared in silence at Ben, who was still leaning against the wall by the door.

Was he positioned there so he could keep tabs on what was happening inside and outside, or was he nervous, justifiably upset about someone dying on his property?

Jeff shook a cigarette from the pack and offered one to Ben. Jeff's hand was shaking as handed it to him.

Whoever the fuck you are, he thought.

"Thanks," Ben said as he slipped the cigarette into the corner of his mouth.

When he flicked his lighter and held the flame to Ben's cigarette, Jeff studied the man's face in the sudden brightness. He didn't see anything behind the distant, glazed eyes. Then he lit his own cigarette and, leaning his head back, blew a cloud of smoke up at the porch ceiling.

"This is some fucked-up shit, huh Evan?" he said as the nicotine rush went to his head. He put emphasis on the name but didn't notice any reaction from Ben…or Evan…or whoever he was.

"Amen, brother," Ben said, exhaling noisily.

Jeff let the cigarette dangle from his lower lip as he folded his arms across his chest and cocked his butt up onto the porch railing. The wind had lessened but was steady now. It swept the smoke into the night.

"So what do you think's going on?" Jeff asked.

Ben was silent for a long time. He cocked his head to one side and scratched his cheek.

"I wish to fuck I knew," he said. He sounded so sincere.

Jeff took another puff and let the smoke out slowly through his nose.

Now was the time, he knew, to see if he could crack Ben, but Jeff had his doubts. His lack of sleep made it feel surreal to find himself in a situation like this when all he'd been expecting was a quiet reunion of camp friends.

It was almost impossible to believe that *someone* was out to kill them.

"I—uh, I think I know," Jeff said.

"Know what?"

"Know what's going on."

"Really."

Ben took a long drag on his cigarette, but Jeff didn't like the way his was affecting him, so he snapped it out into the darkness. It hissed and was extinguished when it hit the wet ground.

"Yeah. I do," Jeff said.

He didn't like the way he was winding up inside. He remembered the feeling of anticipation he always got when he was up at bat. Year after year, Mike was the star of their tent's team, but Evan had always been a good player, too, and Jeff had felt driven to compete with them. Every time at bat, though, he got terrible butterflies in his stomach. It was like that now…only worse.

"I went for a walk a while ago." Jeff lowered his voice as though in the confessional with a priest.

The Wildman

He tensed and waited to see how Ben would react. If he had a gun, what was to stop him from using it right now? Then he could go inside and finish off Mike and Tyler before they had any idea what was happening.

"Doing a little snooping around, were you?" Ben asked.

Jeff couldn't read Ben's tone of voice. It was tight and higher than usual, a curious mixture of nervousness and agitation. When Ben took another puff, he sucked hard on the cigarette so the glow lit up his face, giving him a leering, devilish look.

Jeff was keenly aware that he was probably blundering into something he might not be ready for right now, but once he'd started, there was no turning back. Before he accused Ben of anything, he wanted the other guys here to witness what he said and how Ben reacted. Easing the dining hall door open and keeping a wary eye on Ben, he stuck his head inside and called out, "Hey! Guys! Come out here a second, will yah?"

"What the fuck are you doing?"

Ben moved away from the door toward the edge of the porch. He looked like he was coiling up, getting ready to run or fight.

"There's something I want to ask you about, but I want the others here when I do."

Jeff's pulse was hammering so hard it squeezed his throat as he waited to hear or see signs of activity from inside.

"Yo!" he called out. "Hey guys!"

"Just a sec," Mike shouted from inside, but before Jeff could respond, Ben made his move. A blur of motion in the corner of his eye drew his attention, and the night exploded with pain as something hard—harder than a man's fist—slammed into the side of his head. White stars sizzled across his vision, and he rocked back on his heels. His legs almost gave out as the night slammed down with a roaring *whoosh*. He staggered backwards, waving his arms for balance, but he was barely conscious when the backs of his legs bumped against the porch railing, and his momentum carried him over the edge. He hit the ground, landing on his back, hard enough to knock the wind out of him, but he didn't lose consciousness. Pain and shock numbed him, but the cold air quickly brought him to full consciousness.

An instant later, the night exploded.

A bright white flash accompanied a loud snap, and something whistled past his ear before hitting the ground with a dull *thump*.

Jeff looked up at the porch and saw a dark smear of motion. Still dazed, he realized it must be Ben, and he had just shot at him.

"You fucking asshole!" Ben shouted.

Jeff knew he was taking aim at him again, so he rolled over on his hands and knees, and scrambled away toward the side of the building.

"What the fuck's going on out there?" someone shouted from inside. It sounded like Tyler, but the ringing in his ears made it impossible for Jeff to know for sure.

As he crawled away over the saturated ground, he cringed, waiting to hear another shot and feel the bullet tear into him.

You never hear the one that kills you, he thought, so even though the sound of the second shot made him flinch and almost piss himself, he was filled with a surge of relief as he staggered to his feet and ran around the side of the building.

"*Look out!*" he shouted as he turned the corner and started running toward the woods. "*He's got a gun!*"

Another bright flash lit up the side of the dining hall the instant a third shot rang out. The bullet clipped a tree trunk close to Jeff's head, kicking up splinters of bark that sprayed his face but didn't do any serious damage. He guessed—he hoped-Ben couldn't see him in the darkness. That was his only chance.

Cowering behind one of the pine trees and panting to catch his breath, Jeff looked at the glowing windows of the dining hall. Hopefully Mike and Tyler recognized that some serious shit was going down and would take cover…or else come out to help him.

"*Be careful, you guys!*" Jeff yelled, cupping his hands to his mouth. "*He's got a gun and wants to kill us!*"

Through the dining hall windows, he saw a flurry of motion. Shadows cast by the firelight shifted crazily across the windows like a dark kaleidoscope. Jeff had no idea if Ben had gone into the building or had jumped off the porch and was coming after him.

Who does he want to finish off first? He wondered as he turned and headed off into the darkness.

Chapter Eleven

Wide Game

JEFF KNEW NOW for certain that Ben had figured out he had found Evan in the infirmary.

He would have to come for him first.

He also knew that, with the ground as wet as it was, he would leave tracks any idiot with a flashlight could follow. And Ben, while he might be crazy, certainly was no idiot.

His best chance of survival, he decided, was to strike off into the woods, avoiding the muddy paths as much as possible. He had turned his back on the dining hall and was entering the woods when three shots rang out the night. They were muffled in the darkness, but he turned around in time to see the last of the muzzle flashes as it lit up the inside of the dining hall.

"Sweet Mother of God," he whispered, realizing Ben must have gone back into the dining hall and finished off both Mike and Tyler before coming after him.

It made sense.

They were isolated on the island with no way off unless someone found a boat or was desperate enough to swim the mile or so back to the mainland. It would be difficult if not impossible to swim that far in water that had to be close to freezing this time of year.

As for the boat, Jeff held little hope he could get to it and use it. Ben must have done something to kill the engine so they'd think they were stranded here. Jeff held out a slim hope Ben hadn't permanently destroyed the engine. How else would he get off the island once he had done what he set out to do?

Ben had to keep his options open.

If the boat really was useless, then he had to have another boat or some way of getting off the island. Jeff had to find out what that was and use it to his advantage.

But right now, Ben was hunting for him. He had to survive.

Not being armed, Jeff would have to elude Ben and try to get off the island. Now that Ben had killed both Mike and Tyler, he could take his sweet time and stalk him at his leisure.

Crouching in the darkness, Jeff surveyed the dining hall for any signs of activity. He tried not to visualize what must have happened there. Mike and Tyler, no doubt having been confused by the sounds of gunfire outside, probably didn't have time to react before Ben came in and shot them both. There was a slim chance one or both of them had escaped, but that didn't seem likely. Ben probably walked in there as cool and calm as could be, took aim, and shot them both in cold blood.

Bleak despair filled Jeff.

He shivered as cold night air misted his face and ran in trickling streams down the inside of his raincoat. He still had his flashlight, but he had dropped the birch stick on the beach when he had helped pick up Fred.

"Come on. Pull it together. Slow down and think."

He tried hard to focus, but the situation seemed hopeless.

Jeff believed now that Evan had been telling the truth. Ben had tied him up and left him out in the infirmary, but Evan wasn't of any use to Ben any more. Ben would be gunning for him, too. Jeff would have to get back to the infirmary as quickly as possible before Ben got there, found Evan, and killed him.

But Jeff knew he could be walking right into a trap if he went out there now. He wished he could think of some way to save Evan, but he couldn't come up with any options.

Without a weapon beyond sticks and stones, what chance did he have against someone with a gun?

He had to think…think…

This was like the "wide games" they used to play as campers. Sometimes certain tents would challenge other tents; other times, it would be all of the campers against the counselors and staff; but basically, it was a camp-wide game of hide-'n-seek…only this time, the stakes were a damned sight higher than a free ticket to the snack bar.

All was silent in the dining hall.

The only sound was the steady patter of water, dripping from the trees and plopping on the ground. The orange glow of the firelight inside the building seemed to mock Jeff as he shivered in the cold, but he couldn't risk going back there. Not now. Even if one or both of his friends were wounded or being held captive, perhaps as ransom, there was nothing Jeff could do to help them now.

No, Mike and Tyler were on their own.

As far as he knew, no one had left the building.

So what was going on in there?

Was Ben gloating over the corpses of his supposed friends?

Was he rifling through their belongings, looking for something of value?

Or was he reloading so when he came after Jeff his pistol was fully loaded?

Come on, man! Think... think!

There had to be *something* he could do…some way he could outsmart this guy and get the upper hand.

"Hey! Jeff!"

The voice, coming so suddenly out of the surrounding darkness, startled Jeff and made him jump. The echo made Ben sound much closer than he was. Jeff peered into the darkness, straining to see if—somehow—Ben had snuck up behind him.

"I know you're out there!" Ben's voice echoed in the night. "You might as well give yourself up now! You're not going to get away from me!"

Jeff could tell by the direction of his voice that Ben was on the side porch, hidden in darkness.

"It won't do you any good to run, you know! Come on out. Let's talk."

There's nothing to talk about, Jeff was tempted to shout back, but he wasn't going to be tricked into giving himself away.

He wished he knew what had happened inside the dining hall. He shivered at the thought that both Mike and Tyler could already be dead—like Fred. But even if they weren't, he wasn't about to give Ben the upper hand.

But they must be dead.

Why else would Ben be calling for him and no one else?

Then again, if they had heard his warning, it was possible one or both of them had gotten out before Ben came in with pistol blazing.

He decided to hope they were alive until he knew differently.

But hope was all Jeff had left as he drew back into the forest and started moving slowly and quietly away so Ben wouldn't hear him.

He wanted to go straight out to the infirmary, but he knew—especially if Mike and Tyler were dead—that's where Ben would go, too. Maybe he should stay close to the dining hall. If Ben left, Jeff could go inside and find something to use to defend himself. He could grab one of the cooking utensils Ben had used for meals, maybe a carving knife or something.

Anything.

"Don't worry," Ben called out, his voice filling the night. "Mike and Tyler are fine. I swear to God they are."

"Like hell," Jeff whispered.

"Let's sit down together and talk this thing out."

Ben sounded so calm now, totally reasonable and rational, but Jeff caught an edge of desperation in his voice, too.

"I mean—where are you gonna go, right?"

No answer.

"Come on. Let's talk."

While Ben kept yelling, Jeff used the diversion to move deeper into the woods. He made his way around to the back of the building so he could see the side porch. Behind the dining hall, the lake was lost in a dense fog bank. Jeff was sure the clouds were breaking up overhead. Stray moonbeams shone through the breaks, casting harsh shadows across the ground.

Jeff clung to the deepest shadows under the trees, but he had the unnerving sensation that—somehow—Ben was like a cat or an owl, and could see in the dark.

With the luminous backdrop of the lake and fog behind him, Ben's silhouette stood out sharply against the night. He was crouching slightly as he swept his pistol back and forth, and peered into the darkness.

If I only had a gun.

Jeff knew there was no way Ben could let him or any of them survive. Even if he hadn't had anything to do with Fred's drowning, he had taken three shots at Jeff as soon as he even hinted that he had found Evan.

"Hey! You!" Ben shouted.

Jeff saw Ben turn toward the dining hall door and wave his pistol.

"Get the fuck out here. See if you can talk some sense into him."

The rusted spring on the screen door twanged as it opened and then slammed shut. Another figure came out onto the porch. Jeff knew by the bulk that it was Mike. He was leaning to one side as though hurt.

"Go on," Ben said, his voice mild but firm. "Tell him to come back so we can figure this out."

For several seconds, the only sound was the heavy thud of Jeff's pulse as he waited for Mike to say something. The only sound he made was a low, watery sigh that might have been real or might have been the night playing tricks on Jeff's hearing.

"Go on! Tell him!"

The Wildman

Ben waved the pistol at Mike. Even so, he didn't say anything. All he could manage was a soft whimper before he doubled over as if in pain.

Jeff was worried Mike was hurt so bad he was bleeding to death right there in front of him. Ben sure didn't seem to give a damn.

"So, you won't cooperate?"

Jeff heard a high, wavering crackle in Ben's voice as he leveled the pistol at Mike's head.

"Do you want to die? Is that it? You think you're being a hero or something?"

Mike bowed his head and shook it from side to side. Jeff squeezed his fists in frustration, wishing there was something he could do to help, but if he revealed himself now, it would just mean he would end up dead, too.

"Jeff…" Mike's voice was tight with pain. "You…you gotta do what he says."

"You hear that, Jeff? I swear to Christ, I'll kill him if you don't come out right *now!* I know you can hear me. I'll give you a count of three."

Fighting back the urge to come out of hiding, Jeff cringed even more in the shadows.

He felt like a coward. No amount of telling himself Ben had every intention of killing them all no matter what he said or did would convince him that he wasn't letting down his friends.

"*One!*"

Ben took a step closer to Mike, who cowered away from him. The gun was raised and aimed at his head. Sweat ran down Jeff's face and into his eyes, blurring his vision.

"*Two!*"

Mike cowered, collapsing onto his knees as though in prayer. Even at this distance, he could hear Mike snort as he broke down and cried.

"Come on, man," Mike said in a low, shattered voice. "He means it. He's gonna do it."

Jeff drew in a raw breath and opened his mouth to call out, but before he could make a sound, Ben shouted, "*Three!*" An instant later, a single shot rang out.

A bright white flash illuminated the underside of the porch for an instant, leaving a blue afterimage that streaked across Jeff's vision. He watched, stunned, as the impact of the bullet slammed Mike's body back against the wall. It made a loud thump when he dropped to the porch floor and lay still.

"See what you made me do?" Ben called out. "I didn't want to kill him, but you made me do it. I'm as serious as a fucking heart attack, Jeff, so…" He let out an exaggerated sigh. "All right, then. Have it your way. Stay where you are. Or you can run and hide if you want. Sooner or later, I'm gonna find you. I mean—where you gonna go, right? I'll run your sorry ass down, and when I do…oh, I promise it won't be quick and easy like it was for old Mike here." His cold, humorless laugh filled the night. "No-sir-ee… You're gonna take a long time to die, Jeff. A *long* time. Just ask Evan."

Stunned by what he had witnessed and wishing he could believe it hadn't really happened, Jeff was trembling as he huddled in the damp darkness. Water falling from the trees pelted the ground around him. The throbbing rush of blood in his ears and his own frantic breathing were the only other sounds.

This isn't real… This can't be happening, he kept telling himself, but it was all too real.

Mike was definitely dead, as was Fred and probably Tyler.

That left him and Evan, who would no doubt die as soon as Ben got out to the infirmary to finish him off. Then it would be just him…unless he could come up with a plan to stop Ben.

With the afterimages of the muzzle flash still wavering across his vision, Jeff struggled to collect himself. He was already so cold and wet he was past miserable. What he had just witnessed had stripped away the last vestiges of civilization from him. He had been reduced to a savage, a wild man, and he would fight with as much or more savagery than Ben had just shown.

Gritting his teeth and telling himself to ignore the cold and damp and pain, he moved into the woods, melting into the wavering shadows cast by the moon.

All of his senses were opened up now, wider than they had ever been before. He inhaled the smell of wet, rotting mulch…the cold, antiseptic sting of the ozone-tinged air…the resinous pines and brush around him…and he felt the hot charge of blood surging through his veins. The raw, primal force of nature filled him with savage energy.

I am the wild man, he thought, chuckling softly to himself as he moved away from the dining hall. *I am the lord of the forest… I am Hobomock, the demonic spirit of the wild… and nothing… nothing and no one can stop me!*

❦ ❦ ❦

All of Jeff's senses were heightened as he made his way deeper into the woods. He barely felt the cold dampness of the night now. The clouds were tearing apart, driven by a cold north wind. All around him, the pine trees swayed back and forth with a loud clacking of branches that sounded like rattling bones.

The Wildman

Moving as silently as a shadow, he cautiously made his way toward the infirmary. Now more than ever he felt compelled to save Evan from this nightmare. If that meant he was going to have to kill Ben, then so be it...all the better, in fact.

The layout of the campgrounds was imprinted in Jeff's memory from childhood, but he wasn't sure he could trust it. So much had changed over thirty-five years. Trees had grown up and died; buildings had rotted and collapsed; familiar landmarks he had used while wandering around camp at night no longer applied. He was going to have to trust his primitive instincts.

But what about Ben?

Was he so confident in his superiority, especially because he had a weapon, that he would assume he had the upper hand and not think things through as carefully?

Would he rely on old habits, or would he realize the rules of the game had suddenly changed?

Jeff stayed away from the old, well-worn trails. Instead, he wended his way through the woods, moving as much by instinct as knowledge. The pine needles and fallen leaves were wet, so they didn't make much noise underfoot. Crouching low, Jeff weaved between the trees, moving swiftly and silently. He was halfway to the infirmary when he caught a faint glow of light off to his left.

A flashlight?

He stopped short and stared into the swelling darkness. Every muscle in his body vibrated with tension. He was ready to respond either with fight or flight.

The beam of light grew steadily brighter, sweeping from side to side, lighting both sides of the trail.

It *had* to be Ben, following him and looking for any evidence Jeff had come this way.

Low mist clung to the ground, twisting in gauzy tendrils between the trees and shrubs. Jeff was confident Ben couldn't see him where he was, but he had to get closer...close enough to get behind Ben and attack him.

As the light came closer, Jeff dropped into a crouch, counting on the brush and mist to hide him. After a few tense seconds, he saw Ben's silhouette. He was wearing a dark raincoat and had his head lowered with the hood pulled over his face. He was breathing loudly, taking short, raw gasps.

Good, Jeff thought, clenching his fists. *He's winded... He's already getting tired.*

Jeff felt so charged with energy he knew he could easily outlast Ben through the night. It was down to just the two of them...plus Evan. But Evan

was in no shape to fight. If he wasn't much better than when he had left him, it was going to be an effort just getting him off the island.

Jeff told himself he'd worry about that later.

Right now, he intended to follow Ben and see what he was up to.

Jeff watched as Ben moved up the trail, heading for the infirmary. He was filled with rage and frustration because, other than brute force, he didn't have any idea what he could do to stop him.

Once Ben was past him, Jeff followed along beside him, keeping to the woods and stepping carefully so he wouldn't make any noise. He wished it was raining so the sound would mask whatever noise he made, but Ben didn't seem to know how close he was and that he was watching him… tracking him.

The night air was bracing. With every breath, Jeff felt another amazing surge of energy fill him. All of his nerves and senses were much sharper than usual; honed to a fine edge. He could hear and see and smell things he had never perceived before. The air was filled with the raw smell of rotting things as the year came to a close. The drops of water falling from the branches all around him glistened as though each of them had an internal light source. Gold and silver splattered around him in a dazzling display that was nearly psychedelic. The trees swayed in the wind, tossed by the wind that whistled through the branches and whispered to him. He believed he was so attuned to nature he couldn't be harmed.

One small, rational corner of Jeff's mind told him he was imagining all of this. His mind, stressed by anxiety and danger and exhaustion, only seemed to be sharper than normal. He was more receptive to the night because he was past the point of rationality.

That's a good thing, Jeff thought as he moved through the forest, never letting Ben's wavering flashlight beam out of sight.

The muscles in his arms and legs thrummed with energy and power. He started to imagine what he would do if—not if…*when* he got his hands on Ben. He would choke him…crush his throat with his bare hands in a surge of savagery and tear him apart with his bare teeth.

He found the primitive imagery that filled his mind unsettling, but Jeff had to be this savage if he was going survive the night.

Because one thing was sure…

Only one of them was going to live to leave the island in the morning, and Jeff was going to make damned sure it was *him*.

Jeff stopped short in his tracks and then dropped into a crouch when, up ahead, the dark hulk of the infirmary appeared through a gap in the trees. The oval of Ben's flashlight beam played across the front of the building. Even at this distance, Jeff heard Ben mutter a growling curse when he saw that the door was wide open.

But where's Evan?

Tension twisted inside Jeff.

How am I going to save him?

Ben leaped up onto the small porch in front of the door and, leaning against the wall beside the open door, raised his hand. Jeff saw the pistol, held high like the cops did it on TV.

Moving as close as he dared without revealing himself, Jeff held his breath, watching and waiting for Ben to burst into the infirmary, his gun blazing. He narrowed his eyes, surprised by the deep, rumbling growl that escaped his lips as he watched Ben…hoping…praying that—somehow—Evan would get the drop on Ben.

Had Evan heard him coming?

Was he ready?

Even now, was he crouching just inside the door… clutching one of the rocks I gave him… ready to fight?

Ben stood there for a long, tense moment beside the open doorway. He shifted his weight from one foot to the other and then, with a piercing yell, charged around the corner. Jeff checked the impulse to use the noise Ben was making as a cover so he could rush forward and attack Ben from behind. Instead, he stood there, holding his breath and waiting.

"*Fuck!*"

That single word filled the night.

Jeff recognized Ben's voice, and he knew Evan wasn't inside. An instant later, Ben burst back out onto the porch. Crouching low, he shined the flashlight all around. The beam skimmed across the water-soaked front yard, tracked by the pistol in his other hand.

"*Fuck!*" he shouted again, his voice echoing from the woods.

Jeff smiled as he watched Ben jump down to the ground and start moving around the side of the building. His head was bowed. The flashlight was focused on the ground. He was clearly looking for any tracks Evan had left, but Jeff was confident the heavy rain had washed them away.

Ben circled around the infirmary and came back to the front door. He paused by the landing, bending over and studying the ground.

It was obvious he had no idea where Evan had gone or what he should

The Wildman

do next. Evan could be hiding anywhere…in the woods, down on the beach, maybe back at the dining hall.

Jeff was afraid Evan wouldn't last long, not if he was somewhere in the woods.

I'll have to find him first, he thought, but he was just as perplexed as Ben about where Evan might have gone.

After a short, fruitless search, Ben started back down the trail, heading toward the dining hall. Jeff dropped to the damp ground behind some bushes to avoid the flashlight beam as it swept back and forth. He wished he could move silently enough to get behind Ben and jump him, but he had to let him go…

For now.

His first concern was finding Evan and making sure he was still alive. Revenge for what Ben had done to his other three friends could wait a little while.

As soon as Ben was gone, Jeff moved closer to the trail, still keeping close to the woods in case Ben doused his light and tried to sneak back, hoping to lure either him or Evan out into the open.

It struck Jeff as odd that he no longer felt the cold and damp. He wondered if he might already be dying of hypothermia and simply didn't recognize it yet, but the truth was, if anything, he felt more alive than ever before. His senses were filled with the raw input of the night and the forest, and he was more in tune with life than he had ever been before.

Keeping to the woods, he got as close as he could to the infirmary. Then, crouching low and sitting on his haunches, he waited as he stared at the dark slash of the open door. Taking slow, even breaths, he listened to everything around him. He told himself he could wait here all night if he had to. His eyes were wide as he tried to pierce the darkness, and his ears were pricked as he listened for any indication of danger.

He wasn't about to risk getting taken by surprise. As tuned as his senses were to everything around him, he wasn't about to overestimate his abilities… or underestimate Ben's.

He lost any sense of time, but after a while, something—a shadow darker than the night—shifted against the foundation of the building.

Is that an animal?

Maybe the raccoon or skunk who burrowed under the old foundation had been frightened away by Ben's shouting and now was coming back to investigate what might be happening to its lair.

Or maybe it was Ben.

Maybe he had circled around through the woods and was coming around from behind the building to see if either Evan or Jeff had come out of hiding.

Jeff held his breath and stared, wide-eyed; every fiber of his being tingled with anticipation.

Before long, he heard a low, scrambling sound like someone or something clawing at the ground.

Jeff was convinced it was an animal, but the shadow suddenly grew larger, rising up, dark black etched against the darkness of the infirmary. Jeff held his breath and waited. Then he smiled to himself when he saw that it was a person.

Still, Jeff didn't move.

He had to know if it was Ben or Evan.

Then a hushed voice whispered in the night, barely audible above the wind overhead.

"*Psst… Hey, Jeff…? You there…?*"

A surge of relief flooded Jeff. Evan must have been hiding in the narrow crawlspace underneath the building. Fortunately, Ben hadn't thought to check under there.

Still, Jeff didn't move.

It was possible Evan had just walked blindly into Ben's trap. As much as he wanted to save Evan, he wasn't about to do anything foolish…not if he could help it.

He watched as Evan crept over to the porch in front of the building. He was holding something, and Jeff realized he had a large rock in each hand.

Evan stepped cautiously up onto the landing and then, leaning into the doorway, checked inside the infirmary. Satisfied that it was empty, he turned around and leaned against the doorframe. He raised his arms as if hugging himself against the cold. Even at this distance, Jeff heard Evan's teeth chatter.

Finally, once he was positive Ben was nowhere around, Jeff broke cover and came forward. Evan didn't notice him until he was less than twenty feet from the infirmary. He jumped and let out a frightened grunt as he raised his right hand, ready to attack.

"Easy there," Jeff said. "It's me."

Jeff took a step back and raised both hands as though surrendering.

"Christ! Don't *do* that! You scared the shit out of me!" Evan paused and swallowed hard. "Where the hell were you?"

Jeff nodded back down the trail and said, "In the woods," as if that were answer enough.

"He was here," Evan said. "Ben came out looking for me."

"I know. I saw him. And it's a damned good thing he didn't find you. He's got a gun, and he'll use it. He already has. He killed Fred and Mike and, I think, Tyler."

"Oh, Jesus. Are you sure?"

"Positive. I saw it."

Evan lowered his gaze to the muddy ground.

"What about Tyler? Where's he?" Evan asked, his teeth still chattering.

"I'm not sure, but I don't hold out much hope for him, either."

Jeff clenched his fists as a sudden rush of indescribable rage filled him. It pounded through his veins and nerves, giving him a surge of energy.

"This guy's totally lost his mind," Jeff said, "and he plans to kill you and me before we can get off this goddamned island."

Evan groaned softly and seemed to fold in on himself. With his newfound perception, Jeff imagined he could see his friend's life force draining out of him. Reaching out and grabbing Evan by the shoulders, he gave him a bracing shake.

"You can't punk out on me now. We're not dead yet, and we're not gonna let him get us."

Evan groaned even louder and turned his head away as if he was too embarrassed to face Jeff.

"What good am I gonna be," he said in a frail voice. "I can hardly walk, much less fight if we have to." He took a whistling breath through his nose. "How 'bout you leave me here and go back to the mainland and bring the police back? I can hide out 'till morning. I'll crawl back under the infirmary foundation. He'll never find me."

"If he does, you'd be trapped," Jeff said. "You were lucky he didn't find you there already. He'll think of it sooner or later."

"But if I can find—"

Before he finished, Jeff gave him another, harder shake.

"No!…There's no way," he said in a low growl. "I'm not gonna let this asshole get me or you the way he got the others, and I'm definitely not leaving you here. You're coming with me whether you want to or not."

"But I'll just hold you back."

There was a crazed, frightened gleam in Evan's eyes that made Jeff wonder if he might have already snapped from the time he'd been locked in a closet without food or water.

How much can the human mind and body take? He wondered. He had a sickening feeling, before the night was over, they were both going to find out.

Chapter Twelve

Illuminations

JEFF HAD NO idea what he should do next. He wanted to get back to the dining hall so he could grab some food and maybe a bottle of rum, but it didn't look good. Evan told him he had collected some rainwater to drink, but his stomach had been empty for so long he vomited it back up after only a couple of sips.

"It's gonna be a while before you get your strength back," he told him, trying not to think that Evan was probably going to end up in the hospital hooked up to an IV for at least a few days.

"So what's the plan?" Evan asked.

"I'm not sure."

"That's not much of a plan."

Jeff stepped to one side so Evan could hook his arm around his shoulder and use him for support.

"We've got to get to the boat. That's our only chance. Even if the engine's fucked, we'll row back to the mainland if we have to.

"As long as Ben hasn't taken the oars."

"Yeah…there's that."

"You don't think he'd think of that?" Evan shook his head. "He's been planning this for a long time. Chances are, he's got his bases covered."

Jeff sniffed with grim laughter and shook his head.

"Yeah, but he hasn't counted on the human element."

Or the **inhuman** *element*, he thought, still confounded by the transformation he'd experienced in the woods. Although his senses weren't as keen right now as they had been, he was sure something fundamental in him had changed inside…some primitive part of his brain that was dormant had been unlocked or re-awakened, and was working in ways he still had trouble comprehending. But he couldn't deny he could sense things that even yesterday, although yesterday seemed so long ago, would have slipped past him without a ripple.

"We'll swim over if we have to," Jeff said. He held Evan by the waist, hooking his fingers around his belt for support. "First thing, though, we have to get down to the lake and see what's what. He's just one man. He can't be everywhere at once."

Evan chuckled and said, "Right. It's not like he's Hobomock or something."

He had said it in jest, but Jeff's immediate thought was, *Yeah, maybe* **he's** *not Hobomock… but* **I** *am.*

He almost said it out loud, but let it drop. On a purely rational level, he knew it wasn't true. It couldn't be. He hadn't been possessed by any Indian spirit or demon. There must be a simpler explanation for what had happened to him. The threat to his own life had kick-started some weird defense mechanism in his brain. It was probably something everyone had, but society or "civilization" buried it so deeply beneath layers and layers of laziness and complacency that we were no longer aware of it…unless or until we needed it.

Like now.

The danger he faced had stripped all of the trappings of civilization from him. He was more in touch with his primitive heritage, and he was confident he could outsmart, outfight, and kill Ben.

It was simply a matter of survival.

"You up to this?" he asked.

Evan sucked in a whistling breath and took a step forward. His muscles had obviously atrophied from inactivity, but all he had to do was keep moving. Put one foot in front of the other. They would deal with whatever came when and if it came.

The wind hadn't let up. It was bending the trees as it blew cold and hard from the west. Even Jeff had to admit that the cold and damp were getting to him. As they made their way slowly along the trail, he couldn't stop thinking about how nice it would be if only they could get in front of the fire in the dining hall and have something to eat and drink. It wouldn't take much for the civilized part of his nature to reassert itself.

Odds were Ben was hanging close to the dining hall and the boat, waiting for them to show up. The boat was their only option of surviving and getting off the island. Ben could hole up somewhere out of sight and be ready when they came.

"How you doing?" Jeff asked. Evan's steps were faltering more and more the further they went. His breath came in short, wheezing gasps that shook his body. With nearly every other step, he stumbled and would have fallen if Jeff hadn't been holding him.

"I…I'm…all right. I'll make it."

"Wanna take a minute to rest?"

Evan gritted his teeth and shook his head.

"If I sit down now, I'll never get up."

Jeff had to admire his friend's fortitude. He wanted to say something about how, even if they didn't make it out of this, even if both of them ended up dead tonight, they had been brave and had tried with every resource they had, and could die satisfied.

But Jeff wouldn't allow such thoughts. They weren't going to die. Thoughts like that worked against them.

They were about halfway to the dining hall when Jeff suddenly drew to a halt. His senses were tingling as he craned his head forward, cocking it from side to side as he listened and waited for something that had caught his attention to be repeated.

"What is—?" Evan started to say, but Jeff shushed him. Moving quickly, he all but dragged Evan off the trail and into the woods. They knelt behind a low evergreen bush, and Jeff eased Evan down to the ground before creeping ahead a short way under the low-hanging branches.

"Stay quiet," he whispered.

As he scanned the trail, every nerve and fiber of his body vibrated. He sniffed the wind as he listened and stared into the well of darkness. To his eyes, the night glowed with an eerie purple iridescence that seemed not to have a distinct source.

Danger is approaching.

He knew that much.

It was a palpable presence in the night, as if the air and the forest were his skin, and something was pressing against it, applying slow, steady pressure.

Moving swiftly and quietly, Jeff darted off into the woods, circling around but always staying no more than twenty or thirty yards away from the path. After he had gone a hundred yards or so, he doubled back toward the trail, knowing the threat was getting closer and was coming toward him.

The night crackled with tension. The wind hissed like angry snakes in the branches overhead. But beneath all of these sounds, Jeff heard something else…the slow, steady tread of feet on the rain-soaked ground.

You don't stand a goddamned chance, he thought, anticipating that it was Ben. He clenched his fists and waited patiently, barely breathing as the footsteps came closer and closer. After a few tense moments, with the night vibrating all around him, Jeff saw a dark figure. A solitary dark silhouette was making its way slowly up the trail without the aid of a flashlight, feeling his way through the darkness like a blind man.

Moving forward silently, Jeff prepared to attack as soon as the person—it had to be Ben—walked past him. The person rounded a turn in the trail, walking past where Jeff was hiding. As soon as his back was to Jeff, Jeff struck. Barely making a sound, he moved up quickly behind the person. When he was only a few feet away, he leaped at him. His arms encircled the man's waist, and the forward momentum propelled them both face-first onto the ground.

Growling savagely, Jeff hooked his right leg around the man's lower body, scrambling to hold him down.

The man thrashed wildly to free himself. His grunts of desperate struggle were muffled by Jeff's weight as it pressed his face down into the mud.

"You son of a bitch," he said softly, surprised that he wasn't filled with insane rage. Instead, a cold, calculating cruelty filled him. He was as heartless detached as a snake striking its prey.

The man beneath him continued to struggle, but his resistance quickly drained away. Before he killed him, Jeff wanted to stare him in the face and watch the light of life expire in his eyes as he clamped his hands around Ben's throat and squeezed the life out of him.

"You really thought you were gonna win?" Jeff whispered in a cold, merciless voice. "You thought you'd get the better of me?"

Feeling Ben sag in his embrace, Jeff shifted his weight off him. Still holding him down with his legs, he yanked his shoulder and flipped him over.

Jeff was stunned when he saw Tyler staring up at him with fear-widened eyes. His tongue protruded from his mouth, and his breath made watery, hitching sounds.

"What the *Christ?*"

For just a second, Jeff wondered if his eyes were playing tricks on him.

What if Ben had learned the magic of the forest and was tricking him with this illusion?

But Tyler groaned as he shook his head.

"What the *fuck* are you doing out here?" Jeff said. He kept his voice low, fearing Ben might be within hearing distance.

When Jeff released him, Tyler tried to sit up, but his hands and feet kept slipping in the slick mud, and he fell. His throat was still making funny gagging noises as he flopped onto his left side and assumed a fetal position.

"For Christ's sake," Tyler gasped. "You don't…you don't have to…fucking *kill* me…"

The Wildman

"I will if I have to," Jeff said as he got slowly to his feet and brushed his hands. Bending down, he helped Tyler to his feet. Once he was standing, Tyler started to wipe the mud from his clothes but soon realized how futile that was and stopped.

"What are you doing out here?" Jeff asked. "How'd you get away?"

Jeff's senses were still honed as he turned and looked up and down the trail, expecting to see Ben nearby.

"I came to find you," Tyler said, still laboring for breath.

"How the hell did you get away? You know he fucking killed Mike, right?"

Tyler took a step away from Jeff. The move was subtle, but it put Jeff on his guard. Something wasn't right here.

"Yeah," Tyler said. "I know. Mike's dead…and Fred, too, but you…we have a real problem here."

"No shit, we do. We have to kill that motherfucker before he kills us."

When Tyler took another step back, Jeff noticed he had his shoulders hunched up as if he was preparing to attack.

"That's why I came out looking for you," Tyler said. He still sounded like he wasn't getting enough air into his lungs. "You gotta talk to him."

"Are you out of your mind? I'm not gonna talk to him. I'm gonna kill him as soon as I get the chance."

"No, no," Tyler said with a firm shake of the head. "It's not like that. You don't understand. It doesn't have to be this way. You can talk to him…reason with him."

Jeff glanced up and down the trail again and then looked into the dark woods. Although Ben wasn't nearby, Jeff could still sense his presence.

He's out there… right now… watching us… listening to everything we say…
Is he already aiming his gun at me? Is he going to shoot me in cold blood?

The night was charged with energy as Jeff and Tyler faced each other less than six feet apart. Jeff didn't doubt he could beat Tyler hand-to-hand, but he didn't want to fight him. All he wanted was to get off this goddamned island with Evan. If he had to hurt or kill Tyler to do that, then he would without a second thought.

"No," Jeff said, his voice a deep, animal growl. "It's *you* who doesn't understand."

"Just talk to Evan. You'll see. He can be reasonable. He's just…he was confused. He didn't mean to kill Mike. The gun went off accidentally."

"Jesus, Tyler! You haven't figured it out, yet, have you?"

"Figured what out?"

"That's not Evan. Evan Pike has been held as a prisoner out here. That guy you think is Evan is really Ben Foster."

"Ben Foster?"

"Yeah. Jimmy Foster's younger brother. And he brought us all out here to kill us because he blames us for what happened to Jimmy."

A look of genuine shock spread across Tyler's face. Then he frowned and shook his head as though struggling to deny the truth of what Jeff said.

"He had Evan tied up in the fucking storage closet in the infirmary. He was going to kill him after he killed the rest of us…even you, Tyler."

"No. No. That's not true. That's not what he told me." Tyler's face contorted with the effort of trying to accept what Jeff was telling him. "He wants to explain how it was all a misunderstanding…a terrible misunderstanding."

"I *saw* him kill Mike," Jeff said. "He pointed the gun at Mike's head, counted to three, and shot him point blank. He shot at me, too. You must have heard the shots. And he's gonna do the same thing to you if you don't help me get the fuck off this island and get the police out here."

"You know where Evan is?" Tyler asked, his voice lifting with hope. He took a step closer to Jeff, but Jeff backed away, maintaining the same distance between them.

"I did." Jeff was surprised how easily the lie came to him. "But when I went back to the infirmary, he wasn't there. I don't know where he is now and, frankly, I don't give a shit. All I want to do is get out of here. Are you with me?"

Tyler's expression glazed over as he lowered his eyes and shook his head as if what Jeff had told him was too much to handle. His body started to tremble, and he looked like he was about to drop.

"I'm telling you, man," Jeff said, resisting the impulse to step forward and help support him. "That's not Evan. He's got you snookered. He fooled all of us. He's using you to trick me into giving myself up."

"No…no," Tyler said, raising his head and glaring at Jeff. His mouth was a firm, bloodless line. "He said you're the killer, and if I helped him find you so he could stop you, he'd let me go."

"He *what*—?"

Tyler took another step closer. This time, Jeff didn't back away. As they glared at each other, neither one of them said a word. Jeff stretched out his senses out to the night, listening…and smelling…and looking …

And the night spoke to him, talking to him in ways he had never experienced until tonight.

The Wildman

He knew that the immediate area was safe, at least for the time being. Ben wasn't nearby, but he wasn't far off.

And he's coming for me.

The thought send a tingling chill up Jeff's spine. He experienced a heady rush that made him feel giddy.

He thinks I'm a fool... He thinks he can trap me...

Jeff snorted and almost laughed out loud. He couldn't let Tyler know he could see what they were up to as clearly as if they were standing in broad daylight.

In a quick, fluid motion, Jeff stepped forward, clenching his right hand into a fist. He cocked it back. Before Tyler could react, he snapped his fist forward. An amazing feeling of exhilaration filled him when his fist connected with Tyler's face, hitting him squarely on the bridge of the nose.

Something in Tyler's neck cracked as his head snapped back. He made a funny little squealing sound as a jet of dark blood shot from his nose. Without another sound, his legs folded up, and he dropped. His body made a loud squishy sound when it hit the muddy ground, sending a fan of mud flying into the air.

Jeff stepped back, knowing Tyler was down for the count. He might even be dead, but he didn't care. The son of a bitch had tried to trick him. He had betrayed his trust, and he had to learn that anyone who got in his way was going to pay a huge price.

But Jeff didn't have time to enjoy his triumph.

A second later, the night around him throbbed with a cold rush of air. His surroundings brightened for an instant, and the woods filled with a muted purple glow.

In that instant, Jeff had the sensation he was flying, hovering several feet above the ground. Something had changed with his vision, and he saw further down the path than he should have been able to. He could see around the twists and turns of the trail as though looking down a long, straight line that led all the way back to the dining hall and beach. Far off in the distance, Ben Foster was moving along the trail toward him. Jeff saw the gun in Ben's hand and the murderous glare of rage in his eyes.

Soundlessly, Jeff turned and ran off into the woods just as Ben rounded the turn in the trail. A single shot rang out, but the bullet whizzed by harmlessly and ripped into the woods.

Moving fast and silently, Jeff went deeper into the woods, feeling himself blend into his surroundings as if he had become the darkness. He was confident Ben hadn't seen him. He was taking pot shots, shooting at any sound or motion.

By the time Ben got to where Tyler was lying unconscious on the muddy trail, Jeff was already circling around to where he had left Evan, hiding in the brush.

They didn't have much time, and he planned to use what they had to his advantage.

❦ ❦ ❦

"You sure you can walk?"

Jeff didn't like the way Evan was so unsteady on his feet, but he was determined not to leave him behind. If Tyler really was on Ben's side, their chances of getting back to the mainland were decreasing.

"I'm good…seriously," Evan said, but when he took his first step, his legs collapsed buckled under him. Jeff grabbed him to keep him from falling.

"I'm still kind of stiff from not moving for so long." He took a deep breath. "I'll be all right once we get moving."

Without another word, they started off through the woods side by side, keeping parallel to the trail but never so close to it that they would be seen if anyone came along. They hadn't gone far before Evan had to stop and catch his breath.

"I can't believe this is all because he blames us for what happened to his brother," Jeff said.

Evan nodded. "As far as I know."

"I can't figure why he didn't kill you when he had the chance. It doesn't make sense to leave you out there like that."

Evan shrugged.

"Maybe he planned to use me as a hostage or negotiating chip or whatever."

Jeff shrugged, not convinced. If Ben planned on confronting all of them at the same time, he would have done it the first night. It made more sense for Ben to pick them off one by one, rather than confront them as a group where they might be able to resist and overwhelm him.

Still, *he* had the gun.

Until they changed *that,* he had the advantage.

Before he was consciously aware of it, Jeff sensed something moving toward them in the dark. He shushed Evan and looked around, letting the night fill his senses. Reaching out as much with his mind as with his eyes and ears, he implored the night to speak to him.

"I think he might have found our trail," he whispered.

"What are—"

"Shsssh."

Branches clattered as the trees swayed in the wind, but beneath that, there was another sound. Again, Jeff experienced a curious disembodied sensation as he stretched out his senses and nerves to feel what was going on around him.

This is magical, he thought, feeling almost giddy, and, at the same time, telling himself, *No… you're losing your goddamned mind… you've snapped because of what's going on.*

Jeff knew, without a doubt, that Ben was moving toward them, walking slowly…cautiously…his gun poised and ready.

"We have to get down to the lake before he does," Jeff whispered. "Are you *sure* you can make it?"

"I don't want to hold you back."

Evan sounded wrung out with exhaustion. He was shivering as he slumped forward, looking like he was going to drop any second now.

"Are you sure you don't want to do this on your own? I'll hide somewhere they can't find me. After you contact the authorities, you can come back and get me."

Biting his lower lip, Jeff considered for a moment but then shook his head.

"I'm not leaving you behind. We either get out of this together, alive, or we don't get out of it at all." He listened for the sound of Ben's footfalls as he closed the distance between them.

"Let's go," Evan said simply.

Walking side by side, they continued through the woods, dodging trees and stopping every now and then so Evan could catch his breath. Jeff kept reaching out into the night, wanting to hear and feel every step Ben took, but the night was silent now. The presence of imminent danger had lessened.

Is Ben moving away from us?

Jeff wondered if his senses were failing him. What if Ben was coming closer, and he couldn't sense it?

It seemed to take longer than it should have, but eventually up ahead he saw a clearing and knew they were near the dining hall. The strong smell of wood smoke filled the night air, but he told himself not to think about the creature comforts inside the dining hall. If they tried to get in there, Ben would have them trapped before they could get away. He had to stay outside, where his newfound awareness would tell him everything he needed to know.

But there were things in the dining hall he needed.

For one, he wanted to get his cell phone and car keys. He also could use some dry clothes for himself and Evan. And if he could, a bottle of rum would help warm them up and fend off the hypothermia they both were close to suffering.

The problem was, he didn't see how he could accomplish any of that without getting caught.

What he needed was a distraction.

※ ※ ※

They moved through the woods until they could see the glow of the fire in the dining hall windows. The mist blowing in off the lake made it all but impossible to see if Ben was lurking somewhere outside, waiting in ambush. There was no sign of danger, but Ben and Tyler could be anywhere.

Jeff's chief concern was the boat.

What would Ben do to prevent them from using it?

Was the motor really useless, or had he choked it out on purpose so they would think it was broken? After all, once he had gotten his revenge, he needed a way back to the mainland.

If the motor really was burned out, was he going to row back to the mainland once everyone else was dead?

If that was his plan, he would have hidden the oars so no one else would find them.

And if the boat was out of the equation, the only option left would be to swim back to the mainland.

In water as cold as the lake must be, that was all but guaranteed suicide. Evan was already in such bad shape he would surely die if he didn't get food and warmth soon. Exposure to the near freezing night was also wearing Jeff down. In spite of the transformation he had experienced in the woods, he knew he was still mortal. He hadn't really *become* Hobomock. He was no Native American spirit or demon who was impervious to the elements.

But then again, neither was Ben, and unless he planned on committing suicide once he'd killed them, he had to have a way of getting off the island.

"I've got it," Jeff said, snapping his fingers.

"Got what?"

"How we're gonna get out of here. But you're gonna have to do something to help. I hope you're up for it."

Jeff stared silently at Evan, trying to evaluate just how much he thought he could tolerate. Evan looked shaky on his feet. His shoulders were slumped forward as he leaned against a tree, gasping for breath.

"I'll do whatever you say," Evan said. "You're the boss."

Jeff couldn't help but smile.

The Wildman

"There. You finally admitted it after all these years."

"Admitted what?"

"That I'm the boss."

Evan sniffed and shook his head. "You'll have plenty of time to gloat about that once we get the hell out of here. So tell me. What do I have to do?"

Chapter Thirteen

Kaleidoscope

THE NIGHT WAS cold, and the wind gusted so strongly on all sides Jeff had a hard time staying on his feet. The sensation of falling was dizzying, and he braced himself, struggling to maintain his composure as he stared at Evan and tried to think what to do.

"It all depends on a couple of things," he said.

"Like what?"

"First off, we have to hope Ben hasn't hidden the oars on us."

"What are the chances of that?"

Jeff shrugged as he stared past the dining hall toward the lake as if he could somehow peel back the mist and darkness to see the boat and whether or not the oars were in it.

"He sure as hell seems to have covered all his bases," Evan said, sounding both nervous and exhausted.

"Not really. If he had, we wouldn't be alive now, would we?"

Evan hesitated before he replied, "I dunno. It all depends on what he had in mind for us."

"That sure inspires confidence."

Evan shrugged. "I'm just saying."

Jeff couldn't help but feel as though they were kids again, taunting each other with their foolish games of one-upmanship. He narrowed his eyes, trying to focus on the problems at hand. They could pretend this was just a joke or a game, but—somehow—Ben had gotten Tyler to take his side, and he didn't want to contemplate what would happen if they caught him and Evan.

"I say we head out to the baseball field," Jeff said. "We can circle around through the woods, skirting where the meeting hall used to be. We might be able to get down to the boat without being seen."

Evan considered the suggestion for a few seconds, then grunted and shook his head.

"I'm not so sure about that," he said.

"Why?" Jeff choked down a rush of anger, telling himself this wasn't just another case of Evan trying to take charge.

"We can't let the boat out of our sight," Evan said. "If he hasn't taken the oars yet, he will now because he's gotta know that's our next move."

Jeff shrugged and said, "The oars are either there or they're not. What difference does it make if he gets them now? He's got the gun. We have to stay out of sight. If he walked up right now and took them, all we could do is watch."

"But we might see where he stashes them," Evan offered. "If he needs them later…"

"What if he takes them into the dining hall? He can put 'em up in the rafters, and there wouldn't be a damned thing we could do about it."

"I know…I know," Evan said.

Jeff was happy to hear Evan agitated like this. It meant he was getting his strength and spirit back.

"Okay. Good point," Jeff said. "So what do we do? Stand around here arguing all night?"

"No. I'll go down to the boat," Evan said simply.

"Whether the oars are there or not?"

"Uh-huh. And I'll take it out onto the water and head away from the island. Ben's sure to come after me. That will give you time to go into the dining hall and get the stuff we need."

Jeff narrowed his eyes as he scanned the open area around the dining hall. It was frustrating not to have that sensation of heightened perception. The night and the surrounding woods seemed perfectly normal. He knew he must have been experiencing an adrenalin rush from the excitement of escape and pursuit, but at the time, it had seemed much more than that. So much more. Now that they had more practical and immediate problems to solve, it was as though his senses had shut down or—at least—returned to normal.

But it didn't matter whether or not he could see Ben or sense where he was. Jeff knew he was somewhere nearby. Even if he couldn't hear or see or smell him, he could feel the murderous rage inside Ben that seethed like boiling lava, seeking an outlet.

"You want a distraction, don't you?" Evan said.

When Jeff didn't answer, Evan jabbed him on the shoulder.

"Well…? Don't you?"

The Wildman

"Yeah, but…" He took a breath. "It's too risky." But even as he said it, he knew there was no way around it. Evan's idea seemed like their best plan.

Hell, it was their *only* plan.

He had to believe it would work out. But as he prepared to spring into action, he told himself—*Yeah… ask Mike and Fred how it's working out for them…*

※ ※ ※

"Ready…Set…*Go!*"

With that whispered command, Evan broke cover and started running toward the beach. Staying in the shadows, Jeff watched, his heart racing and his stomach churning with anticipation.

Evan was just a small, black shape moving against the night and then was lost in the mist blowing in off the water. Jeff was left feeling as though Evan, like Fred and Mike, had been swallowed by the darkness never to return.

For what seemed like much too long a time, there was no sign of activity from within the dining hall. No shadows cast by the firelight shifted across the windows. No one exited the doorway.

Nothing.

"Damn," Jeff muttered, clenching his fists in frustration.

If Ben was watching from the dining hall…if he knew they were out there…he would have responded by now.

Wouldn't he?

Unless he was still in the woods, searching for Evan around the infirmary. Or maybe he was waiting for them at the boat, hiding in the shadows, ready to pounce when they showed up.

The boat was their only possibility of escape, so that seemed most likely. Just wait them out…

And meanwhile, where was Tyler?

If he was helping Ben because he still believed Ben was really Evan or because of some promise Ben had made not to hurt him, he must be around here somewhere, too.

As far as Jeff knew, Ben might already have found Evan and silently killed him. He didn't need a gun. He could have gotten a knife or some other weapon from the dining hall. This very second, Evan might be lying face down on the water-soaked sand, leaking blood that washed away in the runoff rainwater.

Tension and frustration coiled inside Jeff until he could no longer stand it. He broke cover and moved toward the dining hall. No matter what was going on, he had to act fast. One way or another, Ben and probably Tyler were going to be coming for him.

His feet made loud slopping sounds on the muddy ground as he approached the side of the building. Water gurgled as it ran off the roof, overflowing the gutters and pounding the ground into a muddy mess. Jeff went to one of the windows and, easing himself up cautiously, looked inside.

The glow of firelight seemed to mock him. The piles of clothing and bedding, all spread out in an arc around the blaze, looked so comfortable and innocent Jeff found it all but impossible to believe he was engaged in a fight for his life. Seeing what had been so normal until a short time ago filled him with an odd sense of unreality.

Come on… just do what you gotta do, he told himself.

Still, he didn't dare move. Narrowing his eyes, he stretched out his senses, trying to feel where Ben was, but the heightened perceptions were dulled again, if not gone. All he felt now was fear…fear that he and Evan weren't going to survive…fear that Ben was going to outsmart him and kill them both…if Evan wasn't already dead back on the beach.

Fighting a dark wave of despair, Jeff snuck around to the side porch, keeping his back to the building. His heart was racing so fast it felt like the cold hands were wrapped around his throat and squeezing.

He hesitated at the foot of the porch when he looked up and saw the still, silent form of Mike, sprawled on his back next to the railing. Jeff was almost too afraid to walk past his dead friend, but he couldn't waste any more time. Something, he had no idea what, was happening down on the beach. Either Evan had the boat and was preparing to launch, or else he was dead, and Ben was coming for him.

Sucking in his breath and holding it, Jeff stepped up onto the porch. The rotting wood sagged beneath his weight. Rusty nails made dull squeaking sounds as they pulled out of the wood. Jeff couldn't stop glancing at Mike's body, unable to believe his friend was really dead. And Fred was laying stone cold just inside the doorway.

This can't be happening.

As he stepped over Mike's corpse, Jeff half expected him to roll over and grab him by the ankle before pulling him down…down to join him in death.

"Fuck this shit," Jeff whispered as he jumped over the body and quickly entered the building. He didn't even pause to note Fred's body, where they had laid it in the hallway by the restroom door.

The smell of wood smoke tingled in his nose, almost making him sneeze. The blast of warmth embraced him as if he had just stepped into a hot sauna,

The Wildman

but he didn't have time to luxuriate in the heat. He had to grab what he needed and get the hell out of here before Ben caught him.

As he rounded the corner into the main dining room, the sudden brightness after being outside in the dark for so long stung his eyes. He stumbled over something on the floor and almost fell. Wheeling around and dropping into a defensive crouch, he expected to see Ben standing there, gloating over how easily he had fallen into his trap.

What he saw instead was worse.

Much worse.

Tyler was sitting on the floor, his back against the wall, his legs splayed out in front of him. His head was hanging at an awkward angle to one side.

It was obvious he was dead.

A wide wash of liquid as dark as used motor oil covered the front of his jacket. His face was as white as bone. Even the orange glow of the fire didn't make it look warm. His tongue was hanging out of the side of his mouth like something he had been trying to eat and then spit back up. His eyes, wide open and glistening in the firelight, stared sightlessly at the floor. Even so, Jeff felt as though Tyler was looking straight at him, silently accusing him and pleading, asking *Why… why did this have to happen to me?*

"Because you fucked up, my friend," Jeff whispered as he knelt down beside Tyler. Shivering at the touch, he closed his friend's eyes. There was nothing more he could do for him.

Tyler's throat had been sliced from ear to ear. The blood no longer flowed from the wound, but it was still warm and sticky to the touch. He couldn't have been dead long.

So it was down to the three of them—him, Evan, and Ben. The odds were still in Ben's favor, but Jeff would see if he could change that.

But if he has a gun, Jeff thought, *why didn't he use it to kill Tyler?*

Why slit his throat?

Is he low on ammunition… or maybe out?

Or did he not want to reveal himself with a gunshot?

Or had he enjoyed cutting Tyler's throat?

These thoughts sent a chill through Jeff that bit deeper to the bone than the foul weather outside. If he had been any doubts before, this gruesome example of how far Ben would go made it clear just how dangerous the situation was.

Jeff took a shuddering breath, wincing at the stink of death that filled the room. Then he stood up. He had to move fast.

Keeping in a low crouch so Ben wouldn't see him through the windows if he was outside, he went over to his pile of things and quickly rifled through them. His hands were shaking out of control, and his teeth were chattering as he grabbed his car keys, cell phone, and wallet, and stuffed them into his pants pockets. He ran to the corner of the room where they had stashed their supply of booze and grabbed an unopened bottle of rum. Before sliding it into his coat pocket, he couldn't resist breaking the seal, screwing off the cap, and raising the bottle to his mouth.

He took a bigger gulp than expected. The liquor ran from the corners of his mouth and filled his chest and belly with blast furnace warmth so strong it staggered him. He narrowed his eyes, allowing the flickering glow in the room to shatter into thousands of wavering points of light.

He took another, smaller swig of rum, telling himself it was all he could allow himself. He had to stay sharp, focused. His hands were still shaking as he grabbed a clean, dry sweatshirt and T-shirt, shucked off his wet jacket, and slid the fresh clothes on. He considered putting on some dry pants. The one he was wearing were so saturated they practically slid off his hips, but he didn't dare take any more time than absolutely necessary. He rolled up two pairs of pants and two pairs of dry socks, and stuffed them inside his jacket, zipping it up and hoping they would stay dry enough until he and Evan had a chance to change into them.

As he turned to leave, he noticed the cooking utensils Ben had used to prepare their meals. After a quick search, he saw that the heavy carving knife was missing.

Of course it's gone!
That's what Ben used to slice Tyler's throat.

Jeff shivered but resisted the temptation to take another shot of rum. He looked around one last time, feeling like there was something he was forgetting, but didn't see anything else he could use. He didn't want to overburden himself with too much stuff, anyway. If he and Evan got the drop on Ben, they could come back and take all the time they wanted to eat, drink, dry out, and warm up in front of the fire before they went to the mainland and notified the cops about what had happened out here.

"First things first," he whispered, and his first priority was to find Evan and see what they could do about getting the boat.

❦ ❦ ❦

Jeff felt as though he had been inside the dining hall for a long time, at least an hour, but in truth it must have been less than five minutes.

A lot could have happened in that short a time, though.

Ben hadn't come for him, so that meant he likely was down on the shore, waiting with the boat. Darting from tree to tree and keeping to the shadows, Jeff ran to the beach where, earlier today—

Was it really today and not a couple of years ago?

—they had beached the boat after their aborted cruise around the island.

Jeff was all the more convinced Ben had faked the engine failure as part of his plan to isolate them. It might be a vain hope that they could get the boat going, but he clung to it, thinking, *maybe… just maybe…*

The raging wind tore through the trees overhead, making the branches click as they swayed wildly back and forth. Gusts of wind drove into his face, chilling him. The rushing sound of wind filled the night, masking all other sounds. As Jeff looked around, hoping to catch some sign of Evan, he wondered why he no longer had that intense feeling of altered senses.

Had it been an illusion brought on by anxiety and tension, or had it been real? Had he been in touch with something magical or supernatural?

It was easy to imagine he had been transformed, that somehow Hobomock or some other ancient force of the forest had taken him over and given him the strength and perceptions he needed.

Now, it was gone, faded away, and he was what he had always been—a mere human who, even though he was out of shape and unprepared for this, was fighting for survival.

As he stared at the mist covered lake, he wished he could get back in touch with whatever that feeling had been. He wished he could feel and hear and see and smell the night, but now, when he stared into the misty night, all he could see was darkness. A cold, terrible fear wrapped around his heart like a snake and squeezed.

There was nothing he could do for Fred, Mike, or Tyler, but he *had* to survive…he had an obligation to live and save himself and Evan, if he could. If it came down to it, he knew he would sacrifice Evan, too, but he prayed it wouldn't come to that.

As he approached the beach, he knew his options were limited. He would go down to the water's edge and then move up the beach until he came to the boat. The mist closed in around him, and he could see no more than thirty or forty feet in any direction. All he knew was, the boat was up ahead. It had to be. The only real question was, who would be there when he got there, Evan or Ben?

As he ran, his feet sank into the wet sand and kicked up grit behind him. Waves stirred up by the wind hissed on the sand. He ran in a low crouch, thinking he would offer as small a target as possible if he bumped into Ben first. Before he saw anything, though, he heard a sound from up ahead.

A loud hissing, grinding sound and a faint splash.

It sounded like someone sliding something heavy, a boat perhaps, across the sand.

Please… please be Evan, he thought desperately as he slowed his pace and approached more cautiously. Through swirls of mist, he saw the dark bulk of the boat up ahead and someone—he couldn't tell who it was—moving around on it. He resisted the urge to call out. If it was Ben, the only response would be gunfire.

He stopped short and, scooching down, watched as the person struggled with an oar, trying to push the boat out onto the lake. Waves slapped against the side of the boat, rocking it as the person struggled to cast off.

Jeff didn't move as he watched and waited.

It *had* to be Evan.

Ben would have no reason to be taking the boat out.

But if it was Evan, where had he gotten the oars?

Ben wasn't so stupid he would have left them on the boat…was he?

Maybe, in all the confusion, he hadn't had time to take them.

Jeff stared into the swirling fog as it congealed in thick, white clots. He imagined he saw several figures, darting elusively in and out of view.

Is that Ben, or is it the unsettled spirit of Jimmy Foster?

Come on, Jeff told himself. *Get a goddamned grip!*

No matter how much he tried to tell himself his imagination was getting carried away, he was all but convinced he could sense if not actually see presences nearby.

If it's the ghost of Jimmy Foster, is he angry… or sad… or lonely?

Maybe he was trying to communicate with Jeff and tell him how, after being out here all alone for so long, he was glad someone had remembered him and come back to join him.

The fog muffled whatever sounds Evan or Ben was making on the boat. All Jeff could see was a dark silhouette looming out of the mist. He got a quick, horrifying image of Charon, the boatman, preparing to ferry him and Evan across the River Styx to the Land of the Dead.

He's come for all of us, Jeff thought as the damp cold reached inside his coat. *For Mike and Fred and Tyler… and Evan and me!*

Jeff was riveted where he stood, unsure if he should call out to the person on the boat or wait and see what happened next. Maybe Ben was moving the boat to hide it someplace else so they wouldn't find it. Or maybe Evan was trying to get away so he could meet Jeff where they had agreed to meet.

It wasn't long before Jeff got his answer.

The Wildman

The harsh, hissing sound of someone running on the beach filled the night. Off to one side, between him and the boat, a figure appeared, running swiftly toward the water's edge. A split second later, a flash of white light followed by a report of a gun split the night.

The figure in the boat dropped down. Something clattered loudly when it hit the floorboards of the boat. Jeff didn't know if Evan had been hit or was ducking for cover. Less than thirty feet from the boat, Ben drew to a stop. He stood knee deep in the water with waves washing over his feet. Steadying his arm by holding his right arm at the elbow with his left hand, he took careful aim and then shot again, once…twice.

Bullets whined as splinters of wood blew up from the gunwales of the boat. Evan stood up unsteadily. The boat was rocking wildly from side to side. A moment later, he pitched over the side, followed by a loud splash. The momentum of his fall kicked the boat so it spun around in a wide, lazy arc.

Jeff wished he was close enough to see if Evan had been hit or not and, if he had been hit, how badly, but it didn't matter. In his weakened condition, Evan wouldn't last more than a few seconds in the ice cold water. The waves would sweep over him, and—like Jimmy Foster thirty-five years ago—he would go under.

So, Jeff thought grimly, *Jimmy will have company on this stretch of deserted beach after all.*

Evan's ghost will keep him company, and Jeff knew, if he didn't get off the island tonight, he would also join them.

Talk about a camp reunion, he thought with a sinister chuckle.

He was sure Ben didn't know he was standing about twenty feet behind him. He was still focused on the boat, watching it drift away from the shore, carried along by gusts of wind and the currents that swept around the island. The mist closed in, and within seconds, the boat was gone from sight.

Jeff stared helplessly after it, positive that, even if a bullet hadn't hit Evan, he was gone…forever.

All their efforts were wasted…had been for nothing.

It was just a matter of time before Ben hunted him down and killed him.

But even with the boat gone, Jeff couldn't give up. He wouldn't allow it. He had to survive tonight so he could tell the authorities what had happened out here. All of his friends, now dead, had families and loved ones who would want to know how they had died. Jeff's son would definitely mourn his loss, and his elderly parents would be inconsolable. He hoped even Susan would feel a pang of grief once he was gone.

"No," he told himself. "That's *not* going to happen."

Even though his words were whisked away by the wind, he was filled with determination to get off this island.

And the boat might still be his answer.

It was out of sight, vanished as if it never existed, but Jeff hoped the wind would keep it close to shore. Riding the currents would bring it out to the tip of the island.

Jeff's only chance was to get out to "The Pulpit" before Ben did. He had no idea if the oars were still on board or not, but that didn't matter. Even if they weren't, he would paddle back to the mainland using his hands if he had to or just drift until the wind carried him to shore.

Jeff started backing up slowly, praying Ben wouldn't notice him. He was still standing in water, the water halfway up to his knees as he stared into the wall of mist. Jeff tried to see if Evan's body was floating in the lake, but the mist was too dense. He didn't see anything that looked like a body.

Jeff wondered if he should try to sneak up on Ben and take him from behind now, but he didn't dare try. He was too weakened after running around in the cold and damp. He was no longer confident he could take Ben in a hand-to-hand fight.

Besides, it didn't matter.

Ben still had the gun.

He had fired three shots. Jeff had no idea what kind of gun Ben had, but if reloaded recently, he should have at least three shots left before he'd have to reload again.

Moving backwards slowly and hoping the swirling fog would mask him before Ben saw him, Jeff left the beach. It was difficult to judge distances in the fog, but once he was about a hundred yards away from Ben, hopefully out of sight, he started running.

And he knew exactly where he was going.

He ran back toward the dining hall and then doubled back before heading off into the woods. He wasn't as familiar with the trails beyond the perimeter of the campgrounds. His only hope was that Ben didn't know them any better than he did.

His heart was pounding hard, and as he ran, he took in slow, even breaths to steady his nerves. The cold air burned inside his chest like liquid fire, and every muscle ached. He was already past the point of total exhaustion, but he would rather die of exposure than submit to Ben.

His feet made loud sucking sounds in the mud as he ran, but he was confident Ben had no idea where he was or where he was going. He crossed the open area where the meeting hall used to stand and crossed the service road that led to the ball fields and into the woods. Once the darkness of the forest enclosed him, he felt more secure. The sensory acuity he'd experienced before seemed to have come back, at least a little.

It was a distinct possibility Ben was heading to the same place he was. Ben was no fool. He had proven that. He no doubt wanted to retrieve the boat as much as Jeff did.

Or maybe he had already given up.

Maybe he had another way off the island and would use that.

Jeff had no way of knowing, and he didn't care. His only focus was to get to "The Pulpit" and see if the wind and lake currents had carried the boat closer to shore. Chances were it had already drifted far out of sight, but he had to try.

This is like climbing a tree when you're being chased, he thought with a sudden sinking in his stomach. One rule he had learned playing wide games at camp was: *Never climb a tree because then you're trapped.*

It was the same with the tip of the island.

If he got out to "The Pulpit," and Ben was behind him, he'd have nowhere to go…no place to run or hide.

He was betting everything on being right. As much as he was tempted to say screw it, the boat's already gone, and turn around and go back into the woods, he didn't.

He couldn't.

The further he went from the campgrounds, the denser the underbrush became. As he dodged and weaved between the rain-soaked trees, exhaustion burned in his legs and arms. His neck was as stiff as an iron bar, and his face was bathed with sweat. The night became a whirling kaleidoscope of shadows and darker shapes that twisted and twined around him in a frightening frenzy.

Jeff staggered through the woods, knowing or at least suspecting that he was well past exhaustion and possibly losing his mind. He wasn't surprised that he didn't grieve much for Tyler, Fred, and Mike. After all, he had hardly known them. But Evan's death left a numb hollowness in the center of his chest.

I should have done *something… I could have* saved *him,* he kept thinking, but he tried to force such thoughts from his mind because they would weaken him. He had to stay sharp so he would survive.

After running until he couldn't any longer, he paused and leaned against a tree, panting so heavily his breath steamed in the night. He peeled back the sleeve of his raincoat and glanced at his wristwatch, surprised to see it was only a little past nine o'clock at night.

Had his watch stopped?

Was it broken?

He shook his arm and tapped the crystal. When he looked more closely, he saw the luminous second hand was still sweeping around the watch face.

How could it be only nine o'clock?

If someone had asked what time it was, he would have guessed it was close to morning…or at least well past midnight. He knew he'd been stressed past the point of rational thought. That was the only possible explanation for why he'd had that psychedelic experience of feeling as though all of his senses were much sharper than usual.

He leaned over, bracing both hands on his knees, and labored to catch his breath. He knew he had to keep running, but he didn't think he had the strength. If he could just get out to "The Pulpit" where he thought, *he hoped and prayed*, the boat had drifted.

Leaning his head back, he looked up at the night sky. Clouds were racing by in thick, twisting luminous clumps that alternately covered and uncovered the face of the moon.

Jeff chuckled to himself when, once again, an odd, indescribable sensation welled up inside him.

The year was heading into winter when life all but ceased, but something… a powerful force was pulsing all around him in the darkness.

Is this what Hobomock is? Jeff wondered. *The spirit of the wild?*

Maybe Hobomock wasn't an Indian demon after all. Those were just scary stories his counselor had told them to frighten them. Instead of the usual ghost stories or urban legends like "The Hook," Mark had concocted stories from the bare bones of some ancient Indian legends he'd heard.

No matter what he or anyone else called it, Jeff couldn't deny there was *something* dark and mysterious moving in the dark forest. It prowled like a hungry beast, stalking him. It wasn't just the threat of Ben coming after him…it was something else…something more…something so large and nameless and powerful he couldn't even conceive of it. It wasn't really evil. If anything, it was so far beyond human scope it didn't take notice of any pitiful human beings.

Whatever small, rational parts were left of his mind, Jeff knew he'd never be able to understand or explain what he was experiencing.

It wasn't just the feeling of spirits in the forest. There was a sense of danger…of impending doom…of powers and beings beyond his feeble capacity to understand. But even if he couldn't comprehend them, he knew the world did. The world was aware that winter was coming, and that death was a natural conclusion to life.

Jeff fully accepted that he might die tonight, and on a deep level he was at peace with the idea that Ben would find him and kill him.

He was aware that this feeling might involve some kind of prescience.

Maybe his role now, his obligation in life, was to accept things the way they were. Life was so much bigger than he could possibly imagine or comprehend. The surge of life and death, of powers moving far beyond his understanding and control seized him, making him tremble. He couldn't think about them for long without feeling as though he was tumbling backwards in an endless fall into a deep, dark well.

You're losing it, ole' buddy ole' pal, he told himself.

But then another, fainter voice in the back of his mind whispered, *No you're not… you have to keep trying… it's your responsibility to live…*

Jeff gasped and shook his head, shivering as he wiped sweat from his face. Dampness saturated clothes, making them feel like dead hands clinging to his skin…dead hands that dragged him down and wouldn't let go. He imagined thousands of leeches, clinging to his skin, tearing at his flesh. He could feel the blood, streaming down his sides in wide ribbons. Weighted down by the darkness and gloom around and inside him, it was an immense struggle not to give up hope.

Where there's life there's hope, he told himself.

Ben was out there in the darkness, searching for him. As Jeff turned and looked behind him, the peculiar feeling he'd had earlier that night returned in full force. His vision and sense of hearing were suddenly amplified. He inhaled deeply, filling his lungs with thick, damp air. A warm spark of life glowed in the center of his chest, growing stronger.

Raising his hands in front of his face, he clenched them into fists, squeezing them until his wrists ached. His skin was slick with moisture and glistened as though coated with oil. He watched as shimmering rainbows flowed across his skin. Muscles, veins, and tendons throbbed beneath his skin, and he was infused with an uncanny sense of power.

Far off in the distance, he felt as much as heard and saw someone thrashing through the dense underbrush.

It was Ben, but Jeff no longer feared him. He accepted that he might die tonight, but ultimately, none of it mattered. It was all part of life. The only difference was, unlike Mike and Tyler and Fred, he wasn't going to accept it meekly. He definitely wasn't going to let death creep up on him unawares.

He would resist to the end.

Ducking low, he moved through the brush toward the shoreline. This far from the campgrounds, there was no beach, just a jumble of granite boulders and scrub brush that ringed the island. He had no idea how far it was to the tip of the island, and disappointment filled his heart when he thought that the boat most likely had already blown past the island and was far from shore. But he moved forward with grim determination, positive that even if he was trapped on the tip of the island, he would fight like a cornered rat to the last ounce of strength remaining in him.

❦ ❦ ❦

Trees and bushes whipped past him in the darkness, swatting his face and hands like stinging lashes. Before long, his face was bleeding from dozens of tiny slices. The blood mixed with sweat as it streamed down his face and neck. He licked his lips and tasted the coppery tang of blood. Up ahead, he could hear the rushing waves as they crashed against the shore. He knew he was close to "The Pulpit."

Behind him, he could also feel Ben's presence closing the distance between them. The night vibrated with dark energy that, Jeff feared, would soon drag him under, no matter how hard he fought back. He jolted to a stop when he suddenly broke out of the forest and saw the hulking silhouette of "The Pulpit" looming black against the night.

And there, on the shore, washed up and lying among the rocks like it had been placed there especially for him, was the boat.

Jeff couldn't believe his eyes.

The boat rocked violently back and forth, making loud grinding against the rocks as waves battered against it. White collars of foam flew high into the air and were whisked away by the wind. The boat was rapidly filling with water, but Jeff was confident it would float. He listened for a moment and heard Ben coming up steadily behind him.

The rocks on the shore were wet and slick as Jeff scrambled down to the boat. Ice cold water numbed him when he waded out into it, but he ignored the shock as he struggled to push the boat off the rocks and into the open water. He turned it around so the bow was heading into the wind and surf.

And there, lying on the floor of the boat athwart the seats, was a single oar.

"Thank you, Evan," he whispered to the sky as he gripped the gunwales and heaved himself up into the boat. He groaned as he collapsed onto the floor and for a while just lay, breathing deeply and shivering as he stared up at the sky.

The Wildman

I'm not going to make it, he thought, and as if in answer, a gunshot suddenly rang out in the night.

A bullet clipped the side of the boat just as a second shot sounded and sent splinters of wood flying. Jeff heaved himself off the boat's floor. He had no idea if he had been hit or not. He was in such a state of shock that, for all he knew, the bullet could have passed clean through him without him feeling it.

"You won't make it, you son of a bitch!"

Ben's voice was almost lost beneath the roaring wind and waves that crashed against side of the boat.

Jeff looked back at the shore. After a moment, he saw a dark figure scrambling up onto "The Pulpit." The boat rocked wildly from side to side in the surf, less than fifty feet from the rock. If Ben got up there in time, he'd have a clear shot at him.

Jeff slipped the oar into the oarlock while looking around for the other oar, but it was nowhere in sight. It must have fallen overboard when Evan was shot. Jeff grabbed the oar from the oarlock and, sitting close to the port side, started using it like a canoe paddle.

It was difficult if not impossible to paddle into the wind. He could only imagine what kind of target he presented to Ben. Looking frantically over his shoulder, he saw Ben perched on "The Pulpit." He cringed as he waited to see the gun flash and feel the hot sting of the bullet when it hit him an instant before the report of the pistol rolled through the night.

When it didn't come, he wanted to believe Ben had run out of ammunition or couldn't see him, but then, from the top of the rock, a bright flash cut through the mist. The bullet hit the water less than three feet from the boat, followed by the report of the gun.

Jeff dropped to the floor of the boat, but he quickly realized that had been a mistake. As soon as he stopped paddling, the boat turned in the wind and started drifting back toward the island. He would have to risk getting a bullet in the back if he was going to paddle away from here.

With his jaw set in grim determination, he strained at the oar, moving it from one side of the boat to the other to keep moving in as straight a line as possible toward the mainland. He had no idea where the dock and paunch ramp were. His only concern was to get out of range. Then he could worry about finding the dock and his car, and driving to the nearest town to report what had happened.

The wind was hard and cold, blowing straight into his face and cutting like a thousand tiny razors. Water slopped up over the sides of the boat. At least three inches sloshed around on the floor, soaking Jeff up to the ankles. He was so numbed by the cold and exhaustion he hardly noticed it.

Even when the fog closed in and he was out of sight of the island, he couldn't stop thinking that he was going to die tonight no matter what he did. If Ben didn't shoot him, the cold was going to kill him. He hoped dying of hypothermia, if it came to that, would be as pleasant toward the end as he'd heard it was.

That, or maybe he'd drown.

That's what he should do.

Why not just say fuck it and drop over the side of the boat and sink? From everything he had heard and read from people who had almost drowned, there was an unbelievable feeling of relaxation toward the end. Once your lungs were filled with water and the lights dimmed in your oxygen starved brain, it was supposed to be downright euphoric.

With thoughts like this sifting through his mind, Jeff kept paddling, shifting the oar awkwardly from one side of the boat to the other as he cringed, waiting for a bullet to hit him.

You never hear the shot that kills you.

At least there was that mercy.

Ben did fire several more times, but either he missed by quite a distance or else the wind and waves were too loud for Jeff to hear how close the bullets came. Looking back, he saw another couple of faint muzzle flashes through the mist, but the sound of the gun was all but lost beneath the howling wind.

"I just might make it…I just might make it," he kept saying as he strained on the oar.

He could no longer feel his hands, and his neck and shoulders felt as though cold iron rods had pierced them. His teeth chattered loudly no matter how hard he tried to clench his jaw to stop them.

A surge of panic filled him when he realized how much water had collected in the bottom of the boat. It was now halfway up to his knees and rising fast.

There must be a serious leak. Maybe a bullet hole was taking in water. Again, a surge of panic filled him. He had no idea how close he was to the shore. The wall of dense, luminous gray fog surrounded him. The only thing keeping him oriented was the water churning around his feet. If it weren't for that, he would have free floated in a dimensionless, eternal darkness.

It was easy to imagine he was already dead. He could no longer feel any part of his body. He only kept paddling because his body was functioning on automatic. He started crying, tears streaming from his eyes, burning his face as the cold wind whipped his breath away. Exhaustion wrung out every fiber of his being.

But I made it, he told himself. *I got away!*

He may not know where he was, but he was heading for the mainland. He suddenly panicked, thinking he may have lost his car keys and cell phone. He was only slightly reassured when he slapped his upper thigh and felt, or thought he felt, the bulge of the keys and phone in his pants pocket. He reached into his jacket pocket for the bottle of rum and smiled grimly when he clutched the cold glass but then was crest-fallen to realize the bottle had broken. Rum as well as rainwater soaked him. The jeans and socks he'd stashed under his jacket had fallen out at some point, but still, all he could think was—*I did it… I'm gonna make it, goddamn it.*

He tried to imagine what Ben would do next. As far as he knew, Ben was trapped on the island and would have to stay there until the cops arrived in the morning.

How's he going to explain those three bodies?

How's he going to explain it when—and if—Evan's body washes ashore with a bullet in it that matches Ben's pistol?

It's all over… and I won!

All he had to do was get to the shore and find his way back to his car. He doubted his cell phone would work after getting soaked, but he would drive to the nearest town with the car heater on full blast to thaw himself out.

And then he'd get some food. He couldn't imagine how incredible a cup of coffee and hot bowl of soup was going to taste. He smacked his lips, luxuriating in anticipation of the sensations real food would give him.

And clean clothes… clean, dry clothes…

What would it feel like to put on something clean and dry after this?

He imagined the soft caress of clean cotton against his skin. Moaning softly, he raised his hand and caressed his cheek, thinking it was as soft as silk.

An icy tremor made his body shudder as he pictured all the comforts he would experience soon…but before he could sink any further in his delirium, the boat lurched to an abrupt stop. A harsh, grinding sound filled the night, rattling Jeff's teeth as the sudden halt threw him forward. The oar fell from his hand into the water and drifted away out of sight as he pitched forward. He didn't know he was falling until his head slammed against the side of the boat—*hard.* White stars sprayed across his vision as he dropped face-first into the water on the floor of the boat and lost consciousness.

Chapter Fourteen

Helping Hands

THE HULL OF the boat buckled and boomed like thunder as it wedged between two large granite rocks in a small, sheltered cove under a stand of tall pine trees.

Jeff was lying facedown on the floor of the boat, his body bent at the waist over one of the seats. One hand was hanging over the side of the boat, dangling like fish bait in the churning water. His face wasn't completely submerged, but the waves kept rocking the boat from side to side, sloshing water over his face. Barely conscious, Jeff listened to himself snort and sputter, mistaking the sounds for gusts of wind blowing overhead. He imagined the water was someone's hand, repeatedly slapping him across the face. It was just enough to keep him from pitching all the way down into unconsciousness.

Please… just let me lie here for a while… so I can rest…

His mind was spiraling deeper into the darkness that waited to embrace him. If he could just get a little more comfortable, he thought, and if whoever was slapping him across the face would fucking *stop* it, the worst of the pain would pass, and he would be released.

The sound the boat made, crunching against the rocks, reminded him of someone grinding their teeth. He remembered how Evan had done that when they were kids, keeping everyone in the tent awake into the night with the sound.

But Evan… he's dead now… right?

But this wasn't someone grinding their teeth. It was too loud for that. It was something else…something he should be paying attention to because if he didn't—

I don't want to die.

—if he didn't, things were going to get a lot worse.

When a wave lifted the stern of the boat, he flopped forward, his face going under water again. A cold, stinging rush tingled the insides of his nose and throat. When he opened his mouth to tell whoever it was to *stop* grinding their teeth, icy water gushed into his throat, gagging him. Sputtering and spitting out lake water, Jeff rolled over onto his left side, wedged open his eyes, and looked up at the sky.

A solid mass of black clouds unloaded a dense spray of water into his face. Still coughing and choking, he slapped his face with both hands and struggled to orient himself. Events from last night—

Was it really only last night?

—rushed over him in brilliant flashes of terrifying images that seemed distant and unconnected to him, as if he were remembering events someone had told him.

An image of Tyler's sightless eyes and pale, white face with a bib of blood spewing across his chest hovered in front of him…and Fred, sprawled face-down on the beach…and Mike being thrown back as the night exploded with a bright flash and an ear-shattering explosion…and trees…and darkness spinning against the night sky…and freezing wet…and stinging cold…and an insane run through the dark woods that were alive with strange sights and sounds and smells.

All of these images and more etched the night like acid, casting weird, shifting lights that threw sudden shadows, stark and terrifying.

Jeff saw Ben, his eyes blazing with fury, coming toward him like a snake, ready to strike, but suddenly he had the distinct impression he wasn't looking at Ben. Drifting in the night, he saw other figures, fleeting and less distinct. Jimmy Foster stared at him with hollow eyes, cold and dead. He made a subtle gesture with both hands as though beckoning to Jeff, pleading for him to join him. He looked so sad…so terribly alone. He needed company on these cold, bleak, endless nights.

And then another figure appeared. A huge, black silhouette that seemed to be cut out of the night shifted in and out of focus until—finally— it assumed a huge, demonic shape that towered above Jeff where he lay. Red eyes blazed like angry coals, piercing him like lances. Jeff felt an odd duality as if—somehow—he had become this demon and was staring down at this pitifully frail human lying crumpled in the bottom of a fragile wooden boat.

Some part of Jeff's mind was aware that he was dying, but as much as he wished he could let go and embrace peaceful oblivion, he clung desperately to life, struggling against the darkness that swelled up all around him like a

towering tsunami that was about to crash over him. With the last vestiges of life flickering inside him like the dying flame of a guttering candle, he raised his head and made a feeble gesture toward the nearby shore.

There were figures in the forest, too. He recognized his mother and father. Both of them stood in the deepest shadows of the trees, holding their hands out to him, waving him forward, urging him to join them. His mother smiled with a beatific smile.

"I'm coming," he whispered in a raw, crackling voice that squeezed all the air out of his lungs.

When he inhaled again, the freezing dampness of the night filled his chest like a gush of cold water. Again, he coughed and sputtered, thinking it was possible he had already fallen overboard and was sinking down to the slime-covered bottom of the lake.

The lowering sky suddenly opened up, and a torrent of rain lashed against him. Each drop that hit his shoulders and back stung like a tiny bullet. Crazed with pain and fear, Jeff somehow found the strength to get up onto his hands and knees, and lurch forward. His legs slammed against the boat seat hard enough to make him cry out. His hands dragged across the wooden thwarts of the boat, leaving his palms bristling with splinters.

The boat heaved violently from side to side as he crawled to the bow. The dark slash of land in front of him was closer…so close, but Jeff couldn't find the strength to get out of the boat and onto solid ground. His arms and legs ached and vibrated with exhaustion. He had been pushed well past his limit, and there was nothing to do now except let go.

Let go… fall asleep… drift away to where the pain and cold will be gone.

But he couldn't let go.

He couldn't give up.

Not after coming so far.

Even if all of his friends were dead, his efforts would be wasted if he surrendered.

He made pig like grunting sounds as he heaved himself forward. The rocking boat made the sky and land pitch crazily around him. He'd stop every now and then, convinced he was already falling, but then—miraculously—he felt someone touch him. Strong, solid, warm hands slipped under his arms and legs and belly and lifted him.

Jeff looked left and right, unable to see what was going on, but all he saw was a dense, black smear. He could no longer distinguish land from water or earth from sky. He had no sense of direction. He was flying…falling… drifting… tumbling into darkness. He was swimming in the rain-filled sky…

he was crawling through chest-deep water…he was scuttling like a crab over rain-slick rocks that scraped his hands and knees raw.

You have to make it… You have to make it, whispered a small voice in the deepest reaches of his mind.

His hands plunged into cold water, splashing his face and reviving him with a sudden shock. But he was so far gone, he had no idea if he was moving or lying still. The dark band of the shore in front of him appeared to be closer. The uncanny sensation of unseen hands lifting him and keeping his face above the water got steadily stronger.

His left hand clamped around something rough and round. It felt like a gnarly wrist, but whatever it was, it was immobile, and he held on with the last shred of strength. It must belong to whoever was carrying him toward the shore even though he couldn't see anyone beside him.

The dark swatch of land drew steadily closer, but the world still shifted in a crazy twirl. He had the distinct impression he was motionless, and the land was sliding silently toward him. Whoever or whatever he was holding onto was cold and lifeless, as stiff as wood. It took a long time to realize that's exactly what it was.

A gnarled piece of wood.

He was clasping a tree root that had grown out into the water.

It took more energy than he thought possible to muster, but he dragged himself forward another few feet until he was out of the water and on the beach. Clawing at the rocks and wet sand, he lurched forward, inch-by-inch. His legs were useless weights, dragging behind him, and he chuckled when a line from Dickens' *A Christmas Carol* popped into his mind.

"I wear the chains I forged in life."

Is that what my body is? He wondered. *The chains I forged in life?*

The gritty sand rubbed his hands raw, but he was past noticing any pain. He let out a resounding bellow before he collapsed, face first, onto the first solid land he'd felt in—

How long?

He had no idea. All he knew was that he had never expected to feel anything solid underneath him again.

You're not home free yet, buddy, a voice in his head whispered. He was amazed how some part of him could remain so calm and rational sounding under such circumstances, but then again…maybe it wasn't him.

Maybe one of the people who had carried him to shore was talking to him.

His mind and body were screaming that he was finished and would just as soon die where he was rather than suffer any more.

He was on land, but he had no idea where the dock and parking lot might be. For all he knew, the wind and waves might have carried him to the opposite shore or back to the island. He would die wandering in the dark until the cold and damp finished him off.

He patted his upper right thigh with the flat of his hand, but his body was so numb from the cold that he wasn't sure if he could feel the bulge of car keys in his pocket.

What does it matter? I can't make it.

He'd never survive long enough to find his car and get out of here, and even if he did, how would he ever be able to drive? His arms were lead weights dragging him down.

Still, the sensation was strong that someone he couldn't see was urging him on. As he crawled forward, he couldn't believe his arms and legs actually worked. Someone or something had to be supporting him, dragging him away from the water's edge and into the shelter of the trees.

Once he was under the tall pines, the downpour cut off as sharply as if someone had turned off a spigot. Rain splattered as it fell, hissing as it swept in harsh gusts across the lake's surface, but he was protected under the trees.

Waves of exhaustion rolled over him. All he wanted to do was lie down, curl up somewhere, and sleep. Yes, sleep. Every breath made his chest and back scream with agony. He was sure several ribs were broken along with half a dozen other bones in his body. The knife-sharp pulsing in his wrists and neck made him wince, but he could no longer feel his hands or feet. When he leaned against a tree trunk and tried to pull himself to his feet, the sensation of being outside of his body and watching this pathetic attempt to stand returned, stronger than ever.

You can make it... you have *to make it,* the voice in his head said again, and Jeff actually felt a spark of hope that he *was* going to make it. He would because he was no longer in charge of his own body. Someone or something else was making him move. Like a puppet. An indescribable energy surged inside him and around him, making his arms and legs move.

The world was spinning around like an insane carousel as he hugged the tree and pressed his forehead against the rough bark. He was only dimly aware of the stinging pain and the blood flowing down his face, but the pain—like the hands he couldn't see in the dark—pulled him closer to awareness of who he was and where he was and what he had to do.

He groaned as he steadied himself on his feet, determined to move forward. He had no idea where he was going or what he intended to do. He was surprised he didn't fall down after taking the first step, but—somehow—he kept his balance. Tears streamed from his eyes, blurring his vision as he made his way through the woods, thrashing like a wounded animal, continually bumping into trees and stumbling over unseen rocks and roots. Several times he fell, but somehow he found the strength to get up and keep going.

When he looked to either side, he still saw indistinct shapes, shifting back and forth, darting in and out of view as they tracked him. A few times, he caught the cold stare of eyes that burned with red fire as they watched him. He wondered if these were the ghosts…not only of Jimmy Foster, but of everyone else whose lives the lake had claimed. The hissing rain as it fell through the trees all but drowned out any other sounds, but he thought he heard several voices, whispering to him. He couldn't tell what they were saying, but even if they were just inside his head, they drove him on into the night.

☙ ☙ ☙

Was it pure luck, or did some force he was only vaguely aware of guide him in the right direction?

Jeff was too far gone to even contemplate what was really happening to him. It took him a long time standing there, swaying drunkenly on his feet, to realize that the dark mass of the launching ramp angling up out of the water was no more than a hundred feet in front of him.

That's impossible, he thought with a soul-deep shiver.

It had to be an illusion…a hallucination he was having moments before he died.

Sometime in the spring, he thought, some fishermen or boaters or maybe a group of hikers would stumble across his body. His flesh would have rotted away by then. Crows would pick his bones clean and, in the warming days of spring and summer, maggots would feast on his remains until his bones were stripped clean. He shuddered to think that it would be a long time, if ever, before his body was identified.

And what about Ben?

Would he ever get off Sheep's Head Island, or would he die out there, starving to death when winter came?

Or did he have an escape plan?

He sure seemed to have every contingency covered, so why wouldn't he have a fallback plan?

But what if he didn't?

Maybe he didn't want, or need, one.

Maybe he came into the weekend with such confidence that he would kill everyone that he never intended to leave the island alive. If he wanted to kill them to get revenge for his brother's death, once he'd accomplished that, what more would he have to live for?

Or maybe Ben had a terminal disease…maybe that's why he had done all of this in the first place, and he was content to die now that he had done what he'd set out to do.

In the end, what difference would it make?

How important, really, were any of their lives?

In the great scheme of things, he, Ben, Mike, Tyler, and Fred all counted for little…if anything.

No one would miss any of them for long. The world would go on just fine without them.

No… whispered the voice inside his head. *You've got to get back… you've got to make sure people know who did this and why.*

The thought galvanized him, stiffening his resolve to make it to the launching ramp and up to the parking lot where the cars were parked. There was no way his cell phone would work, so he would have to drive out of here. First, though, all he had to do was get to his car…get it started…and turn on the heater so he could thaw out.

He hoped it wasn't already too late.

His hands and feet were so numb they might as well have been amputated. As he took a few tentative steps forward, he was sure his legs would fold up, and he would fall down, only this time he wouldn't be able to get back up.

I've fallen down and can't reach my car.

It felt like walking on stilts as he started along the beach toward the launch ramp. He reached an open stretch of beach where there were fewer rocks, but he kept stumbling in the mucky sand and tripping over his own feet. Gritting his teeth to keep from crying out, he moved one foot in front of the other.

Left…right…left…right…

No matter how hard he tried, though, the launch ramp didn't look to be any closer even after he had gone for what felt like more than a mile. The world seemed to telescope. He wondered why the figures in the woods—the ones who had carried him out of the boat and whispered to him, encouraging him—seemed to have abandoned him now.

Did they know he would find the strength to make it on his own?

Or had they deserted him because they could see he wasn't going to make it?

The slow, dull throbbing of his pulse was making his head spin. Each pulse was weaker that the last. His knees buckled as a terrible pressure was bearing down on him. It took every shred of strength to keep moving forward.

The Wildman

The rain was coming down in a downpour. Visibility was cut to practically nothing as he slogged along the shore, staying close to the lake and taking advantage of any stretches of open beach. He staggered forward, no longer even sure if he was even headed in the right direction.

Is this how it all ends? Is this how it all ends?

That simple question rose in his mind and kept repeating itself until it practically drove him insane.

He thought he probably lost his mind back on the island when he had those feelings of being in tune with something utterly supernatural. Or maybe on the boat, when he finally made it ashore on the mainland and was so far gone he imagined people lifting him out of the boat and carrying him onto land. There couldn't *really* have been people or anything else out here to help him.

He was on his own, and he would do it on his own or else die.

"I'm losing it bad," he muttered, and he laughed a high, cackling laugh as he slogged onward through the night, listing from side to side like a drunk. If anyone was out here tonight, he would scare the bejeezus out of them. They'd run off, terrified, instead of staying to offer help.

The wind blew strong off the water, carrying a chill Jeff knew would kill him before long. He vaguely remembered the dangers of hypothermia and, even if he'd had the right clothes—a waterproof coat and insulated pants, he wasn't going to make it through the night unless he got to the parking lot and into his car.

But he didn't think he'd make it.

The launch ramp still wasn't any closer. Was he lying on the beach, staring at it and imagining he was walking toward it?

It didn't matter.

It was lost in the swirl of rain and mist coming off the lake. For all he knew, he could have walked past it without even noticing it. He was so far gone he could have walked past a house with its light blazing and not recognized it for what it was.

But he kept moving forward, struggling to attune his senses to the night so he could once again experience that heightened awareness of what was going on around him. There were things in the night that most people never had the slightest clue about, but he had seen and heard and felt them.

But where were they now?

Why hadn't they come to his aid now when he needed them most?

No matter how hard he strained his eyes and ears, all he could see and hear was the pouring rain as it cascaded from the sky in blinding sheets that masked even the slopping sounds his feet made in the wet sand.

Tears gushed from his eyes and ran in hot, searing streams down his face, mixing with the rainwater. His throat closed off, making it all but impossible to breathe. His face was as cold as marble, and heat radiated from the top of his head as if it were a furnace.

He hesitated, swaying on his feet, then took another few lumbering steps forward. Then he paused again. His breath billowed like plumes of smoke in the cold air before being whisked away. Every bone in his body felt as brittle as an eggshell. But he kept moving forward a few steps at a time until, moaning, he pitched forward and landed facedown on the sand. His head smacked against a half-buried rock, sending a spray of white stars streaking across his vision. When he raised his head and looked down the beach, the black slash of the ramp appeared through the mist.

His body was shaking out of control as he struggled onto his hands and knees, and lunged forward. He didn't get far before his arms gave out, and he crashed onto the ground again, this time getting a mouth full of sand. Someone somewhere nearby let out a long, agonized moan. It took him a while to realize he had made the sound. He raised his head again and saw more clearly that the boat launch was in fact closer.

He had no idea where he found the reserves, but he got onto his hands and knees again and, after taking a long time to catch his breath, started to get to his feet. The world swung around him in a slow, sickening spin that lifted his stomach. The night was a smear of black against darker black, and rain hit his face like thousands of icy pinpricks.

Not far now... Not far now... he kept telling himself, but the boat launch might just as well have been the moon. The hard, black wedge of cement looked solid and real enough, but he expected it to dissolve into the mist as he took another few steps closer.

Not far now... Not far now...

He whimpered as he placed one foot in front of the other and then, holding his breath, struggled to keep his balance. The earth was spinning wildly out of control. He held his hands out like a man trying to keep his balance on a tightrope.

Not far now... Not far now...

Another step. Looking ahead, he saw that the dark shape rising out of the water was still there. If anything, it looked more solid...more substantial.

I can't believe I'm going to make it, he thought, fighting a giddy rush of excitement that threatened to spill him over again.

But as he moved haltingly forward, step-by-step, a paranoid thought suddenly struck him.

The Wildman

What if I didn't really make it? What if I'm already dead? What if I'm imagining all of this before I fade away? What if none of this is real?

But the cold rain lashed his face, and the mist blowing in off the water carried a strong fishy smell that snapped him back to reality—or at least his version of reality. He forged ahead, taking short, halting steps in time with his labored breathing.

To his left was the gentle upslope of land that led to the parking lot. There weren't many trees, so he hoped he really was looking at the parking lot and not imagining it.

His legs trembled and burned with exhaustion as he turned his back to the lake and started up the slope. It seemed impossible to climb. His feet dragged in the sand, leaving behind deep, scalloped marks. Finally, somehow, he made it off the beach and onto the dirt driveway boaters used to back their boat trailers down to the lake. Rocks and gravel crunched underfoot.

It's Hobomock… gnawing on the bones of his prey, Jeff thought with a deep shudder.

And I'm next!

The incline wasn't very steep, but it felt to Jeff like he was climbing Mount Everest. He leaned forward, his hands outstretched in front of him, almost touching the ground for support. The mist obscured the cars at the top, and Jeff had another paranoid thought that—maybe—somehow—Ben had all of the cars towed or disabled in case any of them escaped from the island.

Just keep going… you're almost there… just keep going…

He trudged onward, grinding his teeth as he slid one heavy foot in front of the other. His shoulders slouched forward, and he lowered his head, imagining that he was a bull, charging up the slope.

But he drew to a sudden halt when he saw something shift in the mist on the top of the hill.

It wasn't much.

Just a hint of motion.

It was there…and then it was gone in the blink of an eye.

He stood there panting heavily and trying to peel back the darkness and mist. After a terribly long moment, he heard the faint scuff of feet on gravel. He hadn't moved. He knew he hadn't made the sound.

Standing perfectly still, his heart racing as fast as a bird's in his chest, he looked up the slope.

Maybe his foot had slipped and made the sound without him knowing it. Maybe what he thought he had seen was the mist, thickening and thinning in the wind.

He waited, his body tensed. If he had to face any danger now, he didn't have the strength to resist or run.

He was satisfied to die where he stood rather than face another challenge.

After a moment, his pulse began to slow. The chilly air no longer burned in his chest when he inhaled and prepared to continue up the hill. If he was going to survive, he had to get to his car now. Any more time spent in the damp and cold was a death sentence.

An amazing sense of relief mixed with disbelief that he had actually survived filled Jeff as he moved closer to the summit, but just as he was congratulating himself for making it, a voice spoke, filling the night.

Chapter Fifteen

Without End

"I KNEW YOU'D COME here if you made it," the voice said.

Jeff froze in mid-step until he started to lose his balance and almost fell before he finally placed his foot back down on solid ground.

For a terrifying moment, he wanted to believe he had imagined hearing that voice. He was so far past the point of exhaustion he knew he was susceptible to all kinds of visual and auditory hallucinations. All he could think was he had to get some place warm and safe or else he was going to die.

His shoulders hunched and pressed forward, constricting his chest as he blinked his eyes against the rain and looked up to the crest of the hill. He was about halfway up the slope, but at the top, silhouetted against the night sky, was a black figure.

A deep roll of laughter filled the night as the figure shifted forward. Jeff rubbed his eyes, hoping the vision would go away; but even as he started taking short steps backwards, shifting his feet without lifting them, the figure resolved more clearly.

And then the voice came again.

"You're a lot tougher than I gave you credit. The others…?" There was a loud harrumphing sound of derision and then the person spat onto the ground. "They were cowards. Weaklings. I assumed you were, too, but I've got to give you credit, Jeff. You've got sand."

Who the hell are you? Jeff wanted to shout, but he already knew. He knew as certainly as if he were looking at Ben in broad daylight.

And even though it was dark and the rain made it just about impossible to see clearly, Jeff knew Ben's gun was aimed at him.

"Are…you…real?" Jeff said through chattering teeth that diced every word.

He didn't know if his voice carried far enough for Ben to hear him until another deep rumble of laughter rolled down onto him like a landslide. It was all too easy to imagine this was Jimmy Foster's ghost, come to mock him or Hobomock somehow materializing and coming to torment him before destroying him.

The problem was, as much as Jeff wanted to deny what was happening, he knew as surely as the icy grip the night had on his bones that Ben had found him.

But how?

"I...I don't want to die." Jeff's voice was all but lost beneath the steady sound of the downpour.

"What's that you say?" Ben leaned forward and cupped one hand to his ear. "I didn't quite catch that, Jeff."

He started walking down the slope toward Jeff, moving a few steps at a time. He was wearing a hooded raincoat that made him look like a huge statue carved out of the night. All the darkness, all the terrors of the forest had congealed into this one horrifying figure.

"You'll never make me beg," Jeff said through clenched teeth. He stiffened his shoulders. "I know who you are...I know what you're doing."

"Oh, really? And pray tell. What is that?"

"No." Jeff shook his head so hard his neck made a loud snapping sound. He flinched, thinking Ben had fired at him, and he hadn't heard the shot that had just killed him. He put his hand to his neck, amazed that he didn't feel a stream of blood.

"What's that?" Ben's voice hit a high, hysterical note. "You're gonna have to speak up. I'm having a little trouble hearing you."

Ben took another few steps closer, moving silently down the slope. Jeff chanced a quick glance over his shoulder, but all he saw was the dark, flat surface of the lake and the black angle of the launch ramp jutting out of the water. He imagined turning and running into the lake if only to confound Ben, but he knew he wouldn't survive the shock of the cold water. He had reached his limit. Truth was, he had passed it long ago. It was a miracle he'd survived this long. He should be proud of what he had accomplished even if it meant the next few minutes were to be his last.

"I said I'm not going to beg for my life."

Jeff's voice sounded stronger now. Even he was surprised by the firmness and determination he managed to muster, but all it seemed to do was amuse Ben, who kept moving slowly, inexorably forward. As he got closer, Jeff saw the pistol in his hand.

"Hell, I don't expect you to beg," Ben said with an eerie calmness in his voice. "What's that line from *Goldfinger*? 'No, Mr. Bond. I expect you to die.'" Ben's voice suddenly twisted into a high, shrill screech. "*That's what I expect!*"

When Jeff reached the bottom of the slope, he stopped on the dirt road. He shifted his weight from side to side, preparing to run…somewhere…anywhere.

"That's my only plan, Jeff. To kill you. You're the last one."

"And once I'm dead…what then?" Jeff was amazed how—somehow—he found the courage to challenge Ben. He couldn't break now. He had to go down defiant to the end.

"After you're dead—?" Ben paused, and then a high, maniacal laughter filled the night for a few seconds before fading away with a dull echo from across the water. "After that, I could just about give a flying fuck." The odd flatness in his voice had returned and was tinged with a note of wistfulness.

"I know you're doing this because you think we were somehow responsible for what happened to your brother," Jeff said. "But don't you see? There was nothing we could do."

"I thought you said you weren't going to beg?" Ben said with derisive snort.

"I'm not begging. I'm just telling you…there was nothing any of us could have done. Christ, Ben. We were kids. You can't—"

A flash of light filled the night, followed a split second later by the report of the gun. The bullet ricocheted off the ground with a loud whine inches from Jeff's left foot.

Jeff flinched, thinking for an instant he'd been hit, but then he realized he hadn't…

Not yet… he's toying with me.

He looked left and right, desperate to find someplace to hide, but he knew he didn't have the strength to run. His only sliver of hope was the thought that Ben wasn't immortal, either. He must be nearly as exhausted as Jeff. If he could just get away somehow…

But there was no cover within fifty feet on either side. He'd be gunned down before he took three steps.

"I know it won't change anything if I tell you I'm sor—"

Another shot split the night. The bullet zipped past Jeff's ear, sounding like an angry hornet before it plunked into the lake behind him.

Jeff turned to one side, hoping to make a smaller target. Maybe Ben hadn't reloaded recently…maybe he'd run out of bullets, teasing him like this.

"It's way fuckin' too late for apologies, Jeff." Ben said, still using a low, even tone of voice that sounded perfectly rational. "When my brother died, do you know it killed my mother, too?"

"No, I—"

Another shot rang out. The bullet grazed Jeff's left shoulder, tugging on his raincoat like someone behind him trying to get his attention.

"Shut up! I'm talking!" Ben screamed, and again his voice echoed in the night. Then he continued in his low, perfectly calm voice again. "She went into a really bad depression. Can you fuckin' blame her? Her son was dead! She started drinking heavily, and then…then she killed herself a year later. On the anniversary of Jimmy's death, actually."

"I didn't know th—"

Another shot, and this one hit Jeff's right arm, just above the elbow. He spun to one side thinking the bullet hadn't hit him. Either that, or he had gone into immediate shock and couldn't feel a thing. His left hand was shaking as he reached up and felt the tear in his raincoat, but there was no blood…no wound.

Good, he thought as a sour taste flooded his mouth. *I don't want to feel it when I die.*

"I got Mike and Tyler and Fred and that bastard Evan because I couldn't get that son of a whore Mark Bloomberg before he fucking died."

Jeff started to say something but caught himself, knowing all it would earn him would be another shot that—this time—might not miss. He stared at Ben.

"A heart attack!" Ben said. "He died of a fucking heart attack! At his age?" Again, his voice rose to a high pitch, but then it immediately dropped low again. "So it's down to you and me, and if I've counted right, there are two bullets left in my gun. One for you…and one for me."

"You don't want to do this."

"How do you know?"

Ben stopped his slow, steady advance and raised the gun, this time taking careful aim at Jeff. His hand was steady as he drew a bead, but before he fired—from behind Ben—Jeff saw a flurry of motion. He cringed, waiting for the muzzle flash and the sound that would reach his ears only after he was dead. But the motion at the top of the hill became clearer. For a flickering second, Jeff felt a surge of hope.

A car had appeared at the top of the hill. Its headlights were off, but it was rolling slowly forward, its tires crunching on the gravel as it came.

"You don't want to kill me, Ben," Jeff said, hoping to distract Ben. "Honest to God. You don't."

"No. Honest to God I *do*," Ben said, his flat tone of voice now sounding all but dead. Nothing was going to stop him…nothing except…maybe…that car at the top of the hill.

Jeff was rooted where he stood. It was too late to run or hide, but he shifted his weight to one side and dropped to his knees, looking past Ben just as the car reached the crest and started rolling down the slope toward them.

Jeff narrowed his eyes, praying that Ben wouldn't hear the tires on the gravel until it was too late. He coiled up, getting ready to leap to the side and make a run for it.

The car grew huge against the night sky as it reached the tipping point and then, moving forward, started to gather momentum on the down slope. Jeff wanted to keep talking as loud as he could to keep Ben distracted, but Ben suddenly wheeled around when the car was less than twenty feet from him.

The night exploded with two flashes as Ben fired twice at the oncoming car. There was a shattering of glass and a loud buzzing sound as the bullets ricocheted off into the night.

It didn't do any good.

The car was moving too fast now, and Ben didn't have enough time to get out of its path. Jeff heard and felt a loud snap in his knees when he jumped out of the car's path. He hit the ground hard, twisting his ankle on the uneven ground. Then he went down, wincing with pain, but he watched what happened next, seeing every detail as if the world was moving in slow motion.

The car's headlights came on, filling the night with a blinding, white glare. The twin beams pegged Ben like searchlights as he scrambled to get out of the way. Before he could, Jeff heard a loud thump and then saw Ben go down underneath the front bumper. The car heaved heavily to one side as it rolled over him, and there was a loud crunching sound of bones breaking punctuated by a short yelp that ended with a short, watery gurgle.

Jeff watched as the headlights shined out across the lake, lighting up the swirling mist with a near supernatural glow. In the twisted strands of fog, indistinct figures shimmered and weaved above the headlight beams.

The car reached the end of the ramp, slowing down only when it plunged into the water. With a huge splash, fans of foam flew up into the sky from both sides of the car. Then, still rolling forward on the launch ramp, it went under. The headlights glowed for a moment under the water and then winked out silently, plunging the night into a dense darkness that vibrated with weird energy.

He's dead! He's gotta be dead!

Jeff got up stiffly and hobbled over to the motionless figure sprawled on the ground. He pried the gun from the dead hand and tossed it aside. Then he knelt down, leaning close to check the damage.

The tires had flattened Ben's chest. His eyes bulged from his head, two huge orbs that glistened with a weird iridescence. Thick streams of blood, as black as ink, ran from his mouth and nose. A wheezing, bubbling sound of air escaped from his crushed lungs. His left leg was twitching so badly the sneaker he was wearing flipped off.

Down by the lake, the car was still moving forward, much slower now as it sank off the end of the launch ramp. It took a long time before it registered on Jeff that someone must be in that car.

Jeff hardly noticed the stinging cold as he ran down to the lake and dove in. A stream of bubbles was rising and breaking on the surface as waves lapped against the shore. In the dark, it was all but impossible to see who was in the car. After treading water for a second or two, Jeff took a deep breath and dove.

He couldn't see a thing underwater, and he found the car only by accident when he slammed into it. His hands were so numb they were almost useless as he felt around for the driver's door. It wasn't long before his lungs were starved for oxygen. Feeling as though it was a cowardly thing to do, he placed both feet underneath him on the roof of the car and kicked off, propelling himself back to the surface.

I'm gonna die if I go back down there, he thought, but an instant later, he drew in another breath and dove.

This time he landed on the hood of the car. From there, it was easy enough to find the driver's door. The car was still sending out streams of bubbles that broke across his face. He hoped there was an air pocket inside the car where he could get more air before he tried to drag the driver, whoever he was, out of the car and up to the surface.

One of Ben's shots had shattered the windshield, and the car was filling up fast with water. If the person in there was still alive, if one of the bullets hadn't already killed him, they just might have a chance.

Jeff found the door. Bracing both feet on the car frame, he triggered the latch and pulled back as hard as he could. There was an amazing amount of resistance, almost too much for him. He was about to give up and swim back to the surface when the door slowly yielded. Just about out of air, he reached inside and felt around until the driver's hand brushed against his face. For a terrifying instant, he thought the person was already dead, but then the fingers clasped onto his forearm and squeezed.

Jesus! He's alive!

Reaching into the pitch-black interior of the car, Jeff wound his arms around the person. The body flopped in his arms without resistance, feeling much lighter than he'd expected. Jeff panicked when the grip on his forearm relaxed, but he got his feet beneath him, pushed off the car, and kicked hard, swimming for the surface.

His lungs were on fire. The weight of the driver was weighing him down, but he struggled until his head broke the surface. The rain was still pouring down, and when he threw back his head and inhaled, his mouth filled with as much water as air. Rolling onto his side, he angled his body so the driver's head was also above the surface. White-capped waves washed over them. By the way the body hung loosely in his arms, Jeff was positive his rescue attempt had been in vain.

Maybe I'm a goner, too, he thought as he looked at the shore.

It wasn't far away, but Jeff was convinced he couldn't make it back to land. His strength was fading fast, but as much as he tried to prepare himself mentally for death, his body fought against the waves as he struggled toward shore. His grip on the person kept slipping, and he had to readjust it time and again, but he kept swimming until—somehow…miraculously—his foot scraped the bottom of the lake.

He couldn't believe he'd made it. Had he imagined feeling solid ground under his feet? He didn't know or care. He just kept moving forward until his other foot touched something solid. It was the underwater portion of the cement launch ramp.

Sputtering and shivering, Jeff dragged the all but lifeless body out of the water and lowered him gently to the ground. He turned the unconscious man's head to one side to keep the rain off it, and as he did, he saw who it was.

"Jesus," he whispered.

He had no idea how Evan Pike had made it back to the mainland or into the car. He was too far gone to think about it or care.

❦ ❦ ❦

Fifteen minutes later, after a tremendous struggle to carry the unconscious man up the hill, Jeff and Evan were sitting in Evan's car with the engine running and the heater on full blast. Evan sat behind the steering wheel, and

Jeff was slumped in the passenger's seat. Rain rattled against the roof and bounced off the hood.

Jeff had no idea how long it had taken him to get Evan to his car and get him inside. The night had an elastic quality that kept stretching and bending.

Shouldn't it be dawn by now? He asked himself as he rolled his head to the right and looked out the side window.

Maybe this storm's so intense it's blocking out any hint of daylight.

He glanced at the illuminated dial of the clock on the dashboard but couldn't believe it was accurate.

How could it be only one o'clock in the morning?

No goddamned way!

Both he and Evan were shivering in spite of the blast of warm air that filled the car and steamed the windows, erasing the night outside.

"You gonna live?" Jeff asked, rolling his head against the headrest and looking at his friend.

Evan's eyes were closed, and he looked for all the world like he was dead. The only hint of life was the faint stirring of his chest, rising and falling as he breathed. His face was as white as bone; his lips were a bruised purple that made him look like he'd been drinking grape juice. Jeff had no doubt he looked no better than Evan.

"You with me, bud?" he asked, giving Evan a feeble poke that made his head loll from side to side. "Don't punk out on me now. Not after what I've been through to save your sorry ass."

"My sorry ass?" Evan said in a low, choking gargle. "Who saved… whose…sorry ass?"

"Okay. Maybe you got me there."

Jeff chuckled and then took a deep breath as he settled his head against the headrest again. He tried to ignore the pain that made every muscle and joint ache at the slightest motion. It felt like he was being torn apart by some incredible torture device that was grinding his bones to powder.

"I can't believe you ran my car into the lake," Jeff said after a while. "It's gotta be fuckin' destroyed."

"Yours was closest to the ramp," Evan said weakly, not bothering to open his eyes. "I'm surprised neither one of you heard me when I broke the side window to get inside. That'll teach you to lock your car."

Jeff shook his head but didn't say anything.

What could he possibly say?

Even though Evan had totaled his car, he was right. He had saved his life, and he was grateful for that.

"We gotta get you to a hospital," Jeff said after a long silence punctuated only by the steady sound of rain on the car and the two men's heavy breathing. If anyone had seen the car, steamed up like that, they would have assumed a couple had driven out here to make out during the storm. Jeff found the sounds almost soothing, now that he was at least warm, if not dry.

He thought they should rest here first. Maybe sleep if they could. It was all too easy to imagine letting himself slip away into unconsciousness now, but a small, rational corner of his mind was telling him they had to get help if they both were going to live. He couldn't get this far and then die of hypothermia.

"How'd you do it?" Jeff asked, listening to his voice drag like an old-time record on slow speed.

There was another long silence. Jeff would have been convinced Evan had died if it wasn't for the low, soft hissing of his breathing.

"How'd I do what?" Evan finally asked. He kept his eyes closed and his head titled back.

"How in the hell did you get to the mainland before either me or Ben?"

Evan snickered softly, his shoulders shaking loosely beneath his drenched clothes.

"When he shot at me, when I was taking the boat, I dove into the water, hoping he'd think he had killed me." Evan sounded totally exhausted. His teeth were chattering even though the car was as hot as a sauna.

"I must've gotten disoriented in the dark, and once I started swimming, I figured I'd be better off staying away from the island."

"But you could have drowned. Christ, I can't believe you didn't drown. The water's gotta be close to freezing."

"I thought I was gonna drown, too," Evan said with a shrug.

Jeff patted the pockets of his raincoat, felt the bulge of his cell phone, and took it out. The light didn't come on when he flipped it open, and the screen was half filled with water, making it looked like a carpenter's level.

"No way this sucker's gonna work," he said as he clicked it shut and dropped it to the car floor.

Evan moaned and, opening his eyes to slits, indicated the glove compartment in front of Jeff's knees with a feeble wave of his hand.

"Mine's in there," he said. "Hand it to me."

Jeff was stunned. He gave Evan a long, slow look before he leaned forward and opened the glove compartment. The cell phone was lying on top of a registration folder and some Dunkin' Donuts napkins.

"Why'd you leave it here?" he asked.

He didn't like the faint stirring of suspicion he felt. As he closed his hand around the cell phone, he turned and eyed Evan carefully.

"I knew it wouldn't work on the island," Evan said simply. "The reception's shit out there, but sometimes it works here." He held his hand out and shook it impatiently. "Come on. Give it to me."

"No," Jeff said as he flipped the phone open and looked at the lighted screen. The battery was half charged, and the signal strength indicator was showing three bars. It might be enough.

"I'll dial," Evan said, sounding more insistent.

Jeff ignored him as he thumbed the button for the directory and saw the list of Evan's contacts. As weak as he was, Evan made a grab for the phone, but Jeff turned away from him and thumbed the directory button down…and down…until he came to the names starting with the letter **F**. After *Feeney*, *Fecteau*, and *Fidler*, he saw an entry for *Foster*. He tapped the button once to get the information.

"Give me the goddamned phone," Evan said.

His voice was edged with agitation, and Jeff could understand why. Listed under *Foster* was the first name *Benjamin* and a phone number with a Massachusetts area code.

"What the fuck is this?" he whispered, but he kept his body turned away from Evan so he couldn't see the phone's screen.

"What the fuck is what?"

Jeff couldn't believe what he was seeing. His heart skipped a few beats, and in spite of the heat blasting from the air vents, his skin went deathly cold.

"You *knew* it was him," Jeff said.

"Knew who was who? What the fuck are you talking about?"

But Jeff could hear the lie in Evan's voice. He was suddenly positive that, no matter what he said, Evan would deny knowing Ben Foster…or maybe he would insist this was a different Ben Foster.

"So what was it? Were you in cahoots with him? The two of you planned this whole thing together?"

"I have no idea what the hell you're talking about." Evan said, but he was unable to hide the edge in his voice and the frantic look that lit his eyes when he opened them and looked at Jeff.

"You knew all along he was Jimmy's brother?"

Jeff's body began to convulse as blinding anger filled him.

"You knew all along, and—what? You brought him out there to the island so he could get his revenge on us?"

Evan stared at him, his eyes wide with shock, but he said nothing.

"He must have had an escape plan—a backup." Jeff grabbed Evan by the collar and shook him hard enough to make his teeth clack. "Does he have another boat? Is that what happened? You both came over here to finish me off?"

"No…No…It's not like that at all. I swear to God, I never…I never even made the connection with his name. It never crossed my mind that he might be Jimmy's brother."

"That's fucking bullshit!"

Jeff stared out at the dark lake and listened to his pulse, hammering in his ears.

"You've lost it, man. You're out of your goddamned mind. I swear to Christ, I never—"

"You couldn't have swum over here. The cold would have killed you for sure. I know what happened. He promised not to kill you if you gave up the rest of us? That's it, isn't it?"

"You're talking crazy."

Evan was trying to sound calm, but Jeff could see the stark terror rising in his eyes.

"In the dark—did you even know who I was? Jesus, were you trying to run *me* over instead Ben? Is that what happened?"

"You've lost your mind. Exhaustion…exposure have really gotten to you. You have no idea what you're saying, so look. Just calm the fuck down and give me the phone."

Evan lunged at Jeff while, at the same time, reaching down to the floor and slipping his hand under the car seat. Jeff caught the motion, and he wasn't surprised when Evan raised his left hand, holding a gun. Just as he was started to bring it around to aim at him, Jeff lashed out with the hand holding the cell phone. That instant, the gun discharged with a flash and a deafening thump that made Jeff's ears ring. The passenger's side window exploded, inches from his head.

"You lying sack of shit," Jeff shouted as he clenched his fist and drove it with every remaining ounce of strength he had into Evan's face.

There was a satisfying crunch of breaking teeth and bone as Evan's head snapped back hard against the headrest. A mist of blood shot from his nose like a spray gun, and his eyes rolled back to expose the whites. Trembling with fury, Jeff clenched his fist, cocked his arm back, and punched him again… and again…and again until—finally—Evan let out a low, gurgling moan and sagged back in the car seat. His head was cocked to one side, resting at an awkward angle on the car seat. Blood streamed from both nostrils and the corners of his ruined mouth. His eyes were half-opened, but they gazed sightlessly at Jeff. The whites were an odd yellow shot through with tiny broken blood vessels.

Tears filled Jeff's eyes and streamed down his face. He muttered something unintelligible, but what he said was punctuated by sharp hitches in his chest as he reached across Evan's chest, snapped open the driver's side door, and pushed him out onto the gravel parking lot.

Evan hit the packed ground hard and rolled over once before coming to rest with one arm draped across his chest. Rain pelted him as he lay on his back, staring sightlessly up at the night sky.

Jeff struggled to catch his breath as he stared at the motionless figure. He had no idea if Evan was alive or dead, but he didn't care. His body was shaking out of control as he raised his bloodstained hand in front of his face and clenched it into a fist. The blood sticking to his fingers made a sick, squishy sound. He knew his hand was broken. The pain reached all the way to his shoulder.

I've gotta get help, he thought, but he couldn't find the strength to move.

It would be much easier, he thought, to close the door and sit here with engine running. Even with the passenger's window blown out, he would either warm up or the carbon monoxide would get into his bloodstream and kill him.

Either way, what did it matter?

Nothing mattered any more, as far as he could see.

They had started out with five—five supposed friends—and now, only he was left.

Would the police even believe his story?

Or would they suspect he had been the killer all along who had lured these four innocents out to Sheep's Head Island to their deaths?

And in the end, what would it matter?

He had already lost everything that mattered to him—his wife, his son, his life, if you could call it a life. He didn't sell houses. He was a paper pusher and a money grubbing moron. Although everything that had happened on the island already seemed like a terrible dream, he remembered—for a short time—he had been really alive out there. The spirit of the night had filled him some strange energy...a power that made it all too clear that his life—until this weekend—had been empty...hollow...without meaning.

No one would miss him if he died now, and he was content to know he had won. He had beaten Ben Foster at his high-stakes game, so even if he died now, he could die knowing he had won.

The Wildman

His hand was still trembling as he relaxed his fist and reached for the steering wheel. The effort was almost too much, but he managed to shift over to the driver's seat. Evan's foot was still hanging inside the car, but he kicked it out onto the ground.

The rain was still coming down hard. He watched with an uncanny detachment as his hand took hold of the gearshift and slipped it into reverse. He released the emergency brake and stepped down on the gas. The tires skidded on the wet gravel, but they found purchase, and the car crept backward. He snapped on the headlights and watched them wash across the slumped body of Evan Pike, lying in the middle of the road.

"Goddamn yah," he whispered.

His breath misted the windshield, obscuring his view for a moment as he backed the car around and shifted into drive. Then he stepped down hard on the accelerator. The tires spun on the gravel, squealing as he drove off into the night.

※ ※ ※

You could say it all ended when Jeff reached across Evan's chest, opened the car door, and shoved him out onto the dirt road, but that wouldn't be strictly accurate. Too many things happened afterwards to make that particular event a clean cut conclusion to this story.

Jeff lost any sense of time as he drove into the night, the car rattling and bouncing on the rutted dirt road. He didn't have much, if any, awareness of where he was headed. All he knew was that he needed to find someone he could tell what happened and who might be able to help him. He also needed to get warm and put on some dry clothes and eat something substantial. Hell, even a Granola bar would do. If he didn't eat soon, he was going to die... although that thought no longer held the terror it once had.

He was barely conscious when the car careened into the parking lot of a Rite Aid pharmacy in the town of Arden and screeched to a stop at an angle that cut across two parking spaces. One front tire was up over the curb, and he had just missed hitting a Rav4 parked nearby. After killing the engine, he opened the door and all but fell out onto the asphalt.

He was amazed he had made it this far.

His plan was to go into the pharmacy and get something to eat and drink. He had his mind set on an energy drink and Granola bar, but he never made it. Harry Shannon, the owner of the Rav4, found him sprawled on the pavement with his legs still inside the car.

After the police cruiser and ambulance arrived and took him to the hospital, everything became a blur of bright lights and confusing sounds as dozens of people—doctors, nurses, orderlies, and policemen—hovered over him, asking too many questions. He had the impression he replied to each question in clear, sensible sentences, but then he began to have his doubts because the same people—or maybe it was different people—kept asking him the same questions, over and over again until he was ready to scream. Finally, someone shot him up with something, and he drifted off to sleep after being reassured that he was perfectly safe now.

As he faded away, he remembered being asked if he wanted someone to contact his next of kin, but he didn't remember what he answered. As it was, Susan never showed up at the hospital that night or for the three days he was there. She didn't get in touch until he was back home, recuperating. His parents called him and sent him a get well card, but they weren't able to make the trip to Maine from Florida. Matt came home one weekend, and it was great to see him. He would have stayed longer, but it was heading into midterms.

You could say the story ended when David Blake, the police captain in Arden, and a rookie patrolman named Russell Dawkins drove out to the boat launch at the first light of dawn. The clouds had passed in the night, and the day was breaking sunny and unseasonably warm. The cops half suspected everything Jeff had told them had been the ravings of a man delirious from exposure, because they didn't find Evan Pike's body where Jeff had said he'd left him for dead. No body. No footprints in the still-wet dirt of the parking lot or on the road leading down to the boat launch.

The policemen began to reassess when, further down the boat launch road, they discovered Ben Foster's body and saw Jeff's car, submerged in the lake. Dawkins spotted a few traces of blood on the road. Closer to the lake, it looked like there had once been a significant quantity of blood on the road, but the rain overnight had washed most of it away. The state Crime Investigations Unit would bring out their fancy forensics stuff later. The boat Jeff had told them he had paddled with one oar from Sheep's Head Island was, indeed, pulled up on the shore where he said it would be. Only then did the police become concerned about what they might find when they made it out to the island.

When they did, it was much worse than either of them imagined. It sure looked to Blake and Dawkins as though what Jeff had told them was true.

You could say it all ended later that winter, once the authorities concluded their investigation. By January, Jeff had recovered from the wounds he'd sustained and from the effects of exposure, but he was never the same after that. He testified at the hearings in December and then, that same week, quit his job at Bayside Realty. He sold the house in Westbrook. It was too big for a man living alone, anyway. He planned to live off his severance pay and the profit from the house sale until he decided what he wanted to do next.

At this point, you very well might think the story is over. Jeff would feel some vindication for being proven right, and he would be glad beyond belief he hadn't become a victim or a suspect for any of the killings. You'd be perfectly justified in thinking he was satisfied when all the evidence the police found on the island validated his version of events.

But there was one key element that never came to light, or until it did, Jeff, at least, would never feel as though this story was over.

It would never be over for him until they found or accounted for all of the bodies. Tyler, Fred, Mike, and Ben were all accounted for, but in spite of a rather extensive search, no one found any trace of Evan Pike. The police did all they could with dogs and divers and search parties, but they all came up dry.

There was plenty of speculation about what might have happened to him. Some of the locals dismissed it by saying scavengers must have dragged Evan's corpse off into the woods and finished him off. But if that were the case, why had Ben Foster's body, in the same immediate area, been left untouched?

Other folks were convinced Evan wasn't dead when Jeff rolled him out of the car. Maybe he had been so hurt he got disoriented and wandered down the slope and fell into the lake, where he drowned. If that's what happened, these folks declared, his remains would most likely show up come spring, once the ice that blanketed the lake from November to April finally melted.

Other people suggested that Evan may have been conscious enough to try to walk back to town to get help, and that maybe he got lost in the woods where if not this year or next, maybe *some* year a hunter or a group of hikers would come across a pile of decaying bones. If they were lucky, there would be enough to identify him.

And of course there were other people who had some fairly peculiar ideas about what might have happened out there. If they're right, then this story will never end. It wasn't long before talk about what had happened on Sheep's Head Island that weekend took on the charm of folklore.

Not long after ice-out that spring, when fishermen were plying the waters of the lake for rainbow trout and bass, there was talk that if you took your boat close enough to the island—especially around sunset—you might catch a glimpse of a ghost, lurking on the shore near where Camp Tapiola had once stood.

The story is, this apparition's hair is snow white, and his long, gray beard wafts in the wind like smoke from a chimney fire. His eyes flash with murderous rage whenever anyone comes within hailing distance of the island. Some folks say it's not a ghost at all. They say a crazy hermit, a wild man who has lost his mind, lives out there, subsisting on roots and berries and whatever animals he can catch and eat.

Of course, these stories about ghosts on the island bring to mind the death that happened out there thirty-five years before, which is when this story really may have started. There is plenty of talk, especially from older people who remember what happened back then, that maybe what they're seeing is not an old hermit at all. It's the ghost of a lost, lonely child who still watches and waits for his friends to come and join him.

And as long as people even half believe these stories…as long as people repeat such tales, you could say this story will never really be over.

The End